# Dark forest

Disillusioned ... Disaffected ... Dangerous ... just some of the labels police chiefs are attaching to Phil Todd.

He was the force's high flier, a rising star. A blast from a killer's shotgun lames him. Parting from his long-time lover leaves him embittered. The loss of the grandmother who raised him adds to his emotional pain.

He is seeking a medical discharge from the service with compensation for his crippling wound. The woman lawyer he engages offers him an assignment as her inquiry agent on a missing person case.

It takes him into the cut-throat world of commercial drug manufacturing and sets him against a powerful multi-national company and politicians with secrets to hide.

On bleak coalfields and in a threatening, fog shrouded forest, he must work alone, trusting no-one, not even the flame-haired, hot-tempered lawyer who hired him.

*Dark forest* introduces Phil ('Sweeney') Todd, Frank Palmer's new character, taking over from Detective Inspector 'Jacko' Jackson, happily retired and writing his long awaited crime novels.

What critics say:
'One of the best delineators of the criminal landscape.'
Philip Oakes, *Literary Review*
'A tender as well as angry writer.' *New York Times*

## Also by Frank Palmer

# PREFACE

22 March

Dear Jacko,

Enclosed are the tapes, completed as promised. In all, they make around seven hours of listening.

I'm no writer. I have just tried to recall it as it happened, so the whole yarn is a bit rough around the edges.

Some correspondence is attached which might be useful.

Don't forget you gave your word that you'll change the names. The honour of three special ladies is involved here.

In haste,<br>Sweeney

# DARK FOREST

Frank Palmer

Constable · London

First published in Great Britain 1996 by Constable & Company Ltd,
3 The Lanchesters, 162 Fulham Palace Road, London W6 9ER
Copyright © 1996 by Frank Palmer
The right of Frank Palmer to be identified as the author of this work
has been asserted by him in accordance with the Copyright,
Designs and Patents Act 1988
ISBN 0 09 475900 6
Set in Palatino 10pt by CentraCet Ltd, Cambridge
Printed and bound in Great Britain by
Hartnolls Ltd, Bodmin

A CIP catalogue record for this book
is available from the British Library

For Carole

Special thanks to Paul Barwick, of the Forestry Commission, for his guided tour of Sherwood Forest.

The East Midlands Combined Constabulary and its cases are fictional. So, too, are the companies, the constituencies, all the events and, with one exception, the characters in this story.

Dennis McCarthy, the celebrated presenter with BBC Radio Nottingham, agreed to a cameo role. Sadly, just a few weeks before publication, he died suddenly. The scene reflects my admiration and affection for a unique broadcaster. The active encouragement he, his wife Marjorie and daughter Tara always gave me will never be forgotten.

# 1

*Tuesday, 4 January*

Distant voices float up the fog, voices from a grave. Heavy footsteps, zombies getting closer.

Now, he orders himself. Make your move now.

A leg collapses, then the ground beneath. An avalanche picks him up and sweeps him down; a helter-skelter on a bed of sharp stones.

Red ignites the grey a split second ahead of a dull explosion and fiery pain. Chill, pain, searing heat, pain, deathly cold.

Hands grip his leg. Don't let it come away.

Blood coats his palms and oozes through his fingers.

Don't let them cut it off. Please. Give it a chance. Don't amputate. Please. Don't cut it off. Please. Please. Please.


No need to reach beneath the green duvet to feel, just to touch it. It's still there – for all the good it is.

So grey is the light through the thin curtains, a double take is required to read the bedside clock: gone eight.

Nine hours' sleep and out of fuel already. That dream always drains every drop from my emotional tank.

No reason to reach across the bottom sheet with my left hand. She's not there to touch, to feel alongside. No cause to get up. No point in trying to doze either.

I used to have this certain sleeping draught. We'd be together on this sun-kissed island. To get sex out of the way, I'd imagine we'd been in the sack all afternoon. Now it is almost midnight, a shadowy moon, a vesper of a breeze. The sea lazily slaps the white sands. We have eaten too much and drunk too much. We are in each other's arms in a wide hammock gently swaying to and fro. Never used to fail. Never works these days.

I try never to think of her. So I'll just lie here for a little while and think of her.

The bedside radio trumpets a catchy tune, faded for a gravelly male voice. 'Tuesday is our "Where are they now?" spot when we reunite long-lost friends and relations. So ring us on *Afternoon Special* . . .'

Afternoon? Have I slept that long? Not all morning, surely? The clock shows nearly nine. Has it stopped?

A different male voice summons up the AA for a traffic check. What I've heard is a trailer of forthcoming events.

A woman cheerfully lists the familiar blackspots and tailbacks as the nation returns to work after Christmas and New Year weekends that merged. Every day for months has felt like a bank holiday to me. I wonder when I'll get back to work, wonder if every day is like this for the unemployed, nothing to get out of bed for.

The lead news is about the latest political scandal – a minister who knocked single mothers while knocking up a mistress. An opposition MP accuses him of hypocrisy. The litany of local crime and road crashes follows, nothing major. The weatherman forecasts heavy rain most of the day.

The bedside phone rings. 'Mr Todd?' A woman's voice, not hers, the one I want to hear, long to hear. 'Jordan Associates here. Could you slip up to see Michelle Fogan around ten?'

'OK,' I reply, and ask no questions, replace the receiver and get out of bed, stiffly, as always.

In the tiny bathroom, the right spot on the shower dial is impossible to find, as always. The water comes out thinly and slowly, too cold or too hot, depending on which bit of plumbing is in operation next door. A flushed lav and you scald. A hot bath and you freeze. Today is Tuesday but feels like Monday, wash day next door, freezing. No shampoo this morning, and the waterproof stocking ('Makes you look like Nora Batty in *Last of the Summer Wine*,' she once joked) has been discarded now the skin graft has finally taken.

Shaving in a cracked mirror makes me wish I had washed my hair, which she often poked fun at ('So blond and fluffy; powder it and wear a beauty spot and you could dance the minuet.'); much darker, duller, flatter today.

I wear my one suit, deep brown, for the first time since the funeral. A lemon tie matches it better than black.

I am dressed for work for the first time in eight months.

My route out of the city centre routinely gets mentioned on the AA traffic check. Rush-hour should be over but vehicles that always seem to breed in the rain still tail back; yellows from sidelights, reds from brake lights, not many greens from traffic lights.

To the left, behind a cemetery, is the Forest. Just ahead is Sherwood. Both must be deeply disappointing to tourists on the Robin Hood trail. The Forest is a pancake-flat playing field; Sherwood just another suburb with terraced back streets.

Not quite four miles are built up all the way. Twenty minutes should easily do it, door to door. Ten of them go at road-works.

In a pitch for some trade from tourism, Arnold was once called 'Gateway to Sherwood Forest' but the only greenery comes from the plastic bags of rubbish piled high on kerbsides, the debris of Christmas, awaiting collection.

The offices of Jordan Associates across the deserted market square fit the law firm's split personality – modern biscuit-coloured brickwork in Victorian design, all sharp angles and narrow windows. From previous visits last month, I know a handy place to park behind the Co-op.

'Ah, Phil,' says the dark young woman in a warm ground-floor reception-cum-waiting room. An impatient expression disfigures an extremely attractive face. 'Good.' Now she's pleased to see me. 'Ms Fogan is waiting.'

'Sorry, Natty.' First-name terms were forged hanging around to see Old Man Jordan, once for almost an hour, for less than ten minutes.

She leads the way into a room I've not seen before – light and tidy compared with the oppressive book-lined office of her boss.

The sight of Ms Fogan sitting behind her desk almost stops me in mid-limp. Long loose red hair falls over the shoulders of an emerald green silky blouse, collar up like Eric Cantona's. A pale face is much freckled. Tired greeny-blue eyes hint at late nights over the festive season.

Four files are before her, one as thick as the Bible. Only two have my name on the front covers. She opens none, just folds tiny,

11

white hands, nails long and painted blood red. 'Mr Jordan has handed you on to me.'

Bad news, this. I need Peter Jordan on the case. He's senior partner here, the one with the contacts and clout, the one I have to be close to. My dismay is showing.

'I handle most of the medico-legal stuff these days,' she says, nodding me to a straight-backed chair opposite her.

That's hard to understand, I think, sitting down. Old Man Jordan is the district coroner as well as head of the firm, and you can't get much more medico-legal than that dual role. Just lately, I have learned to accept bad news with a weak smile, very forced. 'Fine.'

She opens the thick file. 'See you've changed your address.'

'Renting,' I reply. She looks across at me, expecting more, so I have to explain that my lady and me have parted.

'Putting your place up for sale, too?' She seems to be touting for business, as if I haven't given her firm enough. A don't know is shrugged.

Talk of property prompts a switch in priorities. She closes one file and puts a thinner one on top, opening it on my latest letter requesting Jordans to probate my grandmother's estate. 'Got her house up for sale?'

Yes, I confirm, but the place has no central heating. It's only expected to fetch around sixty thousand pounds.

Her head stays down. 'One way and the other you've had a rough time.'

Inwardly, I second that and am thankful she hasn't said, as so many have: 'Eighty-one was a good innings.'

She anticipates no problems with the three small insurances located clearing out the house. 'We'll handle it.' We smile thanks at each other.

The files are reshuffled. She read up over the holidays, she begins, and her reading of my case is this:

There I sit, thirty-eight, my promising career over. The police authority's offer is disgracefully low. She's toyed with the idea of telling the press. 'Wounded hero short-changed' and all that, but is holding back because it isn't a final offer.

The problem is the force's insurers. Their doctors are saying that eventually I'd get more use back in the leg. 'The more use, the less compensation. They're playing the long game.'

Three times I have sat before her boss, Jordan. Never had his assessment been this frank. He'd been more interested in my

12

motive for quitting the police force than my injury. Ms Fogan, I suspect, belongs to a different breed of lawyers – pro-civil rights, anti-establishment.

'You didn't make it to the hospital last month, I see,' she goes on, rather reprimandingly.

I made it all right, I protest. Before the doctor could get down to the examination, a phone call took me to my grandmother's hospital bedside. 'Ten days there, ten days afterwards clearing up.'

'Sorry.' She doesn't look chastened. 'And the ending of your . . . er, relationship . . .' she is speaking tentatively. 'Has that anything to do with your injury?'

Did it stop me getting my leg over, she means; grounds for upping the compensation claim, along with limited mobility and no participating in sports. Well, yes, as a matter of fact, I concede to myself, for several weeks, and, after that, only with difficulty but with lots of laughing foreplay.

She won't want to hear this, or how it ended on the day of the missed hospital appointment, rushing home to pack a case, opening the morning's mail without looking who it was addressed to, finding myself reading a letter from a man she met while I was in traction, unable to put it down till I'd finished. I don't want to, mustn't, think about this. 'No.'

It must have come out sharper than intended, because she again says: 'Sorry.' She packs up the papers, predicting settlement by the end of the financial year.

A third, unmarked file is shuffled to the top. She slips out a letter which she slides across the desk. 'Remember that?'

My head is down now, no need to reply immediately. 'Harbour Heights Residents Association, Sydney, NSW,' says the letterhead. It is addressed to Jordan and wastes not a single sentence before fawning. 'You have been recommended by a neighbour with friends in Sherwood who speak highly of you.'

Then to business: 'We are gravely concerned about the well-being of our janitor who has failed to return from a trip to England last summer.'

A missing persons case that's known to me is outlined in brief. The president of the tenants' association wants to engage Jordan Associates to do what the police failed to do – find him.

Beneath a neat signature is a list of enclosures – CV, correspondence, photo and a bank draft for two thousand pounds drawn on association funds. These she hasn't pushed in my direction. I turn the paper, not expecting to find anything, merely to indicate I've read it.

'Well?'

This time I have to reply, but don't state the obvious that I was in hospital when the story, such as it was, made the media. 'I saw a bit about him in the evening paper.'

'What do you make of it?'

Anxious not to make too much of it, playing the long game, I shrug. 'Maybe he doesn't want to be found.'

'Possible, I suppose.' A moment's muse. 'How would you go about it?' A small smile. 'Given your police experience.'

'For starters I'd phone Heather Hann in the Missing Persons Unit.'

She nods at a green phone to tell me to help myself.

'Not me,' I hurry on. 'I'm on sick leave.'

'And you don't want headquarters to know how active you are. Good tactics.' Wearing an approving smile, she picks up the receiver and dials a number I dictate.

She gets Sergeant Hann straight away, introduces herself, reads out the letter from heading to signature and asks, 'Have you anything useful on this?' Her face registers annoyance at the reply. She puts down the phone. 'Says she'll call back.'

'You could be anyone phoning up,' I explain. 'They got screwed by some private investigator a few weeks back.'

She nods curtly. 'Know about that, do you?'

Before I can tell her what I know, the phone rings. She asks a lot of questions, but doesn't note many replies, not too impressed by what she's hearing. When she replaces the phone, she relays, 'They went through the motions – state records, mortuaries, hospitals, and all that, but that's all. She didn't sound too interested.'

Heather Hann was a drinking pal of mine, but I don't rush to her defence. 'He's fifty and free to do what he likes. Had he been a young kid, they'd have pulled out more stops.'

She arches an eyebrow. 'Are you interested in having a look?'

More than interested, actually. Thrilled. Like a longterm recession victim about to land a job. I try to show only surprise. 'Me?'

'You were CID.'

For five years, before going into Special Ops, I confirm, playing hard to get. 'Don't you have a regular inquiry agent?'

Had, she says flatly. 'Name of Dunphy.'

I cluck, part sympathy, part mocking.

She asks what I know about him.

A booted-out bobby turned private investigator, the one I'd just mentioned, I tell her. According to the grapevine, he'd posed as a still-serving officer, to get some confidential info from the head-quarters computer, and is now awaiting trial charged under the Official Secrets Act.

She nods gravely. 'He's *persona non grata* here.' She pauses. 'Well?'

Technically, I point out, I am a serving policeman, still on basic pay. Then, 'What's the going rate?'

Fifteen pounds an hour, she says. She fingers inside the file – the bank draft, I guess. 'With expenses, this would fund about a month's work.'

'It would all go on single person's tax,' I grumble. 'Besides, it's moonlighting. Against police regs.'

A cunning smile. 'Not if I don't pay you till the start of the new financial year and, with luck, you'll be out of the police service by then. There's no regulation to stop a person doing an unpaid good deed, now is there?'

I say nothing.

'What are you planning when you do go?'

An honest don't know is the only answer.

'Well,' she says, eyes on mine, 'we have a vacancy. Just turn it over for me. Use the coroner's department, if you need a desk or a phone. Who knows what it might lead to?'

Who indeed? I think, allowing myself to be talked into turning it over till the end of this week, to see what I make of it.


Michelle Fogan slides the bank draft out of the file and the file across the desk. Having speed-read it, a flip forward and back is needed to recap, mentally knocking it into order.

She stands, stretches and walks round to my side. A pleated grey skirt ends just below the knees. Her shoes are shiny black. There's a white flash of tight calf muscle between. A faint, sexy smell of expensive perfume hangs on the air as she looks over my shoulder down on to a coloured photo.

The face we're studying is tanned. A half-caste, maybe. Better describe him as of mixed race, I correct myself.

He has thin features, high cheek bones, good teeth, straight dark hair, cut short, greying at the temples, sad brown eyes, white sports shirt opened at a scrawny neck.

Arnold Gillman was born in Arnold. Arnie from Arnold should be easy enough to remember, I decide, permitting myself a small smile, the only one I get on this poignant paperwork.

A British-born war baby, now fifty plus, he went straight into an orphanage. At war's end, he was shipped to Australia. There was a drama-documentary about child migrants on TV recently. Charities emptied their orphanages and packed off thousands of Arnie Gillmans down under. Young, fresh blood for the old Empire, the theory was. Shunting unwanted social problems half-way round the world, a heart-rending scandal, in my view.

Arnie spent ten more years in homes in the outback, then was thrown out into the big wide world. For a quarter of a century, he drifted – sheep stations, factory hand, building sites, never marrying.

Ten years ago he finally settled. He'd helped to build Harbour Heights – and its swimming pool – and stayed on in the janitor's quarters, jack of all trades.

All the time he was saving up for a trip back to the place of his birth to try to find a mother he'd never known. The chance arrived when the Australian cricket team toured England. Lots of cut-priced package trips were advertised in Sydney. He booked for a three-month holiday.

Then came red tape over a passport, not being Oz-born. He turned to the residents of Harbour Heights to help sort it out.

He knew his birthday – 31 August – but wasn't altogether sure of the year and certainly not the place of birth. That was where H. Myers (no Mr or Mrs or Ms), president of the Residents Association, appeared to have come in.

He or she got the gist of his bleak life and badgered the authorities into producing a birth certificate. Arnold, England, 1941, it turned out.

Armed with that, he got his passport and flew out at the end of June, just over six months ago, bringing his birth certificate with him. He sent a postcard of Buckingham Palace to Harbour Heights, dated Tuesday, 29 June: 'Arrived safe. Tiring journey. Heading for Nottingham tomorrow.'

They didn't expect to hear any more, not a great correspondent was their janitor, and only got worried when he failed to return by mid-September.

They called in Sydney police, who contacted the East Midlands Combined Constabulary, who assigned Sergeant Heather Hann. In November she reported back: No trace.

'He is very conscientious in his work and much respected by our members, especially their children,' Myers wrote. 'None of us view him as the sort of man simply to walk out on his job and home where some personal possessions remain. If he is reunited with his family, our best wishes go out to him. Until we are satisfied about his whereabouts and well being, our concern for him grows.'

The association voted at its December meeting to finance a private inquiry out of its funds. An unnamed member with Sherwood connections suggested Jordan Associates as a good local law firm.

'What do you think?' Michelle asks when I fold back the file, bringing the photo to the top again.

'Nice neighbours,' I think out loud.

'Sad story, though,' she says, looking down at the photo.

My eyes find the date and place of birth, the starting point in more ways than one, I tell her.

'So you'll give it a go?' she asks, returning to her seat.

'For the rest of the week,' I agree.

'I need something to report back, you know, so keep in touch.' She is telling me this is no fifteen quid an hour skive, and who's boss.

I promise I will.

To indicate the interview is over, she picks up the Bible-thick file. The cover is labelled 'Grimston v. Hedges Pharmaceuticals'. She drops it with a depressed sigh and a dull thump in front of her.

Plenty of work in that, I presume, wondering how much an hour she charges. 'Thanks for your time,' I say, rising.

'OK.' She doesn't look away from her reading.

2

A short cut would have been to phone my old pal in Missing Persons. But since my private eye predecessor's failed attempt to hack into Special Branch files, the Old Pals Act is out and the Official Secrets Act in. Any officer disclosing more than the time would join the dole queue, the deputy chief constable had let it be known.

Heather owes me a big one – a favour, I mean – but it's much too early in the inquiry to redeem it, so a detour across the northern suburbs takes me to the offices of the registrar, a square, single-storey building in its own small grounds.

At a glass-enclosed counter, a pleasant woman clerk hands over a form. 'Application for birth certificate,' it says in purple letters. I fill in the answers accurately. 'State your relationship to the person to whom the certificate relates.' – 'None.' 'State the purpose for which the certificate is required.' – 'Missing person.'

Five minutes are spent standing and pointlessly studying two big boards with notices of forthcoming marriages. Emma and me might have had our names up here, if . . . Oh, for christsake, I rebuke myself, forget it.

Five pounds fifty buys a short, wide document with red lettering. I forget to ask for a receipt, so engrossed am I in reading this: When and where born: 31 August 1941. Red House, Oxton Hill, Arnold. Name, if any: Arnold. Sex: Boy. A column for the father is crossed through. Mother: Lillian Gillman, knitwear worker. The father's occupation is blank. Signature, description and residence of informant: Alice Gillman, grandmother, 64 Smith Street, Arnold.

These days, of course, they call a baby without a registered father 'love child'. In those days, bastard.

Know what I reckon? I reckon Lil didn't even see her son and Granny Gillman had stuck down the first Christian name that came into her head. And yet Arnie had travelled half-way round the world to find his mum, to talk and try to understand. Belatedly I'm agreeing with Michelle Fogan; a sad story.

Back in the car, I discover that neither street appears in my A–Z of Greater Nottingham. As No. 2 in Special Ops, I'd have tossed the query over to some young cadet, but fledgling private investigators have no gofers.

I drive to the nearest phone kiosk to call the local police station, telling the switchboard operator I'm a stranger who's lost. She can't locate them either.

I phone the local library, repeat the query and have to hang on because Inquiries is engaged. Twenty pence, last of the silver, runs out. Pockets are felt for a contacts book where I've disguised phone credit card digits I can't remember under an old mate's number. The idea was to save me from losing the card. I can't find the bloody book.

A trudge across the road, through the rain, to a corner shop for a cheap pocket notebook with a bright red cover and change for a fiver.

The box is occupied when I get back. Standing there, getting wet through about ten minutes of chatter from a tubby blonde, I decide I'm not enjoying the first fifteen quid's worth of work in this new career.

Back in the dry, fifty pence funds a reconnection. I hear that the Red House, a refuge for unmarried mothers, was demolished in the fifties and Smith Street was pulled down in slum clearance a decade later.

Smelling damp, I head home, if that's what you can call the furnished house I rent; one of half a dozen with fake Georgian bow windows, built less than ten years ago, on what's called in-fill sites in turn-of-the-century terraced streets; two up, two down, variously advertised as town houses or starter homes.

Out of habit, I prod a pre-set button for BBC local radio and catch that *Afternoon Special* trailer again. 'Time for the news at noon,' says the linkman.

What time is it down under? I wonder. 11 p.m. Let's hope the president of Harbour Heights Residents Association isn't in bed yet.


I have a grill and side salad listening to an hour of middlebrow music, lots of golden oldies. Now and then the music stops for chat, listeners just phoning in, lots of golden oldies among them, too.

*Afternoon Special* is aimed at a stay-at-home audience that likes to get a bee out of their bonnet or to share a memory. 'Community broadcasting', my lady ... my ex-lady ... used to call it. 'What local radio should be about.'

She was working there, a general reporter, when she turned up at HQ, wanting an interview on a hunt I was running for a jailbreaker. I was too bedazzled to be too articulate, longed to ask for a date, bottled out.

Next day I cranked up the courage. 'That worked well. Thanks. How about a follow-up?' I spun a yarn about a minor development in the search, the thinnest of sightings. 'Let's meet to see if we can cobble something together.' I chanced it. 'For a drink, perhaps?'

Drinks became dinner, then back to her place. More drinks into

19

the early hours and she demanded my car keys. 'Can't have you breath-tested.' I stayed. 'This is your side of the bed. This is mine.' She put a pillow between us. 'Like virtuous Victorians used to do,' she explained.

Lots of hugging and kissing and laughing, but, surprising myself, the pillow stayed in place. I told her later, when I knew I was in love: 'Thinking I'm a one-night stand man might have blown it for me' and she'd said, 'I'm not much for flings, either.'

That was three years ago, before she left local radio for regional TV, the first step to the top, *News at Ten* as the golden grail; before her out-of-town assignments and meetings – and her fling.

Ah, Jesus, I don't want to think about this and, mercifully, have to concentrate when the gravelly voiced man announces: 'Where are they now? The part of our programme when we reunite long-lost friends and relatives.'

The show's veteran presenter is called Dennis McCarthy and he must have trotted out this introduction every Tuesday for twenty years or so, but there is urgency and enthusiasm in his tone which becomes quite animated when he adds, 'And our first call is from Helen Myers in Australia, a first in itself, I think, in this slot. You there, Helen?'

'Here,' says Helen.

'Must be the middle of the night for you in Sydney?'

'Just gone two.'

'Must be important to get up at that unearthly hour.'

Well, she says in an accent with a trace of Englishness in it, Arnie Gillman is important to the families who live in Harbour Heights.

She sticks closely to her brief. She gives his date of birth (but not place), and his mother's job and grandmother's address. She's vague about how long he'd been in Australia, but positive about his ten years at Harbour Heights, the date of his departure for England, his postcard home, the reason for his trip.

She repeats what she said in her letter to Jordan Associates, about wishing him well if he's found his family, but hints that the Residents Association can't keep the janitor's job open much longer. 'We'd just like to know where he is and what to do with his possessions.'

'Strange,' says McCarthy, stating the obvious.

'Mmm,' says Helen, non-committal.

'Have you reported him missing to the police?'

20

My heart misses a beat. This, my ex-lady once said, was the way local radio should be – live and unrehearsed – but this is a little too spontaneous.

'Oh, yes, but they drew a blank. And they pointed out that he is an adult and a free agent. We'd like him to get in touch, to know he's safe and well.'

Terrific, I think, my heart beating normally again.

She supposes Arnie's grandma will be dead by now, but his mother or other relatives might be alive. 'Maybe they've heard from him. Any help will do.'

McCarthy, who likes to yarn, picks up on her accent and she tells him she originates from Derbyshire, had lived in Sydney for more than thirty years and runs her own recruitment and employment agency. 'Head hunters, they call us.'

This cues him back to business. 'And now you're hunting Arnold Gillman.' He repeats date and town of birth and the address. 'Not a common name and you never know your luck on this programme. We've had tougher tasks than this.'

He becomes discursive again, asking how Helen knew about *Afternoon Special*. From listening in on trips home, she replies.

He manages a modest grunt and wants to know what to do with any information from listeners. 'Will you call back?'

'I've friends still over there and one will be in touch with you to forward anything that's useful.'

He invites her to say hallo to old friends and she reels off love to couples called Mark and Sarah, Phillip and Em and Nick and Karen.

Then he recaps names and addresses and date, tells Helen to go back to sleep and urges listeners to phone in with any clues. He tells her to leave the name and phone number of her friend for messages, says thanks and goodbye. She says thanks and goodnight.

'Well,' he adds, 'that was different. Let's see if we can help Helen Myers in faraway Sydney.'

What a performance, I think. I could kiss her.

# 3

St Bart's Court is a warden-aided residential home where you press a button on a metal plate by the locked front doors and speak into a grille.

Whoever answers is told that Mrs Bradbrooke is expecting this visit. The double doors buzz and, with a click, open on to a foyer lined with pot plants thriving in the heat that always hits you walking into old folk's residences.

Down a carpeted corridor is No. 8, where I knock. 'Who is it?' a woman's voice wavers.

'Phil Todd,' I call softly. 'I phoned you earlier, after you'd called *Afternoon Special*.'

Two locks rattle undone. A small, plump, bespectacled woman opens the door. She leads the way down a short, dark entrance into what's a dining-room, lounge and bedroom in one.

She walks with some difficulty, ankles swollen, feet slippered and splayed. A radio is on a cabinet beside a high bed tight to a lime-coloured wall. A teatime show which has replaced *Afternoon Special* is turned off.

She turns and invites me to sit on a couch with rough bronze fabric. She hobbles towards a green wing chair which faces a blank TV set, the main feature of a wall unit which also displays photos and forced spring bulbs in bud.

'Cosy,' I enthuse, taking in the rest of the room – a polished table with two high-back chairs in front of curtained windows, two sliding doors, one open on to a kitchen smaller than mine, the other closed on to what I guess is the toilet.

Mrs Bradbrooke doesn't respond, not one for small talk. 'You're going well back in time,' she says, sitting slowly, in the chair against which a cane walking-stick leans.

'Which Gillman lady do you remember?' I ask, just as keen to get on with it.

Both, she says. Old Ma Gillman was the harridan of Smith Street; always dressed in black. 'Felt sorry for Lil. Her ma was a Tartar.'

'What about Lil's father?'

'Never lived in the street. Dead, she said. Deserted her, more than likely.'

'So, at the outbreak of war, there was just the two of them?'

She smiles conspiratorially. 'All there ever was.' I cock my head to encourage more. 'We all knew, though it was never mentioned.' A pregnant pause. 'That Lil was expectant, I mean.' A nice old-fashioned word, that. My gran always used it rather than pregnant; too modern, even for pauses.

No stopping Mrs Bradbrooke now. 'Wore loose clothes for long enough. Worked in the mill till she was well on. When it became obvious Old Ma Gillman tried to make out she was putting on weight.' A smirk. 'On wartime rations? I ask you.'

I decide to open up a bit. 'She didn't have Arnie at home, according to his birth certificate.'

'Never knew his name till I heard it on the wireless.' She flicks her head backwards towards the bedside radio next to a mustard-coloured phone. 'Didn't even know it was a boy.'

'How old was Lil then?'

'Just short of her twenty-first.'

Just over seventy now, I calculate. 'Any idea who the father was?'

'I don't want to gossip,' says Mrs Bradbrooke, a bit late in the proceedings.

An ad lib is required. 'Yes, but Mrs Myers in Sydney tells me Arnie came here to England looking for both parents.'

'He'll not find the father. A GI, they said he was. A darkie, too.'

Lovely, aren't they, these pensioners who, like my gran, have never heard of political correctness and are too old to convert to it now. Not that I plan to lecture her. I'm delighted with her. She's just explained the deep tan on the coloured photo of Arnie. We're talking about the right man.

'Her first boyfriend, poor lass,' she continues.

'What happened to Lil?'

'In them days any girl in trouble went to the Red House, a maternity home run by some religious order. She never came home with no baby.'

'But she came home?'

'Lived in the street till Old Ma Gillman died, not before her time. Went back to the mill. Haven't seen her in years. Within a year of her ma's passing, she was married and went away.'

I dread the answer to the next question, but have to ask it. 'Do you know who to?'

'Oh yes.'

Relief floods through me.

'Matt Sharpe,' she goes on. 'Lot older than her. A collier. A reserved occupation in the war, you know.' I nod. 'He worked on the face with my Ernie till he was transferred.'

'Where to?' I ask, topping up on dread again.


Forest Town conjures up clapboard love nests and log fires. It should be the capital of Sherwood with a fairy-tale name like that.

Growing up in the next county on bedtime stories of Robin Hood, I'd imagined the forest stretching for mile upon never-ending mile. It's not like that, I discovered, when I was on a search for a missing schoolgirl. Never was, my guides explained. Life never is, in my experience.

The forest was a succession of hunting estates with open heathland between, cultivated fields now. You can, and apparently always could, travel miles without seeing any more timber than in any other part of rural England.

To get a sense of the place, imagine a Y. Arnold is on the main trunk, Nottingham below it. The left branch runs a dozen miles or so up the A60 to Mansfield, second biggest town in Nottinghamshire; the right stem up the A614 to Edwinstowe woods and the Major Oak, Hood's hide-out. That's if you believe in fairy stories, of course. Personally, I don't any more.

Between the two roads is Sherwood Forest, though you sometimes aren't really aware of it. Around the Major Oak the trees are native and deciduous, dapple shades in summer, golden carpeting in autumn. Much of the rest is pine, big, dark plantations, imported as fast-growing cash crops to replace the oak chopped down for boats for Drake and Nelson and pit props for the Dukes who opened the coalfield.

The Borough of Sherwood, the jurisdiction of coroner Jordan, is much bigger than the forest, stretching from the M1 in the west to the River Trent in the east.

On this trip, I've bypassed Arnold town centre and stuck to the trunk road with its landmark brewery, long frontage, with cameo friezes, the thirties at their best, overshadowed by a massive metal-clad vat, the sixties at their worst. On the square south side of the vat is the brewery's emblem – Robin Hood in green with bent bow.

The road rises through a cutting of sandstone, more red than yellow, to a roundabout where I take the left fork on to the A60.

Soon, more landmarks. On the left is the square brick tower of a water pumping station. To the right at traffic lights is the cop shop and a country pub next to it. The magnificent oak outside the gates of Newstead Abbey appears on the left. Right again, set in woodland, is the orthopaedic hospital where I went last month for that check-up the day when, for the second time last year, the ground was chopped from under me.

Dark now, the pine plantations on either side of the road just shadowy outlines. The rain has not slackened. Vehicles with headlights dipped spray through water running from roadside fields.

Skirting the town centre of Mansfield, not missing much, I know that I'm not ready to face up to her. Professionally, on the other hand, I'm quite enjoying myself.

The place I'm going – Forest Town – is a couple of miles beyond Mansfield on a B road east towards Edwinstowe.

The estate I'm looking for shouldn't be hard to find with the description that Mrs Bradbrooke gave. 'All the avenues are numbered,' she'd said.

Mini Manhattan, Forest Town, it sounds like.


At right angles to the numbered avenues, Main Avenue cuts through the centre of the estate steeply downhill towards what, in the darkness, looks like a large lagoon but turns out to be the green roof tiles of a sprawling factory on the site of the old pit.

There are more poles than trees in Forest Town from the scaffolding around houses getting new roofs, red tiles replacing grey slates.

Just gone five and the council office from which the modernisation scheme is being run is closed.

Nothing better to do, I decide on fifteen quid's worth of door knocking.


The bill has gone up to thirty quid. My hair has got its shower after all. The old brown mac from the car's back seat has dripped water on the front step of many a door. No one who opened them had heard of Matt and Lil Sharpe.

25

I wonder what's on TV, remember it's *Emmerdale*, a countryside soap, and decide to keep on knocking.

The next door is opened by a portly, bald-headed man, a pensioner. 'Sorry to bother you,' I begin for the umpteenth time, 'but I represent Jordan Associates, solicitors, and I'm trying to trace...' When I drop out the names, his face drops. 'Dead,' he says immediately. 'Both of them.'

At last, my heart sings. 'Where did they live?'

He pops his head out of the door. Rain pitter-patters on his shiny skin. He gives the numbers of the avenue and house. 'Sold, what? – five years.'

'Were you friends of either?'

'Why?' he asks suspiciously.

'Because a relative is inquiring. Routine, really. A matter of tracing next-of-kin.'

'Didn't know they had any.' He hesitates, then takes pity on me. 'Come in.'

Inside is warm, the only light coming from a table lamp with a heavy maroon shade and a TV set in the corner. Seth Armstrong is ee-by-gumming at the Woolpack in *Emmerdale*.

'Take your coat off.' More of an order than an invitation. 'Have a cuppa.' The mac is taken and hung behind a door. In a small, sparse kitchen, the talk is of the weather. 'Glad I'm not having my roof done today.'

'Cosier place than mine,' I say, truthfully. 'Homely.'

'Bought from the council. Five hundred quid. Selling for twenty-five thousand now,' he proclaims proudly.

Only when the tea is brewed and poured do we sit at a small round table. The introductions are made without standing again or a handshake. 'John Posnett,' he says. 'Everyone calls me Pozzie.'

Everyone at HQ called me Sweeney after the old TV Scotland Yard series, Sweeney Todd being cockney rhyme for Flying Squad, but I decide not to tell him. 'Phil.'

'Yer,' he says without more prompting. 'Knew Matt Sharpe from a youth.' He'd gone to work at the local pit in the late forties. Matt had already got twenty years in. 'Top man.'

'Manager?' I query.

He pulls a face. 'On the face. The biggest earner. Did his back, oh, late seventies, but they kept him on as an instructor. Cantankerous old bugger. You don't get 'em lasting that long any more. I got finished when the pit shut. Now they're being paid off in their thirties.'

'Did he stay on the estate after retirement?'

'Oh, yes. Wouldn't move far from the welfare.'

I nod my local knowledge. The welfare has nothing to do with state hand-outs. It's what miners' institutes are called, clubs with cheap beer, snooker and concert nights.

Pozzie didn't know Lillian as well as her husband. His wife would have but she'd died. 'A good bit older than her was Matt. She worked at some mill in Arnold. No kids, see.'

I inquire when Matt died.

''85, after the big strike. A staunch union man, he was. Disgusted with us working through it. He joined the industry when collieries were privately owned. Reckoned we'd live to regret breaking the strike. Reckon he was right, don't you?'

I nod, very positively. Notts miners kept the home fires burning during the year-long dispute. Attempts to picket them out caused lots of riots. One striker was crushed to death outside a pit near Edwinstowe. I got a broken rib at the gates of a neighbouring mine.

Again, I don't share this, but I understand. The Government owed its victory to the Notts miners' stand for democracy. Their reward was a stab in the back. Mrs Thatcher's successors were closing down a colliery a month. Those with mineable reserves were being sold back to private owners, the full circle, an act of cynical treachery.

Never, I've vowed, will I let bosses con me with appeals to my loyalty. The only loyalty I owe is to good mates. The only people I care about are the handful who took me for a drink and a chat in these past lonely, eight months, particularly this last miserable month, the pit of pits.

I ask when Lillian died, but he looks unsure. 'Lived here, what? – five years or so after Matt passed away; couldn't manage on her own in the end.' He held out his hands and clawed them. 'Arthritis. Her job, I expect.'

'Where did she go?'

'One of them Laven nursing homes.' There's three or four of them hereabouts, he adds, but he doesn't know which one and had only heard while shopping in the local Co-op that she had since died.

We yarn a while, telly and sport mainly. I'm an expert on both. I know what it's like being on your own – lonely.

Without interrupting the flow of our debate about England's future at soccer and chances on the cricket tour of the West Indies (both non-existent, we pessimistically agree), I ask for and get his phone book. Two Laven homes are listed under Laven Havens. One with 'Admin inquiries' after it is on my way back.

He's sorry when I tell him: 'Time to go', and offers another cuppa as enticement to stay. Reluctantly he stands and returns with my coat, sprinkling the flowered carpet with drops of rain.

He leads me to the door which I notice for the first time is pine, quite new, and I compliment him on the improvements. He pulls open the door. I see that the house opposite has a 'For Sale' board in the small front garden.

A thought strikes. 'The Sharpes – did they buy their place?'

'Yer.' He grins. 'Spouting his socialism in the welfare, then buying from the council when his party was dead set against it. Bloody marvellous.'

'So, after she went into a Laven home, she sold it?' I ask.

'Must have done. There's fresh folk in.'

I thank him again, turn and hear the door close on the night and world.

Don't fancy that myself. Not tonight. There's no soccer on the box. I think I'll keep on working.

# 4

Without wheels, it must be difficult, nigh on impossible, to visit your old gran in this Laven Haven, it occurs to me, spotting at long last a black sign with its name in white curly script.

I'd missed it, lost in a maze of unlit, unmarked country lanes, no one out in the rain to ask the way. In desperation, I pulled up at an isolated phone box and used the credit card number in the contacts book I'd retrieved at lunchtime from the bedside cabinet to call the nearest police station.

The officer who answered asked my whereabouts, which I read out loud from a location plate below the adverts.

'See a ride through the woods behind you?' he asked.

I craned my neck round for a view of a wide avenue between tall, dark pine trees. 'Yes.'

'250 yards through there, but I don't recommend it at this time of year.'

I've followed his instructions – about turn, first right, right again, and can see the name board standing well back among a clump of leafless trees behind a three-bar fence.

A heavily potted driveway opens out into an equally rough car-park in front of a gloomy Victorian building. A low, newish extension has been stitched, not altogether successfully, into its dark brickwork.

A dim lamp beckons to a stone-framed entrance in front of which three cars are parked, the whiteness of a Peugeot standing out.

The door is metal-studded, a black ring for a handle. Twist, then push. The hallway is small and deserted. Opposite are the double glass doors to a large lounge with assorted chairs, all unoccupied, around three walls.

A corridor leads off to the right. I take it, treading as lightly as I can, and tap once on a white door, marked 'Matron'. There's no reply. I do what private eyes are supposed to do, open it and walk in, shutting the door quietly behind me.

There's a well-filled ashtray on a desk in front of a curtainless window. On a smaller desk next to a grey cabinet sits a word processor with an uninteresting menu on display. A typist's chair faces it. On one wall is a cork board bulging with notices and picture postcards pinned to printed alphabetical lists.

With thumb and first finger, I lift up the sheets towards S. getting no further than M.

The door behind me cracks back on its hinges, noisily, frighteningly.

'Stand still.' Shouted, noiser still. 'Keep your hands where they are.'

Only my eyes move, along my shoulder and on towards two barrels of a shotgun. The rest of me obeys, easy to do. I am more than frightened. Everything but my racing heart is paralysed with fear, rooted to the spot. Last time I faced a gun I almost lost a leg. Not again. No more pain, please.

'Police,' I blurt, automatically.

'Shut it.' The shotgun is nipped to the hip of a powerfully built young man, all in black. His feet are set firmly and well apart. His eyes are unblinking. His neck is rigid. Muscles quiver on a square jaw; a hunter sensing a kill.

'Take it easy,' I hear myself saying in a trembly voice. 'Please.'

Over a broad shoulder appears an older face, pale, flabby, glistening with sweat; a face I'm so pleased to see that I speak the first two words that come to mind. 'Jesus. You.'

'What are you doing here?' An Irish accent, stiff with tension.

'Looking for you.' For all that I dislike (no, stronger) despise ex-Sergeant Dunphy, I'm delighted to see him now.

'You won't find me there.' He nods at the notice-board.

'Old habits.' A shrug, weak; the way I feel. 'Got a bit of business to discuss.' I emphasise 'business' hoping he'll substitute 'bribe' for it. 'Privately.'

'It's OK.' He speaks over the gunman's shoulder. 'I know him. I'll handle it. Do a final round.'

The gun is lowered. I blow out and suck in air, my first conscious breath in several seconds. 'Sorry, mate.'

'Try this again and you will be.' A low tone, disappointed. Reluctantly, he backs beyond Dunphy out of the door, soundless. With one final glare, he turns and vanishes.

I dredge up a thin smile and say, quite genuinely, 'Nice to see you, Dunph.'


Liam Dunphy had been a sergeant in Sherwood division, talking a good game in the Burnt Stump, his local. He was never to be seen when we were wading into riots on the coalfield picket lines. Not that he'd have been much use. Then, as now, standing there in the doorway, breathing as heavily as me, he carried the flab of too much boozing.

His contribution to winning the industrial war for Mrs Thatcher came back at the station, in the interview room, playing the hard man. Those days, interviews weren't taped, but written down on forms, supposedly at the prisoner's dictation. On closer inspection, one confession he took on an alleged assault was riddled with inconsistencies, bore more resemblance to fiction than fact.

Been at it for years, the grapevine gossiped; always got away with it because of a powerful old pal high up on the force. The deputy chief constable and Dunphy went all the way back to a double shooting. A superintendent from Sherwood was involved with Dunphy in an even earlier scandal over a confession that didn't stand up. No one was sure which of the two had protected him and fed him inside info to help him start up his new business as a private eye.

No protection, no getting away with it in the sensitive political climate of the mid-eighties, though. Dunphy didn't admit fabrication, of course. Corrupt cops never do. The deputy chief, old pal or not, busted him to constable and returned him to uniform.

Rather than patrol pit gates, he quit and set up as a private investigator, my new employer, Jordan Associates, among his clients.

'What you doing, I asked.' A jowly scowl.

I nod at the door. 'Who's he?'

'Never you mind.' A blunt response, even with the accent of his ancestral West Coast of Ireland, a birthplace that, along with his misconduct, had earned him the nickname of Sligopath.

'Mind if I sit?' I ask, lowering myself into the typist's chair, sticking out my right leg stiffly.

'Feeling dizzy, are you?' He walks in, slowly.

'Wouldn't you be?' I snap, nerve ends still jangling. I yank my head at the door. 'Faced with that.'

'Your fault.' He sits behind the desk. 'Now. What the fuck you doing here?'

'Making an inquiry about an old resident, Mrs Lillian Sharpe.' I lift my head towards the notice-board. 'Just looking to see if I've come to the right place.'

'Why?'

Difficult to tell him that I'm in line for his old contract with Jordans. 'Her son's employers are looking for him.'

'Why?'

More flim-flam required, I decide, anything to talk my way out of this. 'Taken off with their funds.'

He nods at the door. 'Why did you tell him you were still police?'

'To stop him shooting me.'

A harsh laugh. 'So, now you're leaving, you're going private, are you?' If he had any real muscle beneath the sleeves of his creased blue shirt, they'd be flexed now to indicate he didn't like being muscled in on.

I shake my head. 'A one-off. For a friend of a friend. Nothing better to do. What are you up to?'

'What's it look like?' A disconsolate sigh, an embarrassed expression. 'Security. Got the contract here. Consultant.' Sounds better than night-watchman, I suppose. 'I've had a bit of bad luck . . .'

He's wriggling so badly that I let out a little line. 'Heard about it.' I may be out of it now, I add, but I still read the papers and keep in loose touch with one or two of the boys and girls, so I know he's awaiting trial for posing as a serving police officer to get confidential info. 'Cheeky bastard,' I grin.

31

'By-the-Book . . .' the nickname for Deputy Chief Brooks '. . . has it in for me.'

'Me, too.' I tell him about the paltry compensation on offer, but not the law firm handling my claim. 'I'll be out of it soon. Officially. April at the latest.'

'How's your leg?' he asks, a standard question these days.

My standard answer has become 'Fine,' but, after Michelle Fogan's hint not to make too complete a recovery, I play on it a bit. 'Gives me a lot of gyp still.'

'Does it nag when it's going to rain?' He laughs with cheery malevolence.

Quite quick that, I have to concede.

Relaxing a little, we indulge in a where-are-they-now session on mutual contacts, grumble some more about Brooks, the deputy chief, while Dunphy has a cigarette.

Eventually, he asks, 'What about this old crow then?'

'Came in about five years ago'. I don't reveal that she's dead. 'Her son may have dropped by to see her.'

'How much did he nick?'

More fiction required. 'The new swimming pool fund from the tower block where he was . . .' I almost say 'security man', but change to 'janitor' and, clutching a figure out of the air, add, 'Thirty grand.'

His dark eyes glint, pound signs ringing up. 'Are the constabulary after him?'

Yes, and no, I reply. He'd been reported as a missing person, but not as a thief. The tenants were all business types who didn't like publicity.

'What's your bimbo in Missing Persons Unit leaking?' he wants to know.

Heather Hann and I were never lovers. Drink too much together at the HQ local, however, and that's what the grapevine will make of it.

'Come on,' I chide. 'Everyone's clammed up since you got collared. Ask for your own date of birth now and they argue it's Data Protected.'

He smiles rather approvingly. 'What's in it for me?'

It had taken him some time to get round to it, but he had finally read 'bribe' for 'business'. I try not to disclose my delight. 'I've told you. It's a freebie for a friend.'

'You don't turn out on a night like this for a friend.'

'Nothing better to do.'

'Balls. You're bounty hunting.'

I fall back on the going insurance rate. 'Ten per cent, if I crack it.'

'What's in it for me?' A greedy grin.

'I can't get paid till after I get my discharge or the taxman, as well as the deputy chief, will have me. April time's soonest.'

'That'll do.'

I pause, wanting to pitch it about right. 'A ton then, but only for information leading to her son's whereabouts. I'm not a charity.'

He heaves himself out of his desk chair and walks towards me, not light on his feet.

I swivel for a view of him standing before a grey cabinet next to a desk with the word processor. The seat of his dark blue trousers is shiny and baggy. He reaches on top of the cabinet for a box with a see-through lid. Inside, the red and grey sleeves of disc jackets are visible.

He lifts the box off, making it rattle slightly, and holds it to his big, soft belly. Black markers with white words divide the discs. The one nearest to the front is labelled 'Current'. There are other labels, too, but not enough time to note them. He takes out 'Current', and waves it once. 'If she's in any of our places she'll be on this.'

He hovers over me, telling me to vacate my chair. I stand. He sits, rolling himself before the screen, slips the square black disc out of its sleeve, pushes it into the drive, presses a number on the keyboard. I move closer, looking over his shoulder.

Names in alphabetical columns swim on to the screen. My eyes go to the S. then 'Sharp'.

'What name again?' he asks. I tell the back of his head. 'With or without an e?'

'It's spelt different on different docs,' I say, playing safe.

'First name?'

'Could be Lillian,' I reply, opening up more options.

He scrolls down until a block of white rests on 'Sharp A. L.' He flicks another key.

A long, low buzz and a red light flashes and I am reading as slowly as I dare about Alice Lorraine Sharp, widow, date and place of birth, former occupation, previous address, next of kin, other people to contact in an emergency, weekly terms, executor of will, name of family doctor, solicitor and ... I get no further before he speaks. 'Her?'

'No.'

'When she come in?'

I tell him again. 'About five years ago.'

He feels, two-handed, in the box and takes out another disc marked 'Deceased' which replaces 'Current' in the drive. More lists flow on to the screen, too fast to follow, but I wait for the S. then home in on 'Sharpe, L.' Next to it are the letters: HP. The same initials appear after a dozen or more names.

Dunphy makes no move to finger the scroller. 'Wiped.'

'Have a look anyway,' I urge.

He's looking at the screen, not me. 'No point.'

'A ton's a fair point.'

'Wiped, I said.'

'That's her.' Pointlessly, I point at the screen. 'She's on your files. There must be something on her somewhere.'

'She's died.'

I sigh, exasperated. 'What date?' No reply. I raise my voice slightly. 'You must keep records on them.'

Finally, he swings round, face clouded. 'Keep your voice down.'

I try appeasement. 'Just a quick look.'

'I've no access to them.' He nods towards the cabinet. 'You'll have to see Councillor Laven.'

'What about your rake-off?'

'Keep it.'

For several minutes I try begging and more bribery, double his rake-off. All I get are deeply troubled headshakes. 'See Laven,' he repeats. He stands. 'Look. I have to do a round.' He walks to the door, taking a thick, dark anorak from a peg behind it, pulls open the door and jerks his head at the corridor.

'Come on.' Rising, I make one last, cruel shot. 'Don't be Mr Jobsworth. Her son's Aussie, half-caste. You're bound . . .'

Instead of the expected flash of anger, he apologises. 'Sorry.' He locks the door behind us and follows me out.

At the front door, I turn back on him. 'I'll be back tomorrow.'

'Please yourself.' His eyes are down, no longer on me. They are full of fear.

I know because I'm an expert on fear, experienced in it.

34

## 5

Heard of Laven, of course. A political bigwig hereabouts. Such is my lack of interest in government, central and local, I'm unsure who he represents.

Know someone who would know, though. Someone for whom Westminster is the golden grail. Someone who enthuses about politics as I do about sport. Returning down the A60, wipers still busy, I think of her.

She was more than my lover. She was my best-ever friend. We could discuss anything, held nothing back. We were each other's sounding boards for thoughts, ideas and rants. Neither of us needed to feel alone against the world. Like I feel now.

Inside three months, we were together. Not a clapboard cottage, no roses over the door, just a two-up, two-down in a back-street terrace. A love nest all the same.

Friday nights we always went into town. I took her to symphony concerts. She took me to plays. We'd eat out and go home to make love for a long, long time.

We weren't exactly inseparable. The patch covered by Special Ops stretched from the coast a hundred miles inland and that meant overnighting on occasional jobs. She was away more often – London or union conferences by the sea.

Being a chief inspector, living with a journo – even one more interested in political than police affairs – could have stifled pillow talk. So we worked out a pact. Sometimes she'd ask, 'Anything for me?' – a code for me to give out titbits: pending cases to watch out for, background briefings. If I prefaced a tale or some gossip with 'For your ears only' she would never repeat it, let alone report it.

We always holidayed together, once stacking up enough leave for two-and-a-half weeks in Australia and ten days in Thailand on the way back.

The white sands of Koh Samui, sandwiched between light blue sea and dark green trees, is where that hammock vision came from to lull myself to sleep when she wasn't beside me.

Useful, too, in hospital after the shooting. She took a holiday to sit, day in, day out at my bedside, holding my hand, shaving me, emptying my pan, taking turns with my late-arriving mother to run gran back and forth, a fifty-mile round trip.

A gentle return to jogging, the physio recommended after discharge. Most evenings, as summer became autumn, she jogged with me, always a few snail's paces ahead, encouraging me to catch up. 'When I can keep up,' I puffed, 'I'm going to ask you to marry me.'

There. I'd said it. Thirty-eight years old and my first proposal. She stopped, turned, brown eyes happier than I'd ever seen them, and I staggered into her arms, a joyful, panting, sweating huddle. 'Catch up soon,' she whispered.

That morning of the medical appointment, she was on early turn, brought me tea in bed, kissed me quickly, said, 'Good luck with the quacks.'

On my left now is the hospital entrance. 9 p.m., says the dashboard clock. 9.30 a.m. last month when I walked up to reception. 'Message for you.' A yellow slip was handed over. 'Mr Phil Todd. Please ring Emma. Urgent.'

'Sad news,' she said from her newsroom. 'Gran's in hospital.' A neighbour had phoned our home, got no reply, but knew where to reach Emma from meeting her on visits and seeing her on TV. I phoned the neighbour. 'A collapse.' I phoned the hospital. 'She's very poorly,' said the ward sister.

I cancelled the appointment, about-turned to the car and halted at the barrier, wondering whether to make a day trip of it, turn right for Derbyshire, or left for home, to pack a bag and stay over. 'Very poorly.' The sister's words echoed in my head. A long vigil, by the sounds of it. I had to be prepared to stay at Gran's place. I turned for home.

Three or four letters were on the inside front mat, face down. I picked them up and dropped them on the kitchen table, turned on the kettle for a coffee. In the bedroom I packed a bag. Back in the kitchen I made instant coffee, too hot to drink straight away.

On the table was a letter opener shaped like a tiny sword, a memento from a half-marathon organised by the Round Table; Excalibur, Emma had dubbed it.

I sliced open the top envelope, still upside-down. 'Em, angel,' it began.

We often read each other's family letters and postcards from workmates, some of hers from men making rude jokes. They were pinned on the corkboard above my head. We had no secrets, only total trust.

36

This letter wasn't rude. This was no joke. This was ultra-secret. It was written by a man deep into love or lust or both. 'The most memorable day of my life . . . The one I've waited a lifetime for . . . can't wait to kiss again that birthmark of yours.'

She has this mark, like a jellyfish sting, beside her left breast, rather erotic. She's so embarrassed by it that she never sunbathes topless, not even on Koh Samui.

I read it twice, then went in the loo to be sick. I tore off a sheet from the kitchen memo pad and wrote, 'Opened in error.' The other mail was left unopened.

Gran smiled when I bent over to kiss her fevered, furrowed brow. 'Thanks for coming.'

The doctors were honest. If her heart didn't give up, her kidneys would; just a matter of time.

I stayed all day, got back to her home late. Soon the phone rang. 'Hi. It's me.' The standard opening from whoever was making the call.

She asked about gran and I told her. Then, 'This letter. I'm not going to lie . . .'

'Then don't say anything.'

'We have to talk about it.'

'Not now.' And I put down the phone on her.

Next day my much-travelled mum reappeared to share the vigil. Emma caught me in three nights running. 'Let's talk.' 'Too much on my mind.' 'Please.' 'Soon. When it's all over.'

In gran's final week, they made her very comfortable. I fed her soup in one of those plastic containers with a spout that babies are weaned with and Mum spoon-fed her jelly and ice-cream. When they renewed a drip, gran complained, 'I don't know why they bother.'

'Where's Emma?' she often asked.

'Away on a job,' I lied, knowing she'd never see TV.

One night she said, 'There are presents for both of you and Emma in my bottom drawer.' Then she smiled and said, 'If you're wise, you'll marry her.' My mum nodded enthusiastically.

The end came very peacefully. She hadn't spoken for some while. Her breathing became more and more shallow. Then, the early hours of the morning, a little gasp. Then nothing.

*

Among the many calls we made Mum left a message for Emma with her station's overnight desk man. I took the phone off the hook and slept after a fashion.

I stayed there, dawdling over the clearing up. When I was out, Emma and my mother were in contact. 'You're being too hard,' she scolded. 'Listen to what she has to say.'

I'm not inclined to listen to Mother on matters of the heart.

Just a couple of dozen attended at the chapel in the crematorium, Emma among them. We sent separate flowers.

Tea and sandwiches were laid on afterwards in the lounge of a hotel. She talked a long time to Mum, but not to me. 'Ring me soon, please,' she said. She left without a kiss. I'd never seen her eyes so sad.

I dropped off Mum, a longish drive, nothing better to do. 'Go straight home and sort it out,' she urged. Instead, I drove straight back to Gran's place for another couple of days, ringing round to find a rented house. Then I phoned Em to tell her I was coming. She was waiting, standing in the kitchen, when I walked in.

'I feel dreadful,' she said, looking dreadful. 'The time you needed me most and I wasn't there.'

Yes, she said, not weeping, it was true. A drunken one-night stand. Meant nothing.

'Meant something to him,' I pointed out.

I'd made no move to sit down. 'Tell me, when I go away on overnights, do you ever suspect, does it ever cross your mind, that I'm hopping into bed with Heather or any other policewoman or the hotel receptionist?'

Still standing, she shook her head.

'If I did – and you found out – how would you feel?'

'Hurt.'

'And would you forgive?'

'I'd hope to. I'd try to. With a bit of time.'

Time was what I needed, I said, accepting a gift-wrapped get-out. And I got out. Not seen her since. All over Christmas and the New Year.


'Hi. It's me.' It seems so long since I called her that I add, 'Phil.'

'Hi.' She sounds unusually dozy. We ask each other how we are. Both of us are fine, it appears. I lie and say my new place is fine. My leg is fine, too – news to it, because it aches. I'd rehearsed my opening line, index finger hovering over the button for the last figure in our number. 'Can I pick your brains?'

'Business?' She's sharp, even when she's sleepy.

'Semi. Ever come across Harry Laven?'

'The supremo of Sherwood? Often. Why?'

'Just that his name cropped up tonight on an inquiry.'

'You back on duty?' She's wide awake now and surprised.

'No. No. A civvy job.'

'Moonlighting?' A little laugh, mocking.

'Unpaid charity work. Your ears only.'

'Want to tell me about it?'

'Want to tell me about Laven?'

'Over a drink?'

'Over a meal, if you're hungry.'

We arrange to meet in a Thai restaurant that stays open late to catch revellers and shiftworkers like journalists and detectives.


She is waiting by a carved teak table in reception. She no longer looks dreadful, just awful, aged.

She's thirty-two, seems closer to forty tonight. Brown hair and eyes lack their normal lustre. Her complexion is ghostly pale. She forces a wan smile.

An English host in dinner jacket helps her off with her long, white raincoat. She is wearing a woolly, patterned dress, size 14. I know because I helped pick it, and she complained about the weight she'd put on from stopping smoking that jogging wasn't taking off.

'Not to worry,' I'd told her. 'People in jobs like ours should carry a little extra going into winter.' Size 12 would easily fit her now.

We are led upstairs to a window table overlooking an unusually quiet Mansfield Road. She'd devotedly read up on Asian culture and cuisine before our long trip and has cooked Thai regularly since. She does the ordering, asking a waitress in a trailing turquoise skirt for two beers to be served straight away.

When they come, she stoops to take a packet of Silk Cut out of her shoulder bag on the carpet beside her chair. 'Sorry,' she says guiltily, lighting up.

She has always been honest with me and the fact that she hasn't said, 'You look well,' means I look the way I feel. Two people, I tell myself sadly, shouldn't do this to each other.

I ask after her folks and she after my mum. Spoke to her on Christmas Day, I say, and once since.

There's an awkward silence when a selection of deep-fried meats and herbs is set before us. She takes a forkful, dipping it into a lime sauce, before asking, 'What do you want to know about Laven?'

'Anything,' I say, tucking into a salad that is mainly chopped carrot.

'Health chairman of Sherwood Council,' she begins. 'Just got the OBE in the New Year's Honours. A Tory who's going places. Mid-forties. Been on the council fifteen years or so. He made an immediate pitch for the fogey vote – the ageing population. It's an expanding constituency.'

My smile is for her narrative style, and should not be mistaken for understanding. 'How do you mean?'

'Set up pensioners' support groups. Evergreen Clubs, he calls them. Minibuses, day trips to the seaside, concert parties in the winter, second-hand shops to raise money.'

'Is he genuine?'

She looks uncertain. 'What started as a voluntary charity thing seems to have become big business. He's bought up several old country houses, extended them and turned them into nursing homes. He's got a Tory MP on the board of trustees.' She names Perry Cummins, a newish backbencher I've vaguely heard of.

'What was Laven before he set up his homes?' I ask.

'Property developer. Still is.'

'How did he raise the cash to start? Even rundown country houses don't come cheap.'

'Banks, I suppose.'

I understand little about money, just enough to know that in the eighties banks were throwing bags full of money at any entrepreneur. 'Is he a good councillor or what?'

'Very active in the aftermath of the pit closures,' she replies. 'He used his health contacts to bring in industry to replace the jobs lost . . .' her eyes drifted into the distance '. . . but I don't know. Take that HP lab opened at Moorwood. Big grants for what? Fifty jobs. The management is imported. Only a few locals were engaged. White coat, if not white collar, not a redundant miner among them.'

I remember the initials I saw after Lillian Sharpe's name in the records Dunphy brought up on screen. 'HP?'

'Hedges Pharmaceuticals.'

I nod, recalling seeing TV film of their new plant, a smoking aluminium chimney behind high-wire fencing where the pit head used to be.

'And now, of course, he's in line for Euro MP,' she continues.

I cock my head.

She laughs with sudden delight and some of the premature years on her face finally roll away. 'Elections in June. Didn't you know?' I give my head a shamed shake. 'But you know which team is where in the Premier League, naturally.'

My turn to laugh as the dishes are switched and two more bottles of beer are delivered from a bar festooned with wide-petalled flowers.

Her face goes serious as she spoons spicy squid with mush-rooms and onions in a dark oily juice on to a plate of egg fried rice. 'I'm not surprised,' she says. 'We put a lifesize cut-out of the present MEP for North Mids in a shopping mall and asked passers-by who he was. No one recognised him.'

Between hot mouthfuls I give her some, but not all, of the sad details about the missing Arnie from Arnold and the assignment from Jordan Associates. 'I'm doing a bit of devilling for them, just keeping my hand in. The trail took me to a Laven home.' Having worried her enough, one way or the other, just lately, I'm going to play down the shotgun reception I received. 'They were offhand with me, that's all.'

'And you smell a rat?'

Right now I don't want to expand on that, so I decide on a diversion. 'Jordans just want to make sure Arnie, when he's found, inherits anything due to him under his mum's will.' I sigh. 'It's not much of a job. Exercises my mind, though. Saves me from dying of boredom.'

My hope had been that mention of a will might lead on to a question about Gran's house, a safe topic, but she looks alarmed. 'Aren't you keeping in touch with your police pals?'

Oh, yes, I reassure her, and mention the handful I've seen for drinks over the holidays – Jacko Jackson, a retired DI, my partner on the inquiry that ended with me shot in the leg, Heather, Happy, Ginger and Carole.

She knows them from parties and we dwell on them for a little while. This gossip prompts her to ask her usual question. 'Any-thing for me?'

I can't let her go professionally empty-handed, so: 'There's a pending trial which might be worth a piece.'

She doesn't know Liam Dunphy so I tell her of his tainted past service and his job as a private eye. Last November, the 5th appropriately enough, he contacted HQ, posing as a superintendent from Sherwood, called Armstrong.

He gave out the super's code which a clerk fed into the system. Out of it came the complete Special Branch low-down on some union activist. The clerk became uneasy about the caller's faintly Irish accent and kept him talking till the line was traced to Dunphy's office.

'He got nothing,' I go on, wrapping up the story, 'but it caused a big stink, a major tightening of procedures.' It's not the full story, admittedly. I'll complete it for her later, with luck.

'I should think so, too,' declared Emma, a bit of a civil righter. 'It's a serious cause for concern. When's the trial?'

Soon is all I know.

The squid, but by no means all of the rice, has gone now, the beers almost.

I've reached a poignant, personal reason for wanting to be with her. I delve into my jacket pocket. Two small boxes, both in Christmas wrapping, appear in my clammy left hand. I put them on the pink table-cloth.

'Gran bought you this.' I finger one, toying. 'I haven't a clue what's in it.' I nod at the other. 'That's also for you.' Inside is a silver compass, inscribed, 'To see you safely home.' It's not really for taking on more travels we'd dreamt about. It's jewelled, antique, second-hand, for her dresser top.

She is looking down at them, unable to look at me. I know I must go on. 'Every time I open the sock drawer and see them, I feel guilty about not getting them to you earlier. Sorry.'

She is looking at me now. Her eyes are glistening, not quite weeping. 'I didn't get you anything.' She can barely speak.

'I know,' I smile. She was always a last-minute shopper.

Head down, she cups both hands and draws them towards her.

'Don't open them here,' I add, with a hint of panic.

She collects them up, together with her Silk Cut. She bends to stow them in her bag at her feet. She is partly obscured from view for what seems a long time.

'Listen,' she says, resurfacing. 'I don't want to rush this, because I know you need time, but I've enjoyed tonight and . . .'

'Me, too.'

'And?'

'It's a question of confidence.'

42

'Sorry?'

'Well, you go through life thinking everything is lovely, including in the sack . . .'

'It was.'

'Can't have been.' I feel my head shake. 'Nobody, not if they're truly happy, in love, contented, satisfied, call it what you like, gets between the . . .' I let it slide. 'There had to be something missing.'

'Nothing was missing.' She is speaking with great emphasis. 'It was lovely. I was more legless than you when you first came out of hospital. Look. Look . . .' Urgent now. '. . . there's no comparison to make because there was no comparison. I have little memory of it. Honest.'

'Still . . .' I shake my head, the subject too painful.

She waits, but I can say no more.

She smiles and sighs. 'What I was going to say was . . . well . . . fancy an old-fashioned Friday?' She colours slightly, looking all the better for it. 'I don't mean, you know . . . just a night out. Unless you get a better offer, of course.'

'I won't.'

'Well?'

'Fine.'

'Fine.' Her face is not quite radiant with relief. 'I'll look at what's on. I'll call you to discuss. OK?'

'OK,' I say, pulling out thirty pounds, two hours' pay for me. The head waiter is standing with her coat at the street door.

At her car, she turns and kisses me lightly on the lips. 'Don't work too hard.'

I long to tell her I love her, but all I can manage is, 'I won't.'


Knackered after my first full day's work in months, still can't sleep. Tried the hammock. Didn't work. Tried an alternative – walking hand in hand with the love of my life on a river bank, listening to the birds while Beethoven's 'By the Brook' plays in the background. A dark shadow seemed to be following us. Won't bother with the final fallback – dancing a slow minuet to Mozart.

I'll think of work and see if that works.

43

# 6

*Wednesday, 5 January*

Mansfield Road is chocka, the AA girl warns. A government minister with five mistresses is in deep trouble, the news reader reports. Five? I have trouble with . . . Concentrate, you berk. The met man promises more rain.

I get up and shower, feeling terrific. I have something to get out of bed for.

The phone rings as I'm mopping up what remains of a fried egg with bread and butter. It's just a few steps from tiny kitchen through tiny lounge to the downstairs phone on the red-tiled sill of the tiny front window.

A woman checks my name and number before introducing herself as someone from Radio Nottingham. 'Got more information for your friend in Sydney on yesterday's *Afternoon Special*.'

'Hold on a tick,' I plead, retrieving red notebook and pen from the pocket of the brown jacket tossed, slob-like, on the couch around midnight.

A letter had arrived which she dictates: 'This is to inform you that my former friend and work colleague Mrs Lillian Sharpe died in January a year ago. It was my sad task to break this news to her son on a visit here. Please inform your caller from Sydney that he was well, though naturally upset, when I saw him. I am equally mystified about his non-return home. Assure her that I will help in any way I can.'

It's all I can do to stop myself exclaiming: Eureka.

She spells out the signature 'W. Warminski' but, mercifully, gives an address in Arnold, not Warsaw.

Only a detective – and maybe Archimedes – will know just how I feel. This is discovery. Heather Hann, from Missing Persons, the ace operator who trod this path before me, hadn't got a whiff of it. This is a scoop. Exclusive.

Laven, HP, even Emma, are pushed to the back of my mind.


My place is in a side street in the city centre with parking restricted to residents only. After a week or two, you get to know which car belongs to which house and can even work out their shift and social patterns.

Down and across the street is a silver Scorpio that doesn't belong to the usual clapped-out collection which makes my three-year-old Cavalier coveted amongst my neighbours.

Dunphy is sitting behind the wheel, peering over the top of the *Daily Mail*, intellectual for the Sligopath, I would have thought. No one is riding shotgun with him.

I start up and head up the Mansfield Road. He is on my tail. Know what annoys me about private eye films? The way one man – or, increasingly these days, one woman – can trail a target for miles and miles. Tracking is a sophisticated art, involving a team of shadowers, one taking up the chase from the other in radio-linked relay. Any motorist who's been tailed for more than a mile should, in my view, be nicked for driving without due care and attention.

I let him follow me for a couple of miles, stopping and starting in traffic, wondering what worm one day's work has coaxed out of the woodwork. No point in a burn-up, I decide. He'd win.

I need to talk to W. Warminski before tackling Laven and, if the efficient Heather Hann never came across him or her, then pound to a pinch, this dodo behind hasn't either.

On the left is a row of shops that includes a coin-operated launderette and – would you believe? – an Evergreen charity shop. I pull in. Dunphy stops only half a dozen parked cars behind.

I get out and open the lid to the boot which contains lots of black plastic bags. Some are left-overs from countless trips to charity shops or the refuse tip that I made clearing out Gran's home. The rest was taken from the old love nest when, by arrangement, Emma was out. Mostly they are filled with thinning shirts, socks and underwear or sports gear I don't use any more. I pick and mix up a bag and walk across the pavement.

At the back of the launderette a bored woman sits behind a small desk, no customers to supervise. Behind her is wall-to-wall timber panelling, no rear exit. 'Wrong shop,' I gabble, about turning. 'Miles away. Sorry.'

Next door bustles with activity, a woman hanging up dresses on a rail, another serving a customer across a jumbled counter, a man with an armful of coats walking through a back door opened on to a concrete yard where a van stands, back doors ajar.

'Got these.' I offer up the bag to the woman behind the counter.

She flicks her head towards the man. 'He'll take them.'

He puts his load on her counter and takes mine. 'Whatya got?'

'A few sports shirts.' They sound out-of-season. 'Underwear. Some thermals, too.'

I follow him into the yard, through the rain to an outbuilding, piled high with clothing. He's surprised to find me behind him. 'Need a receipt or something?'

'No. No. Just moved house. Pleased to get rid of them.' I nod at an entrance to the back yard, wide enough to let two vans pass. 'I can take a short cut home through there.'

He doesn't say yes or no, as he starts sorting through my and Gran's old underwear.

A circuit of back streets returns me to Mansfield Road, a hundred yards from the parked Scorpio. I shelter in a shop doorway until a blue car with a 'For Hire' sign gets held up in traffic.

I move as quick as I can across the pavement, tap on the passenger window. The driver leans across the seat. 'Arnold,' I request.

He lets me in. Technically, he's not a taxi and plying for hire is against the law. Being of good humour this morning, I'm going to let him off.


A three-quid ride ends in a leafy crescent on a modern estate of houses and one stylish three-storey block of flats, built in deep red bricks, matching grouting between them.

Only after the cab has splashed away do I remember I haven't asked for a receipt to submit on exes. The hang of this job is coming very slowly.

For a semi-invalid, it's a hard, cold climb up two flights of concrete steps.

The woman who opens the maroon door is small, slim and grey, into her seventies. After a long introduction, she invites me into a short corridor which leads to a spacious lounge. She walks so sprightly that I wouldn't want to race her up the stairs.

We sit opposite each other at a polished table in front of a wide window with a sill filled with Christmas cards. 'I'm a bit mystified by it all myself, I must say,' she says. Her accent is not thick Eastern European, but thick and local. She wears a simple blue dress and white cardigan.

'So are the residents of Harbour Heights in Sydney,' I respond.

'So I gathered from the radio.' A troubled frown. 'Not in trouble, is he?'

'They're just worried about him, that's all.'

'I'm worried about the whole business. Can't make head nor tail of it.'

He'd knocked on her door in the summer, she begins, wondering if she could help him. 'With his colour and accent, I thought he was aboriginal at first. As soon as he showed me his birth certificate, I knew who he was, of course.'

'So you knew Lillian had a son somewhere?'

'A child, certainly. Mrs Sharpe and me, we go back to our own childhood.'

Her use of Lillian's married name should not have surprised me. Gran referred to her own lifelong friends with the same formality; out-of-fashion these days when a first handshake means first-name terms. I remind myself it would be regarded as impolite to ask Mrs Warminski's Christian name.

They went all the way back to Smith Street, in fact, school together, then the mill. 'She confided in me that she was expecting. Had to, I suppose. She was off for two months before and a month after. Never even held him in her arms, you know. They just took it ... him away. Doubt whether she knew if he was a boy or a girl. It was like that in those days, the war years. Still, it was for the best . . .'

In view of his institutionalised formative years in Australia this is open to debate, but I don't want to discuss it.

'. . . him being touched with the tar brush and all.' She smiles, not approvingly.

A few years later, Lillian married Mr Sharpe and moved to Forest Town. Mrs Warminski married Mr Warminski, a Polish serviceman, I expect, but I don't cross-check.

'Mrs Sharpe kept on at the mill. There were no children from the marriage. Mine, neither.' A sad expression.

'Until retirement or what?'

'Wish I had my subs books,' she says, mystifying me. She is looking down, searching her memory. 'Let's see. They finished us in '82. Too much competition from sweat shops in the East, they said.'

I am glad my yellow shirt is made in Britain.

'She went voluntarily a couple of years before that. Her hands were beginning to play up.' She looks at her own, which have knobbly joints.

47

'Did you keep in touch?'

Regularly, for the first year or so, for workmates' retirement do's and the final closing-down wake, she informs me, not so much in the last twelve years or so. She hurries into an explanation about not being on the phone and Mrs Sharpe's hands making letter-writing difficult.

A smile now. 'Once a year on Evergreen outings we'd see each other.' Clubs from all over Sherwood converged in buses every summer on Skegness for a day by the sea. They'd team up and swap their news there. She knew about the house purchase, Mr Sharpe's death and Mrs Sharpe's move to the Laven home.

'She didn't like it there,' she continues. 'Wished she'd stayed on in Forest Town and applied for a home help. She was sweet-talked into it.'

'Who by?'

'Councillor Laven. Who else? Know him?'

I shake my head.

'Known him years – since he was wet behind the ears. Not well though.'

'How did you meet?'

'Politics. At polling day counts and events like that. On opposing sides, obviously.'

'What's he like?'

'Not one of us.' A fierce frown. 'All this Evergreen business is as much for him as us.'

'In what way?'

'Him and his staff keep their eyes open going round the afternoon clubs and on outings for recruits to his homes.'

'It's big business,' I agree, not wanting to expand into a debate about the breakdown of the family.

'They charge up to three hundred a week, you know. If you've got the money.'

'And L . . .' I bite my tongue. '. . . Mrs Sharpe had?'

'From the sale of the house. Last place I want to be. Sitting around playing bingo waiting for the Reaper.'

Smiling contentedly, she gets back to Laven. 'He's shifty, you know.' She pauses. 'Still, he is a politician,' she adds, as if that explains and forgives everything.

I inquire if she knows that Laven is standing for the Euro-elections. Yes, she confirms, better informed than me twelve hours ago. He would not get her vote. I steer her back to Lillian. 'When did you know that Mrs Sharpe had died?'

She glances at Christmas cards on the sill. 'She sent one last year, but then didn't turn up at Skeggy last May. I asked someone from the Laven home. They told me she went in a flu epidemic in January, a year as now. Took lots of them, she said.'

'Who did you ask?' I jot down the name of Hettie Brown in my red notebook. 'So why and how did her son Arnie trace you?'

He took a coach from London with the rest of the package tour party the day before the Test in July, she recounts. He'd told a fellow traveller of his quest to find his mum. He showed him his birth certificate, with his mother's address and occupation. At the hotel, they looked up the council's number and phoned to be told that the street and the Red House had gone. Because of his mother's stated occupation on the certificate, they turned to Yellow Pages, looked up trade unions and found the Knitwear Workers' local HQ.

A long-serving secretary answered. Living and working in that trade at that time and place, she ventured, narrowed the field to two possible companies. She suggested half a dozen names, all retired or redundant members. One they called put them on to Mrs Warminski, the subs collector for the union at the old mill.

Christ, I think, ashamed, why didn't I think of that?

'He came on his own the first day the Test was on.' She nodded at the blank TV set. 'I told him what I've told you.'

'How did he take it?'

'Badly. I mean, it was sad, coming all this way, to hear he was too late. To tell the truth, he shed a tear or two. So I made him a cup of tea.' The great British panacea for all ills, I smile to myself. 'Do you want one?'

Thanks, but no, I reply. I'm coming to the end and have more calls to make.

'I told him about the house sale. "Son," I said, "you're next of kin. Get up there and see if anything is due to you. You've a right to what's left."'

Lovely, aren't they, these old-time socialists? They campaign against inherited wealth, unless there's something in it for them or theirs. 'Did he go?' I ask.

'Expect so. Said he would. Don't know for sure.'

'What were his plans after that?'

'Said he wasn't that interested in cricket. It was just a means of getting here cheaply. Had his mother been alive, he'd intended to spend a bit of time round here, like, getting to know her. He

49

wanted her to know he didn't blame her, understood her situation. Never got the chance, poor little waif, to tell her.'

One thing I swear I'll never say in this new job, as all TV private eyes do, is 'One final thing' but I'm thinking it all the same as I wrap up, 'And you never saw or heard from him again?'

She shakes her head solemnly, then brightens. 'Mentioned him to Steve, of course.' She reaches to her left to pick up a card – a black and white woodcut of the Major Oak without its wooden Zimmer frame. 'Season's greetings from Your Local Labour Party,' it says among the branches.

She hands it over. Inside is written: 'To Wendy, with thanks for your help. Steve.' First-name terms, I note; unusually close.

Steve Grady is district secretary for the Knitwear Workers union, she explains, an ex-councillor, chairman of planning for Sherwood Borough until his defeat at the last local election on which she'd helped stuffing leaflets in envelopes.

'Did he know Mrs Sharpe, too?' I ask, giving it back.

'Doubt it. If so, only vaguely. She wasn't very active in the union, apart from paying her subs. Not a member of the party or anything.' A fond smile. 'But she always said that she'd leave a bit to our widows' and orphans' fund because, well, they'd been good to her in her time of trouble. Kept her job open, you know. Gave her a grant. Never forgot their help, she did.'

'Did she leave the union anything?'

'That I don't know. I just mentioned to Steve that there ought to be something in her will.'

'When was this?'

She studies the card, thinking. 'When I saw him at our ward's autumn fair at the end of October.'

'Did he make any inquiries?'

'Said he would,' she answers. 'Don't know the outcome. Haven't spoken to him since.'

'One final thing, ' I say, forgetting myself. 'Where can I find him?'

## 7

A ten-minute wait on the swivel stool, in Matron's poky office, no light on to brighten the damp gloom cast by tall fir trees beyond a rough paddock.

The silver Scorpio was among six vehicles in the car-park in a space marked 'Director', Dunphy and his armed accomplice nowhere to be seen.

Time for an uninterrupted study of the notice-board on the lime green wall next to the grey cabinet, working out tactics. Just one visit here, a couple of routine questions about a former resident, has so panicked Laven that he loaned his car for his security man to snoop on me. Something secret and shitty has happened at this haven, I'm sure of it.

Eventually Laven brings a thin file in with him. He is wearing a plain grey three-piece suit and a dark tartan bowtie. Behind him trails a plump woman in a blue smock with a bosom tag that says 'Matron'.

He walks round and sits behind his desk, where Dunphy lounged last night, ignoring me. She stands guard at the door she'd closed after them.

He sorts through the file. His eyes are yellow-brown, owlish, too big for a thin, lined face, Tenerife-tanned, I judge, from a postcard on the notice-board to which staff shift rosters, an unproductive list of residents and the timetable for a trip this evening to a pantomime are also pinned.

He smooths the back of his hair, brown and neat. Ready at last, he looks up from the file. 'Now, Mr Todd?'

'I called here last night . . .'

'So I gather,' he interjects impatiently.

If he's not going to mention my shotgun reception, neither am I. '. . . inquiring about Mrs Lillian Sharpe.'

'So I gather,' he repeats. He sighs. 'Died, I'm afraid.'

Unlike a CID man, a private detective can't isolate and heavy his targets with sarcasm. They have no powers. They have to creep and scheme. I resist the temptation to reply, 'So I gather.'

He points to an off-white death certificate, a copy of which I've already obtained in a second quick trip to the county registrar's office after a cab had dropped me at my car outside the Evergreen shop.

'13 January. Almost a year ago,' he adds. He doesn't add the cause of death was bronchial pneumonia due to influenza or name the certifying medic as S. Walls MD, the police surgeon. 'Sorry,' he smiles, not at all sorry.

'Did you have a visit from her son?' I ask.

Distracted, he looks at the file as if he'll find the answer. 'She had few visitors, I'm afraid. We were not aware she had close family, were we?' He looks up urgently at the still-standing Matron, who shakes her head dumbly.

'After her death, I mean.' I am wearing my pleasant smile.

'Sorry?' he asks, playing for time.

I speak slowly. 'Did you have a visit here from her son Arnold Gillman on or about 1 July last year?'

He doesn't answer yes or no, but 'Why?'

'Because I'm trying to trace him on behalf of his employers and I think he may have called here.'

He swallows and blinks, not at all owl-like, more like a carrion crow who doesn't like the taste of what he's chewing.

I sit back, as comfortable as I can make myself on such a small hard seat. 'So can you tell me if he called here on or about 1 July last year? You'd recall him. He's Australian, mixed race.'

It's a straight question which should finally pin him down to a straight yes or no. He dodges it. 'We have no record of it.'

'Do you keep records of all visitors?' I persist, cheerily.

'Of course not.' He snorts it. 'They come and go as they please.'

I make a show of thumbing through my red notebook.

'Perhaps then, since his mother had died six months earlier, he visited a close friend of hers . . .' I look up sharply. '. . . Mrs Hettie Brown. Might I check with h . . .'

He doesn't let me finish. 'Poorly, I'm afraid. Isn't she?' He looks at the Matron who replies with a flummoxed expression.

'Very confused,' she confirms, looking it herself. 'Family visits only.'

Laven tries to relax a little. 'Why this interest, Mr Todd? She's been dead a year.'

'In a flu epidemic, I understand.'

They exchange longer looks, deeply worried. 'They happen from time to time in confined communities like ours,' he says quite sorrowfully. 'Look.' He eyes me appealingly. 'If there's a problem, we are here to help.'

I stick to the same fib I gave Dunphy last night and explain the problem is that Arnold Gillman has vanished with thirty thou of his employers' funds.

'Don't see how we can help on that.'

'If I find him,' I answer cheerfully, 'I find the missing money.'

'Wish you well. Sorry we can't help.' He stirs in his chair, wanting to bring an end to our interview.

I sit motionless. 'His employers' view is that, if he's come into his mother's estate, they might be able to take legal action to recoup their money from that.'

He fingers the file. 'She didn't leave much.'

'But she sold a house worth around twenty-five thousand before she moved here. That would go a considerable way to . . .'

'And how do you know that?' Finally provoked, he fixes me with a glare. I imagine his black shoes pawing the carpet beneath his desk, like a bull about to charge.

'From an old workmate of hers. Why?' My innocent face. 'Is there a problem . . .'

Again he doesn't let me finish. 'Much of it went on defraying the cost of her upkeep here.'

I cock my head. It's not a council-run home, he explains, and the state only subsidises residents when they have less than three thousand pounds in the bank.

I perk up. 'Well, three thousand is a start. Plus, hopefully, some insurances.'

'Just an age-old penny one with the Co-op.' He looks down on his papers, pretending to seek confirmation, but really he is trying to keep control of himself.

'Did she leave a will?'

Yes, he says, clearly irritated, but probate isn't necessary under five thousand pounds, just a certified letter of administration.

I look eager. 'That's a lead, thanks.'

He looks very uneasy, almost alarmed.

'A check with the probate registry', I go on, 'will establish if he's taken out a letter of administration. We might trace . . .'

He breaks in yet again, rattled. 'Can't have done. Her modest affairs were settled within a couple of months. Anyway, illegitimate relatives aren't entitled to seek probate.'

'Other than illegitimate sons or daughters,' I point out accurately. I'm no expert on the subject. I'd merely zipped through a booklet from the Lord Chancellor's department which the undertaker handling Gran's funeral gave me. It was one of the few paragraphs that stuck in my mind.

My knowledge has stunned him into silence.

'In whose favour was the will?' I go on.

'I don't quite see . . .' He is speaking very slowly, stirring very uncomfortably now. '. . . what you're driving at, Mr Todd.' Pause. 'Or should it be Chief Inspector?'

Well, well. Dunphy has briefed him fully, rank and everything. 'I explained to your security consultant last night that I am here as a private citizen as a favour to friends.'

The charge, when it comes, is disappointingly weak. 'That doesn't explain – not to me, a humble servant of the taxpaying public anyway – why you should be fit enough to be pursuing such inquiries so relentlessly, yet not fit enough for duty.'

I smile acidly. 'I also explained to Mr Dunphy that I'd be happy to go tomorrow, thereby saving the taxpayer the burden of my sick pay, when the police authority offers adequate compensation for injuries received in the public's service.'

He backs off. 'It was handled by a solicitor,' he replies. 'That's our routine when there's no immediate family.'

I smile cheekily. 'So who benefited under the will?'

He squares his shoulders, his Tenerife tan fast fading. 'I'm quite prepared to tell your defrauded clients that their employee didn't, to save them further expense in this fruitless inquiry, but not who did. That is no business of theirs. I'm sorry I can't be of more help.'

'Perhaps when Mrs Hettie Brown is better she might help.'

'In what way?'

'Well, if, as you say, Arnold Gillman didn't contact either of you . . .' A turn of my head takes in the Matron. '. . . maybe he looked her up, as an old friend of his mother's.'

The small room is silent. He must know I have given him the opportunity to deny he'd ever claimed that Arnie Gillman had made no contact; only that no record of such a visit exists. All a clever man, a shrewd politician, had to say now was: 'I never said that. He did call. I told him what I've told you.'

He is about to shake his head, then changes his mind. Very belatedly and distractedly he partially answers the question about Mrs Brown. 'Perhaps.'

It hasn't turned out to be the bullfight I'd half expected, no blood on the carpet. Not yet anyway. We'll lock horns soon; I'm certain of it.

He is shaking his head. 'Better still, why not write in, stating the information you request, and I'll forward it to our solicitors?'

It's an old bureaucratic ploy to buy time. 'Even better, I could call on them,' I enthuse.

'What's the urgency?'

'Well, we don't want him spending all my client's money, do we?' I lie effortlessly, enjoying myself.

'Residents here have different legal representatives.'

'Just point me to the right one.'

He is shaking his head again, sternly. 'Best if you wrote in the circumstances, I think. I'll see it gets to the right firm.' He beams and wafts his hands across the desk, empty apart from that one file. 'Now, if you'll excuse me . . .'

Rising, I smile across the desk. 'Later, then, perhaps.'


# 8


Well, well, I think, looking in my rear view mirror, back down the rutted driveway, seeing Dunphy running through the rain to a white Peugeot in the car-park.

They're really running scared, terrified I'll uncover what happened to Arnie, his mum or her money. Who's involved? Let's find out.

The way to crack a conspiracy, I was taught in CID, is to feed a titbit of info to one suspect and wait for it to come back to you out of a fellow conspirator's mouth. That proves collusion.

And that being so, there's nothing to lose, maybe something to gain, from letting Laven and Dunphy know where I'm bound. I've the perfect cover for going anyway.

I take him along for the ride, pottering at a steady forty for ten miles or so to make sure he doesn't get lost. I leave the car by the Co-op where I parked yesterday.

On reception Natty is surprised, not unpleasantly so, to see me. 'Ms Fogan's engaged.'

Not to worry, I reply, more than pleased. On the way I'd prepared an excuse for my call and tell Natty what I was told yesterday about a spare desk and phone I could use in the coroner's department. I'd rattle out a memo for her in there.

She directs me down a corridor beyond Michelle's and Old Man

Jordan's offices. At the end of the corridor is a door, marked 'Coroner's Dept'. I tap and walk in.

The coroner's clerk, whom I recognize from my time on Sherwood CID has his bald head down over papers on his desk. 'Hallo, Clarrie.'

'Sweeney!' His shiny face adds extra creases in frowning surprise. 'What are you up to?'

'Miss Fogan said I could use a machine in here to type a memo for her.'

He nods at an electric typewriter on an otherwise empty desk. 'For the use of odds and sods. Help yourself.' A brief smile. 'How's it with you these days?'

I sit. 'You know I'm suing the mob for compo?' If he does, he's not admitting it, so I go on. 'She's handling my case.'

A glance round for typing paper, but Clarrie makes no move to help locate it. He leans back in his swish chair, wanting to yarn about the job. All old cops do. Suits me, but I caution myself not to run off at the mouth.

A heavy-set, dark-suited man, Clarence Ogden is late forties, about to take full pension. His job as coroner's clerk is to be civilianised. He's applied for the civil post. With both Jordan and deputy chief Brooks batting for him, he's bound to get it, according to the grapevine.

From By-the-Book Brooks' point of view, it means one less serving officer on deskbound duties which makes the figures for the Home Office look good. From Clarrie's point of view, it means double take-home pay for doing the same job, the economics of the madhouse that is privatisation.

Retired cops (like he'll soon be) stay in the force's sea-fishing, golf or bowls societies to keep up with the gossip.

Added to which this particular old cop is, like Dunphy, a long-time associate of both Brooks and Superintendent Armstrong, so I'm going to have to be careful what I say. I do not like or trust Ogden. He'll do the gossiping, I vow, not me.

He wants to know the grisly detail of my wounded leg, and the even more grisly fate of the armed killer I was chasing in the fog on a railway line.

All this and the inquest that followed happened south of the Trent, not within his boss's jurisdiction as coroner, so much of the inside story is new to him.

He sums it up. 'And then some rent-a-mouth lefty MP has a fucking go.'

I nod, rather mournfully. Some opposition MP did raise the case in the Commons in one of those late-night or early day motion debates you catch a snatch of on TV, one member on his feet droning on to two other MPs fast asleep on their green benches in an otherwise empty Chamber.

He linked the killer's death on the railway line with a joyrider in a fatal crash during a chase, a rapist who hanged himself in his cell and a nutter shot while waving what turned out to be a toy gun at armed marksmen, effectively accusing the police of killing more people than they saved.

'Never looked down the wrong end of any gun, have they, these bastards?' he adds. Clarrie, you may have gathered, is somewhat reactionary.

In a sense, so am I. I grieve not for dead joyriders or cell suicides. 'If you can't do the time, don't do the crime,' my policeman-grandad used to say. And if I'd been armed on that railway line stake-out, I'd have got the killer before the train and I wouldn't be limping now. So I agree a wholehearted, 'No.'

'Pity it didn't happen in this patch.'

I ask why.

'Perry Cummins would have blasted the lefty bastard out of the water for you.'

I pretend not to have heard of him, almost true until last night when Emma mentioned him over dinner as a trustee of Laven Havens.

Cummins, he explains, is a good egg – the relatively new boy MP for Trent Valley whose west bank covers part of Sherwood. 'Very pro police. Big friend of the deputy's.'

More than I can claim, I say. By-the-Book Brooks is the one blocking my immediate release on health grounds.

Clarrie tuts sympathetically.

Time to introduce a new name, I decide. 'Came across Liam Dunphy last night.' I tell him where.

'What were you doing there?'

'A missing person inquiry for Miss Fogan,' I reply, 'to be set against my legal costs at the end of the case.'

He laughs lightly. 'How you getting on with her?'

'Seems sharp.'

'Too bloody sharp, specially now her kid's teething and she's getting no sleep.'

So Michelle Fogan is a mum, I think with a shock (God knows why I'm shocked) that must be showing.

Clarrie clamps his lips shut, turning off the tap of a mouth that's dripped too much. He seeks refuge in an old, safe subject. 'Dunph's been finished here, you know.'

I disclose that I do know.

'Always was a chancer.'

An odd thing to say about an old mate, so I probe to find out what's gone wrong between them, asking him if he'd seen much of Dunphy about Jordan Associates' office. Not much, he replies, guarded now. The litigation and coroner's sides were kept pretty much apart.

'Did he ever use this office for typing or phoning?' I press.

'Too secretive for that.' He pauses. 'Why? You taking his place?'

I flannel a non-committal answer.

Presently, he says he's expecting his boss and Doc Walls to return from an inquest soon, so it's back to the grindstone. I ask him where to find typing paper. 'Top drawer,' he answers, head down again.

I fill in time pecking out my cover story:

Memo to: Ms Michelle Fogan.
From: Phil Todd
Re: Missing Arnold Gillman.
Inquiries have traced the above subject's mother, Mrs Lillian Sharpe, to a Laven home where she died on Jan 13 last year. There is no confirmed evidence at the home of Arnie having called there during his summer stay in England. My information is, however, that he was informed by a former neighbour of his mother's death.

There remains, therefore, the possibility that he may have sought probate to claim her estate. Can we drop a line to the regional registry seeking full details of the will?

A bit turgid, admittedly, but that's the way cadets were trained to submit reports in my day. It's a clean copy, not a comma Tippexed out, but there's no sign yet of Jordan or Doc Walls, my target on this trip, so I tut, roll it out and start all over again.

The third draft is on its last sentence when Jordan and Dr Walls walk in. Jordan presses down lightly on my right shoulder as he stops by the desk. 'What are you doing here?'

Only then do I allow myself to look up. His wide, healthy smile reveals gaps in stained teeth in a thin mouth. His dark, greying hair is brushed forward to hide the substantial loss of it. Creases filter across rosy cheeks towards bespectacled brown eyes. He's holidayed in the sun since I last saw him.

My own eyes go back to the machine. 'Leaving a note for Miss Fogan.'

'Getting on with her all right?' His hand remains on my shoulder, gripping it slightly, friendly. 'Thought it best if she took over your case. She's our expert in that field.'

The shambling figure of Dr Walls is walking behind his back, not acknowledging me.

Jordan's gold-framed bifocals slip down a prominent peeling nose as he looks over my shoulder at what I've typed. 'Oh.' His hand tightens, then comes away, not so friendly now. 'Nothing to do with your case then?'

He has taken so much time he must have read it more than once. 'What's the problem?'

I ask him what I have not yet typed for the third time. 'Is it possible to get a sight of Mrs Sharpe's will?'

Of course, he says airily, and it won't need a formal letter. 'They're open to public inspection . . .' he looks across the room, addressing either Dr Walls or Clarrie, who are in conversation. 'Where are wills permanently lodged?'

'Manchester,' Clarrie replies.

'We've an agent there who'll dig it out and fax it,' Jordan offers helpfully.

Not what I had in mind. 'I've got a good mate who'll do it, thanks.'

Maybe I sounded ungrateful because he mumbles, 'Please yourself.' He walks beyond me to join Dr Walls at his clerk's desk.

Both are sixtyish, ten years older than Clarrie. Jordan doesn't look it. Walls does. Both are dark-suited, Jordan's smart and well cut to a short, tubby figure, the doctor's fitting where it touched on a tall, gangling frame.

Walls is peering at me short-sightedly but still doesn't recognise me. No reason why he should. Police surgeon sounds a grand title, but they don't operate in theatres. They are the first on-the-scene medics, certifying death. The cause of it is down to patholo-gists, often professors. Most police doctors are ordinary GPs with family practices, or have other contracts as company quacks.

I have met him only twice – both suicide jobs. He struck me as a bumbler. His short-sightedness is not his only handicap. He has a duff left ear which he frequently cups as he says, 'Say again.' He is known in Sherwood division as 'Say Again Sam'.

Clarrie Ogden is briefing them on that morning's death toll. When the conversation peters out, I speak across the room. 'This lady I'm inquiring about, Mrs Sharpe, may have been a patient of yours, Doc.'

Walls peers at Jordan, who looks at me. As they saunter to my borrowed desk, I fish out the death certificate from an inside pocket and put it on the keyboard.

They take up places either side of me, looking down on it. 'Mmm,' says Walls, dwelling on his own signature. 'Influenza.'

I incline my head round and up. 'Remember her?' He gravitates his head gravely. I hurry on, 'I'm looking for her missing son on behalf of Miss Fogan.'

They exchange frowns. Walls clears his throat. 'A year ago. Mmm. I saw quite a lot at that time. There was a bit of an epidemic.'

'Are you the GP for the Laven homes?' I ask.

'Residents are mostly seen by their own family doctor. I'm called there now and then.'

I twist towards Jordan. 'Was there an inquest?'

He looks at Walls, not me. 'Natural causes, yes?'

'All of them,' the doctor confirms.

'No need. Why?' Jordan asks, very bluntly.

'I thought there might be something on file about next of kin.' I hold his steady look. 'You didn't, by any chance, handle Mrs Sharpe's will, as her lawyer, I mean?'

He smiles down without affection or humour. I worry that I'm pushing too far too fast. 'Let's see, shall we?' He heads for the door where he turns. 'Come.'

I get up and follow like a dog, which is all I am really – a hired dogsbody.


'Natalie.' Fawn phone in hand, Jordan is standing behind his big desk in his gloomy office by the time I reach the door.

'Shut, please,' he says, almost snaps, then into the mouthpiece, 'Look for Mrs Sharpe . . .' He looks at me. 'Lillian,' I say. He relays the first name and repeats the last. '. . . in our probated wills, will you, quick as poss?'

He nods me to sit opposite him, a longish limp over thick brown carpet. Still standing, he pokes another button on the phone. 'Step in a minute, if you will.'

He listens, babbling 'but' two or three times. 'A minute, please.' He smiles icily. 'Thank you.' He puts down the phone and sits down. 'Is there a problem here?'

'Well, er . . .' I'm speechless by the speed of his actions and am trying to work out what I've said to trigger them.

The door is reopened. Michelle, in a lemon blouse and another tight skirt, darker grey, walks in, reprieving me. 'Hellfire, Peter.'

'Sorry,' says Jordan, not really apologising.

'I've got this late stuff on Grimston versus Hedges . . .'

'Sorry,' he repeats.

She sighs, exasperated. 'What is it?'

He nods at me. 'Your new inquiry agent,' he says as if introducing me. Circling my chair, she looks sharply at me.

Jordan says with a hurt expression, 'I didn't realise you had hired him as Dunphy's replacement.'

'I haven't,' she protests.

'He's working on that inquiry from Australia.'

She looks sharply – daggers, in fact – at me, but speaks to her boss. 'I actioned it over the hols. I was, after all, duty solicitor . . .'

'Yes, but . . .'

'He's got the experience. He's doing nothing. We need a legman on it.'

What seems like a row about to flare over lack of consultation ends when the phone rings. He lifts it, listens.

I hand over the memo to Michelle who studies it, sulking. She hadn't told her boss about engaging me, I realise. I've dropped her in it.

'Thanks,' says Jordan replacing the receiver. He adds to no one in particular, 'Thank God for that.' Now to me, 'No. Mrs Sharpe wasn't a client.' He explains my query to Michelle. 'I was worried about a nasty conflict of interest.'

Michelle has come to rest, perched on a conference table. Her red hair shines. Her eyes are dull, that up-all-night look. 'Would someone mind telling me what all this is about?'

Jordan cocks his head at me. Over to you, he's telling me.

All this has given me thinking time, but not enough to make it very good. 'Like the memo says, I've traced the missing Arnie's mother to a Laven home.'

She smiles at last, rather maliciously, aiming it at Jordan,

61

addressing me. 'You work faster than Dunphy. Sure, are we, that we've not been tapping into any official computers?'

'No.' Wrong reply, stunned. 'Yes.' And, for emphasis, 'Certain.' I am, and hope I look and sound, horrified.

She softens a touch as I take her down my truthful trail that ends with the news that Mrs Sharpe died a year ago at the Laven home. 'Well done.'

'Naturally,' I continue, 'I went there to see if Arnie had called looking for his mum. I met up with Dunphy last night and this morning I got the bum's rush from Harry Laven.'

They look at each other trying to make some sense of it and then Jordan passes the buck to me. 'What do you make of it?'

'I think – but can't yet prove – Arnie did go. And they're stalling.'

'Why?'

'Could be because they've pocketed what remains of her estate and they don't want her son to know.' They receive this theory in silence. 'In all honesty, I'm bound to tell you that I'm concerned about Arnie's fate.'

'Phew,' Jordan whistles, selfishly relieved. 'I'm pleased I didn't handle her will.' He leans back. 'I've handled a few from there, mind.'

Frowning, I cock my head, my 'how did that come about?' expression.

He catches on. 'One old client went in there and asked me to update her will. Several others flocked around, asking for the same service. A few of them died in that epidemic.'

'Who benefited under their wills?' I ask, point-blank.

'A few made small bequests, but the bulk went to the Evergreen Trust.' He shrugs defensively. 'I went into it with each very carefully. No one had close family. It's not unusual, quite common in fact, for dying people without families to leave nurses and helpmates sizable chunks. But I admit to a certain unease.' He is smiling, far from uneasy.

'If Dunphy's involved, I'm not surprised,' says Michelle, swinging her shapely legs.

'You're being wise, as usual, well after the event,' Jordan responds rather sternly.

'What event?' I ask.

Jordan avoids my question. 'Now you tell me that Mrs Sharpe's son may have disappeared after calling there . . .'

'We should call in the police,' says Michelle flatly, hurtfully ignoring the fact that technically I'm still part of the service.

That's the very last thing I want, so I hurry into pointing out, 'I've no proof he called.'

Jordan spots what Michelle missed. 'What would the police make of it?'

'Without hard evidence, very little,' I reply expertly. 'They can hardly raid a VIP like Harry Laven on a hunch. Think what the press would make of it.'

'If Dunphy's involved, we should definitely call in the police,' Michelle persists.

Jordan's face is deeply reproving. 'Never let personal feelings cloud professional judgement,' he says.

They look at each other unhappily. Jordan stirs uncomfortably as he tries to explain an exchange that's completely gone over my head. 'Not about Mrs Sharpe or her missing son, this.' He sighs deeply. 'It's to do with Dunphy.' He pauses, then plunges. 'He wasn't suspended by us. He's been sacked and won't be returning.'

I have to cross-check this. 'So his departure from here has nothing to do with his arrest and pending trial for hacking into the HQ computer?'

'Oh come on . . .' Michelle is sitting bolt upright, angry. '. . . tell him. He'll find out soon enough when he's worked here long enough. Five minutes with your nosy clerk and . . .'

I get the impression she likes Ogden no more than Dunphy and wonder, fret really, what she is making of me.

'Oh, really.' Jordan is smiling sardonically. 'Dunphy learned, too, and look what resulted.'

'You've seen his record.' She jabs a finger at me. 'He's no Dunphy.'

Totally lost, I throw out hands in the direction of them both. 'Listen. I don't want to come between partners . . .'

'Nor will you,' says Jordan testily. 'Suffice it to say that we had no complaints about his professional work . . .'

'What he means . . .' Michelle is looking at me and flicking her head towards Jordan. '. . . is that we didn't give a shit where and how Dunphy got the info as long as it was quick and accurate.' She turns to her boss. 'And look what happened.'

'It's a set-back, not the end,' Jordan responds somewhat sadly.

A smouldering silence follows, me sitting here totally baffled. I try to prise out more with a CID-style touch of sarcasm. 'Thanks for being so frank with me.'

There's a longer silence now. On her own, Michelle looks as though she'd talk. Jordan's face is set implacably.

I resume, 'So what do you want me to do?'

'Prove Gillman was at Laven's,' says Michelle, eyes glued on her boss's, 'and then we go to the police.'

Jordan nods unenthusiastically.

She has turned to me, but isn't really looking at me, mind far away. 'See me Friday in that pub near the crown court at, say, 1 p.m.' Suddenly she is concentrating. 'And don't worry. If we hand it on to the police, you'll still get paid for all the hours you're putting in.' She smiles conspiratorially. 'Retrospectively, of course.'

Jordan's face has retained a look of puzzlement since she fixed our drinks date. She turns back to him. 'Just heard that I'm first on the Friday civil list with Grimston v. HP. That's why I'm so busy.'

'I see.' He genuinely does see. 'Sorry. How's it shaping?'

'Hedges aren't shifting an inch.'

Jordan smiles encouragement. 'They're taking you right up to the starting line.' He turns to me. 'She's brought us an action over a drug that went wrong. The company has been fighting a rearguard action for almost ten years.'

Michelle slips off her perch, her resolve returned. 'I must get on.'

'Anything else?' Jordan fixes me with an inviting expression.

'Well . . .' I wait while Michelle walks out, still preoccupied, giving me time to frame an awkward question. 'What would the public make of not being told of a virulent strain of flu at large in old folk's homes? Shouldn't there have been an inquest or something?'

'Not if all deaths were certified as natural. Were they?'

I fall back on safety. 'Mrs Sharpe's was, certainly.'

An easygoing shrug to tell me: There are you then.

'Yes,' I go on, 'but shouldn't the matter have been reported to the health authorities, at the very least?'

I was expecting some loyal defence of his old chum, Dr Walls, either singing his praises, or apologising for him on the grounds of his physical handicaps. Instead he picks up his phone. 'Let's see if it was.'

He presses a number, asks Clarrie Ogden for Sam and says, 'That flu epidemic last year at Laven's . . .'

Something is said at the other end. 'Say again,' I presume, because Jordan repeats it and adds, 'Was it reported by us to any health authority?'

He nods now and then, says, 'Fine,' and replaces the phone. 'To Sherwood Council, as a matter of fact.' He doesn't add: where Councillor Laven is chairman of the health committee.

An even nastier conflict of interest, I'd say.

# 9

Outside the Co-op, the Peugeot is still in the slot where Dunphy parked three rows behind me, incognito compared to a white job with red flashes and 'Police' on the roof.

Two patrolmen I don't know climb out as I approach. 'Mr Todd?' one inquires.

'That's me,' I say, chummily.

'Superintendent Armstrong wants to see you.'

Another worm crawling out of the woodwork; more feathers ruffled. 'I'll follow you.'

That polite countenance patrolmen plaster on their faces, like pancake make-up, when they're nicking you, doesn't falter. 'Prefer it if you travelled with us.'

'Why?' I put on a surprised face. 'I can follow. Saves time.'

He looks totally untroubled. 'That was the order. You know what he's like.'

Well, only sort of.

Ten years ago, Armstrong wasn't called Strong Arm for nothing. He was already a superintendent when I joined Sherwood division in the mid-eighties as a sergeant.

Unlike many senior officers, he was on the front line in the coal strike, often one step ahead of the flying pickets, the result of tip-offs from sources he kept strictly to himself.

About the time I made DI and Dunphy quit in a huff on demotion, he'd been fancied for HQ flight deck. Instead, he'd been shuffled sideways into divisional admin.

These days, they claim in the canteen, he only ventures out to bore everyone over drinks in the Burnt Stump, the local next door. For a decade now, he's lived such a chairborne life that they no longer call him Strong Arm, but Seth, after the *Emmerdale* character who's seldom out of his village pub.

Sad, really, what unfulfilled ambition can do to a man.

No one has ever worked out the connection between Dunphy and Armstrong. There was no doubt that the Sligopath was solo when he burnished that fake confession in the strike that ended his police career. Armstrong had been with me at the time, on picket patrol.

But the feeling (no more than that) persists that Dunphy went quietly to protect him from some previous misdeed and, in return, Armstrong feeds him with fast, accurate inside info that earned him fifteen pounds an hour at law firms like Jordan Associates.

Straight away I go to work on that theory, to find out what Armstrong knows. Stiffly I repeat, 'I'll follow you.'

'Sorry,' the patrolman replies, flatly.

'Are you taking me in?'

'Those were his orders, if necessary.'

'On what charge?'

'Suspicion of posing as a police officer . . .'

'Posing! I am a bloody police officer!'

'But not in the execution of his duty, as we understand it.'

I can scarely contain my joy. It has to be Dunphy who told Armstrong about my snooping last night. Or Councillor Laven via Dunphy. I've got a connection between them.

I climb into the back, chuntering. For a mile or two, I sit in suitably smouldering silence and round about the Redhill roundabout I lapse into disturbing thought. A shotgun waved at me last night, a warrant today. Where, how is this going to end?

Not, it seems, at Armstrong's office, I think as we sweep past fenced, wooded grounds that shield his division's main station from public view.

'What's to do?' I inquire anxiously from the back.

'We're to take you straight to his local,' says the driver.

For a very private chat, I presume.


'Ah, Sweeney.' Armstrong's bewhiskered face lights up and his slim body straightens in a settee.

I'm not going to hit him too hard too soon. 'Nice to see you, sir.'

'Friendlier here than there, what?' He swivels his head in the vague direction of his out-of-sight station. He has picked the furthest corner from the bar, no one within earshot.

Without waiting for a reply, he stands, picking up an almost empty glass of whisky from a square, pine table. 'What will it be?'

I ask for dry red wine and, since an arrestee, which technically I am, is entitled to a free meal, a Ploughman's with blue Stilton and sit on a round pink stool, thinking: Odd interrogation, this.

He is looking his age, fifty. His wrinkled forehead is flushed. A couple of swift ones, I suspect, while he waited. His moustache is stained yellow from both scotch and cigarettes. He's on a lot of each, I hear.

Glass in hand, he walks stiffly some distance to a low-ceilinged bar fronted with decorative beer barrels. Like many senior officers, he prefers civvies to uniform about the office. Today's suit is a check three-piece.

He returns with a glass in each hand and announces the bread roll, salad and cheese will follow. 'And how are you?' he inquires as he sits again.

'Cheers.' I tip my glass, take a sip, wondering what card he'll play first – bully or bribe. 'Not bad.'

'Good health.' He sips his drink, more whisky than water, works the tip of his tongue on his 'tache, mopping up any that's missed his mouth. 'Sorry to hear you're leaving.'

I wonder who's told him that I'm quitting. It's not on general release. I wonder, too, if his info has come from inside Jordan Associates. Then again I've not mentioned to anyone there that I blurted 'Police' last night in panic when confronted with a shotgun. Maybe he has two separate sources. Such is my confusion that I don't respond.

'Why?' he asks.

'Why? Know what By-the-Book offered me?' He smiles without mirth at Deputy Chief Constable Brooks' nickname. 'Admin. Christ, I can't even type. It's just taken me three drafts to leave a memo on my compo claim for my solicitor.'

Clever that. It confirms where I've been, but hides the reason. 'I've upset him. Rowed last month. Told him to stuff his paper-work posting.'

'Always was your trouble,' he says, only half-joking.

I have to improvise a bit. 'He thinks I mishandled that train job; told Carole Malloy as much.'

'Lord.' He seems genuinely surprised at the involvement of the head of CID. 'Surely she backed you?'

I shrug a don't know. 'Brooks reckons I could and should have taken the gunman, instead of falling arse over tit, getting this . . .' I nod down at my right leg.

He nods gravely. 'Saw in the *Express* that some Labour MP had a go about it. Mr Brooks doesn't like publicity of that sort.' Armstrong is silent for a second. 'I certainly don't want you to go. There's a post coming up here . . .'

'What?' I sit back and let him lead with the bribe card.

'It's not operational and there's no immediate upgrading . . .' a hapless expression. '. . . er, PR.'

Disgust fills my face.

'Good career move.' He's addressing me in the clipped fashion of a wartime wingco. 'Did a spell in PR myself.'

Fat lot of good it did you, I'm thinking, shaking my head firmly. 'Thanks all the same but . . .'

He's looking a little desperate. 'I think I can fix it with Mr Brooks.'

'When did you speak to him?' I ask idly.

He evades it. 'Be patient on promotion. You university types on the fast track are all the same.'

'Look.' I force a friendly smile. 'I appreciate your concern, but I've made up my mind. I'll go private once I've got my pay-off. It's the in-thing these days.'

He empties his glass, puts it on the table. I gather it up immediately, rising, hoping to signal the end of this particular rubber. 'Another?'

The barman busy, I wait patiently and happily, giving Armstrong time to think through his next move. While I'm away from the table, my lunch is delivered to it. He has not ordered anything for himself.

I head back to our table with a delightful, if dank, view of a sloping cricket field with a tree-topped hill beyond. 'Cheers,' I say again, handing him his refilled glass and, sitting opposite again, noticing how serious his face has become.

'I'm very disappointed in you,' he recommences.

Not knowing if this is a new lead, I just say sorry and break and butter my roll.

'We go back a long way, been very close.'

So close that he never came to see me once in hospital, but I nod a lie. A slice of cheese, soft and smooth, not crumbly, is added to the bread.

'What are you doing tramping around my patch on a missing

person inquiry without informing me?' He's looking very upset now. 'That's not on.'

'There's a crossed line somewhere,' I say, trying to eat at the same time.

'You're not a private detective yet, you know. You're still serving with obligations. What you're doing . . .'

'Who's been stirring it for me with you – Dunphy or Councillor Laven?' I mumble with full mouth.

Though I'm eating, he lights up a cigarette, thinks, then decides not to depart from a script that's beginning to sound rehearsed. 'What you're doing is against regulations.'

I swallow, savouring the creamy, tangy taste, and remain conciliatory. 'Whoever it is has badly misinformed you.'

'Very much doubt it,' he answers sullenly.

'Hand on heart . . .' I put it there, smeared knife in it. '. . . all I've been doing is filling in some spare time looking for a missing employee of a friend in Australia.'

I empty my mouth, the ripe taste lingering. 'Look, even if what Dunphy or Laven has been telling you is true . . .' He frowns, more puzzled than embarrassed. '. . . I could understand Heather Hann in Missing Persons being miffed. It was her case. The missing Arnold Gillman was never down to you.'

'It is our patch.'

'But not your inquiry and never was.' I decide to up the pace. 'You snatch me off the streets . . .'

'Ridiculous.'

'You make me a job offer. You dispatch a patrol with orders to arrest me . . .'

His face is very flustered. 'Just to get you here.'

'To read me the riot act? What's going on?'

He rubs his 'tache with the side of his nicotine-stained index finger, his half-smoked cigarette almost singeing his whiskers. 'Listen, old chap. You're disaffected, disillusioned. I understand that. Don't throw away a good career. You'll be discharged without a penny pension if you go on like this. Certain people are out to get you.'

'Like who?'

He sidesteps it. 'Protect your pension. That's all.'

'But I'm doing nothing wrong.' I put innocent protest in my tone.

'You're making big waves. Upsetting powerful people; a dangerous game. I'm telling you nicely because I like you.' He screws out his cigarette, swallows his drink in one, preparing to leave.

I slide my plate to one side. 'He's been on to you, hasn't he – your old mate Dunphy? Or was it Councillor Laven?'

His face darkens. Had he not swallowed his drink he would have been spluttering now.

'One or the other has,' I continue. 'Only they know I just happened to mention I was still in the police last night.'

I'm not going to mention I'd had a shotgun waved at me. I don't want him making more inquiries, messing everything up.

He is shaking his head vigorously. 'You know consorting with an ex-officer like Dunphy who left in shady circumstances can get you on a fizzer.'

'You're giving me the witch's warning on his behalf, aren't you? Or Councillor Laven's?'

A hurt expression. 'Neither.'

I lean forward, elbows on the table, insolently. 'And there you sit, lecturing me about consorting with a bombed-out bobby.'

He is shaking his head, sadly, not angrily. 'Gossip. Heard it, of course. Rumours. Dunphy's got me in more trouble than you're now in with Brooks.'

'You?' I mock.

'Not funny. Heard about it?'

I shake my head.

'You know Dunphy's awaiting trial?'

Yes, I say, but not the details.

Armstrong is in his element now, holding court. 'Dunphy phoned up HQ, pretending he was me. He gave my code number and asked for some sensitive gen about a chap called Steve Grady. Know him?'

Not wanting to interrupt the flow, I shake my head again.

'Big union man in textiles, friend of mine.'

'What did Dunphy want the info for?'

'Won't say under questioning, apparently.'

'You suspect blackmail?'

'Dunphy's not our pinch. Special Branch did him.'

'Come on. You can't warn me off and keep me in the dark.'

'This is grapevine, OK?'

Unconfirmed, he means, and I nod.

'Dunphy declined to give a statement and is denying every-thing. Grady claims he doesn't know why he was the subject of Dunphy's interest.'

'If Grady doesn't want to complain, it's got to be highly personal,' I venture.

Armstrong shrugs, unsure. 'Brooks had me in about it. He tried to pin several official leaks on me. Just because I've known Dunphy years. Beware of him. He's a bastard.'

First, Clarrie Ogden in the coroner's department warns me off Dunphy. Now Armstrong. Someone doesn't want me close to him. He must be the weak link.

'You know what people say about you and Dunphy,' I say, very quietly, 'what they think?'

He shakes his head very sadly. 'I know what Brooks thinks. He thinks I'm Dunphy's mole. It just isn't true.'

'So what happened?'

'I was in the clear. And you were part of my alibi.'

I don't seek to hide my shock.

'That Handel concert at the Royal. The Fireworks. Saw you with your lady.'

'I didn't see you.'

'You were at the bar. I said hallo to your girl. Wearing a baggy black trousers suit and kipper tie, wasn't she?' It sounds like Emma. 'Did they check it out with her?'

'She never told me.'

He gets back to the narrative. 'That evening my number was given on a records check, but, thank Christ, the clerk rumbled it wasn't my voice.'

'And the caller was Dunphy posing as you?' I cross-check. 'What did he want?'

'Told you.' He mumbles as if he is eating. 'Gen on Steve Grady.'

'About what?'

No response.

'For whom?'

'Some client firm, the theory is.'

'Some firm who's doing what?' I'm having to prize it out of him.

'An upcoming case at crown court.'

'Name of?'

'Can't tell you that.' He's pulling a pained face. 'Look. Only a handful of people were at the inquiry. Very hush-hush. They'll trace any leak straight back to me. I'm only telling you this to warn you what trouble you can drop yourself in.' He leans forward confidentially. 'I'm just advising you. I'm just the messenger and the message is: "Stay well clear."'

I lean forward, aggressively, 'Yes, but who sent the message?'

'You work it out,' he snaps, face closed.

I'm going to have to do it by process of elimination. 'Ever hear from Dunphy these days?'

'Don't want to. And if you're stupid enough to become a private eye, you stay away from him, too.'

I have one last card to play. 'Know who Dunphy's working for now – as a night-watchman?'

'Don't want to know.'

'Harry Laven. Was Laven's name or company mentioned at this inquiry?'

'No.' Firm, final.

'Whose was?'

'Can't tell you.'

'Come on.'

'Don't ask.'

'If I find out from elsewhere, will you confirm it?'

'We'll see.'

He looks at his watch and announces he has a road safety meeting in half an hour. I don't express the hope that he's not driving.

He half stands, then sits again. 'If I can't talk you into staying and you do go solo, bear me in mind.'

I hold my breath, sure he's about to offer the same sort of deal I suspect he had going with Dunphy. 'In what way?'

'You're bound to hear things. Pass 'em on.'

'What's in it for me?'

'Cash. Out of the informants' fund. There'll be no quid pro quo on info. I want no misunderstandings. Right?'

'Right,' I agree. We exchange home phone numbers on sheets torn from my notebook.

'Your lift will await you in the car-park in five minutes,' he says. He rises, nods goodbye. We promise to keep in touch.

Well, I'm thinking in the five minutes I'm sitting alone, he's either straight and much maligned or he's bent and a brilliant actor.


'Back to your car then, sir,' the peak-capped observer queries, opening the back door.

'Leave it where it is,' I reply with an embarrassed grin. 'Your super has treated me to one too many. Home instead.'

Passing by Arnold, I have a happy vision of Dunphy keeping observations on a car that's not going to move for the rest of the day.

# 10

They drop me at the clock tower, all that remains of a Victorian railway station pulled down to make way for a sprawling shopping centre packed with bedraggled bargain hunters mooching around the new year sales.

Much less crowded is a square, grey office block on the other side of nose-to-tail traffic on Mansfield Road. Apart from an elderly woman clerk, the second-floor suite where the Knitwear Workers have their union's regional HQ is deserted.

Mr Grady, she informs me, has added three lieu days to his holiday and won't be on duty till Friday. 'Can I help?'

Maybe, I think, if she is the veteran receptionist who took the call Arnie Gillman made from his hotel and put him on the trail that led to his mum's old workmate, Mrs Warminski.

Then again she might disturb the holidaying Grady with the unwelcome news that a stranger has been making inquiries about a missing son of a late member and a legacy due to his widows and orphans. I want to catch him cold so I tell her I'll catch him later and make a quick exit.

Back on the wet streets, where the white Christmas lights seem to have lost their sparkle, I mingle with the laden shoppers.

My car, it occurs to me, is parked about five minutes' drive from Grady's home. In my mind's eye, I see Dunphy's head against the rest of the driving seat, catching up on last night's lost sleep.

I decide to have a kip myself.

A ringing phone ends thirty quid's worth of sleep. 'Hi. It's me.'

'Hi.'

'Listen,' we say simultaneously, then laugh briefly in unison. 'Ladies first,' I say, more in need of time to blink my brain back into focus than out of politeness.

73

'Why thank you.' Emma sounds delighted. 'This Friday at the Royal. All Mozart, including Symphony No. 29. Remember?'

Remember? So well that my heart misses a slow beat.

We heard it in Paris, the city after which the work was named. Walking arm-in-arm back to the hotel, little more than a pension, near the Notre Dame, I couldn't get the middle movement, a minuet, out of my head. Out loud I deeee-dar, dedar, de-dummed a few bars and, to indulgent smiles from passers-by, we danced a few stately steps.

'Will I ever forget?' I reply.

She asks if I fancy it and I say sure. She volunteers to fix the tickets and we arrange to meet in a bar, a favourite haunt close to the concert hall, just five minutes' walk from this place. 'Your turn,' she says invitingly.

Musical memories remind me of something I had almost forgotten in my doziness. 'Remember that Handel concert?'

'The Royal Fireworks?'

'Yes. Did a superintendent called Armstrong chat you up?'

'Why?'

'Saw him today and he mentioned he'd seen you. You didn't mention him to me, that's all.'

'Should I have done?' She sounds resentful, as though I am checking on her.

'No, no,' I reassure her. 'It would just help pigeon-hole something in my mind, if you'd remembered.'

'What's he like? Tall, thin, RAF moustache?'

'That's him.'

'We just exchanged pleasantries. He did give his regards to you. You were at the bar. Sorry. Was it important?'

'No, no. No problem.' An awkward pause and I badly need a new topic. 'This MP Peregrine Cummins, you mentioned last night . . .'

'Perry, if you don't mind,' she interrupts, voice warm again. 'That's what he likes to be called in this classless society.'

'What do you know about him?'

'Why?' she asks sharply.

I take avoiding action. 'All I know is that he's a new boy Tory MP for Trent Valley.'

'My, my. You have been doing your homework.' Her voice lowers in tone. 'Now answer the question. Why?'

'His name cropped up again in conversation on this missing Aussie inquiry. Now answer mine.'

'Family-wise, sleaze free. A barrister.'

'Never heard of him.'

'Civil, where the money is. Sees himself as a future social security minister, swingeing cuts etc. Ruffled a few feathers in some leaked right-wing think tank report condemning artificially prolonging life. It came out sounding a bit like they wanted to pop a pill in old folk's Horlicks that would . . .' She gasps, very faintly. 'Sorry.'

She's sorry, I know, because she's thinking of me losing Gran, wishing she hadn't been so flip so soon. I also know a flip response will ease any guilt. 'It would certainly cut down on pension pay-outs.'

There's a relieved little laugh. 'He denied it, of course. Claimed it was a discussion paper and blamed the media for misreporting it. They always do.'

More than once she's told me how the government plants untraceable leaks on controversial proposals and awaits public reaction. If it's favourable, they act, claiming all the credit. If there's an outcry, they will pretend nothing was further from their mind and it's all been made up by the media.

I move on. 'Can you save my legs going round to the library and look him up? You know, present and past directorships and, er . . . is there some register?'

'Of members' interests. It's lodged in the vote office at the Commons. I'll get our Westminster man to have a look.'

I ask where I might get hold of Cummins. Parliament is in recess, she says, which means he could be at home in a village on the west bank of his constituency. 'I can phone on some pretext, if you like, to check.'

I say thanks and she asks her usual, 'Anything for me?'

All I have to offer is a medical negligence case coming up at the crown court on Friday morning.

Heard about it, she says, at a forward planning conference. A young Welsh widow is suing Hedges Pharmaceuticals, alleging the husband suffered fatal side-effects from a bronchitis drug when taken ill during the coal strike ten years ago. 'The company's denying liability and every time it gets close to a full hearing they pull a delaying tactic.'

'Are they trying to avoid bad publicity?'

'If so, it's working.' I hear keys tapping. 'They're up another ten at close today. Been bullish for months. They must have something good in their labs, wouldn't you say?'

I say nothing, because I know even less about the City and science than I do about politics.

'Phone you with this tonight, shall I?' she continues.

First thing tomorrow, I suggest, because I'm off to the theatre.

'Heavy date?' Her tentative tone now.

'With a busload of old ladies to a panto.'

We laugh as we say goodbye.


In the darkened bedroom I lie for a minute or two, wishing two days away to Friday when we'll be together, wondering – no, worrying over – how the evening will end.

Rolling off the bed, I don't turn on the lamp. I peer out into the street from behind the curtains.

There's a dirty Nissan Patrol, but no parking permit, on the kerbside opposite. No one's at the wheel, but that doesn't mean Dunphy's not made a vehicle change and is getting better at observation with all the practice he's having.

Not wanting a TV screen flickering, I listen to the six o'clock news on radio, then swill my face with cold water and change shirts in the windowless bathroom to the monotonous drone of an automatic odour expeller.

Downstairs I step out of the kitchen door into a slabbed back yard with plastic pots containing last summer's bedding plants, frosted brittle and brown. The only time I take the air here is to dump take-home curry cartons in a sturdy zinc dustbin to save the whole house smelling all next day.

I pull the dustbin over the slabs to a brick wall topped with trellis. I step on to the white coping stone with my left leg and heave my right leg over the flimsy fence. The left follows nimbly. Palms on the coping stone, I lower myself into a puddle on a dark, unmade footpath which leads to a side street round the corner from my place. Two more side streets and two minutes later I'm on the brightly lit Mansfield Road.


Waiting for the No. 63 in the concrete cold bus station next to the shopping centre, I toy with the idea of getting off at Arnold and collecting my motor. But I'm unsure if Dunphy was in that Nissan Patrol or still staking out the car-park.

'Mansfield,' I request when I climb aboard the red single-decker. 'Return.' The ticket will have to act as receipt for the £3.05 it costs.

The bus starts its long, gradual climb out of town. Just beyond the flat Forest playing fields is a big, modern hotel with saturated flags limp on poles where I once Sunday lunched Gran, so, rather than Em, I'll think of her, easier now with the passing of a little more time, comforting, in fact.

She and Grandpa brought me up in a beautiful, peaceful village in the Peaks, where he was the local bobby. He gave me sport and country crafts, she music, and both much love.

I was born, not in the village, but at a university town where, in the mid-fifties, my mum was doing more screwing than studying. My arrival caused only a temporary lull in both. Like Arnie from Arnold, my birth certificate is also blank under 'Father'.

She dumped me on her folks, went back to college and got a 2.2 in social sciences. A place with her new fella in London was on offer, but declined as unsuitable on my behalf by my grandparents without much argument from Mum. Just as well, as it turned out. Her first marriage was over within two years.

In the flower power sixties she smoked dope and travelled out east and married again in India. She claimed her second husband, a hippy Yank, had paid the local head man two sows-in-gilt for her and Grandpa thought he'd been overcharged. That lasted two years, too.

She often wrote and sometimes visited. We're closer now than we've ever been. Emma's doing, that. There, I'm thinking of her again, but she did bring us together on holidays.

I regard her as a big sister I never had and she, I'm sure, views me as a little brother. She's settled down with a husband boring to the point of tedium while she remains amusingly eccentric and easily manipulated.

I pay not the slightest heed to any advice I get from her, but, yes, I am fond of her, really do like her. Now, my grandparents, well, what can I say other than that I loved them.

Fortyish, they were, when they took me in. Many neighbours seemed to regard me as an unplanned latecomer. Those that knew better made no snide remarks about my illegitimacy – not to me anyway.

Often he took me on his rural beat. By the time I was ten I could identify most game fish and birds, knew how to catch and cook them, and could tell on sight the difference between a traditional 'one for the pot' poacher and a pro who slaughtered wholesale.

His promotion to sergeant came when I was between schools.

His posting was to the south of the shire, the arse end of the county, all clapped-out pits and closing-down mills.

Having lived so long in a station house, they invested their savings into their own home, a detached pre-war house with leaded windows and a walled garden.

It was on a bus like this that I used to travel to the comprehensive school in the nearest town. It was stepping off the school bus one dark evening that she met me to tell me he had collapsed and died, just a year into retirement.

Only once since have I lived through such pain and that period is now, right now; far, far worse than the agony that came with a gunshot wound.

Gran and her music became the big influence in early teens that saw me taking up the clarinet and moving effortlessly from third desk in the school's third orchestra to first desk in the first.

With three As to play with, I turned down Loughborough and sport for Nottingham and music and discovered women and drink instead. Breaking a knuckle keeping wicket – I can feel it now, all knobbly – didn't help finger dexterity either. I left with a bare pass, two grades lower than Mum's, and no hope of making second clarinet in a third-rate orchestra.

Emma – when will she vacate my mind – used to josh me about those three wasted years. Her university was Woollies as a Saturday girl on the sweet counter.

Nothing better on offer, I joined the police; never played in the force band and doubt if I could get much more than a catlike squawk out of my mahogany Boosey these days. Sometimes I day-dream of what might have been had I worked harder, centre-stage playing Crusell at the Proms with that slow second movement, strings only accompaniment, pizzicato.

The locked gates of Newstead Abbey pass by the window and – here I go again – I brought her here for a concert in the gorgeous grounds last summer which was ended after the overture by the sort of rain you only expect to get in India. We sheltered next to a statue of a naked man and Emma said that, if he was Lord Byron, the great local lover boy, his instrument wasn't much to write home about, and we laughed and I smile to myself. God, I long to be with her.

Thick woods either side now, Thieves Wood to the left, Harlow Wood to the right, and coming up are the gates of the hospital where I halted before taking the left home, home to open that gut-

78

wrenching letter. God, if only I hadn't. Does it matter? Does it really matter?

I'd like to think we would have talked about it, if only Gran hadn't been dying in hospital at the same time. I want to believe that I was running from the shock and pain of losing her, and not from Emma, when I holed up alone, like a sick dog, all over Christmas and the New Year.

At the very least I should have had the grace to phone her folks to decline their invite to spend the holiday with her at their home in London.

Instead, she phoned me as I loafed on the brown couch at my undecorated place, watching, but not seeing TV, after a Christmas Day lunch of grilled steak and oven ready chips.

'It's not too late,' she said. 'Drive down now. You'll make the cold ham tea. There's a bed – in the spare room, if that's the way you want it. We could walk and talk in the park tomorrow. Please.'

I steeled my heart and declined again and I know now, deep in that steely heart, that my refusal had more to do with punishing her than easing my hurt feelings.

Does one drunken night of infidelity really matter? My heart hardens again. Of course it matters. What was that line from the Tennessee Williams she took me to? Something like 'If a marriage . . .' and that's what it was in all but name '. . . if a marriage is on the rocks, then the rocks are in bed.'

It's on the rocks, has to be. Otherwise, you don't need a one-night stand, casual sex, a fling, call it what you like. What we had was deep and meaningful. What she chose was shallow and meaningless. There can be no trust in future, no going back.

And now, come Friday, I see myself walking away. And my heart starts to ache with a pain that's different to the hurt that overwhelmed me when I sat in the hospital and watched Gran fade away and the agony I felt holding on to a leg I thought had been blown away. But it's just as bad. To be honest, right now, it's worse.

I blink away these crippling thoughts to focus my mind on the job at journey's end.


Comfortable, are we? OK, then. This is the story so far.

Jack exchanged the cow for a bag of beans which his poverty-stricken mum angrily tossed out of the window. Next morning the stalks had grown up to the sky (well, the fire curtain certainly).

Up he'd climbed into a strange country where he learned from a friendly witch that the wicked ogre had killed his dad and stolen the family inheritance.

Jack hid in the oven and, oh, my God, the ogre smelt fresh meat. Then, what a relief, he dozed off and Jack nicked the hen's golden egg and scarpered home. Now, silly boy, he's donning disguise and planning a return trip.

I am feeling back in my childhood, my grandparents sitting each side of me, all three of us entranced.

The spell is broken when the interval lights come up. A babble of piping, demanding voices, coughs, rustling sweet papers and plastic macs sweeps across the stalls. Several people stand, hand drab street coats and colourful programmes to their neighbours, sidestep beyond contorting members of the audience and head up the aisles to the toilets and the bar.

Among them is Matron, my target when I sheltered ninety minutes ago in the door of a pub across a narrow street from the Civic Theatre, an old palace of varieties, in an impressive row of mixed, yet complementary, architecture – Tudor-style bar, black glass entrance to a museum, the white stone of a turn-of-the-century library; all so stylish that maybe I've underestimated this town.

A house near to full tonight, four hundred or more, many of them teeming out of buses; not an easy stake-out and I'd been relieved to spot her when she led twenty or so in a slow-moving party into the stalls, bossily seating them in a block.

Immediately, she took off a heavy tweed coat to reserve her seat next to the aisle. Then she returned to the spacious foyer – for a quick pee or gin, I presumed – wearing her dark blue uniform so every other theatre-goer could see that she's one of the caring professions.

The ticket I had bought earlier – £6.75, but no receipt again – was taken by the usherette. Inside is all plush maroon and cream, restful. My seat is behind and across the aisle from the Laven home group. Head down, sliding back, I study the programme till Matron leaves the auditorium for another pee or gin.

I stand, tuck my raincoat in the edge of the dark cushion that has tipped up behind me and walk down the aisle.

A few gaps have appeared in the Laven home block, mainly among the menfolk whose prostates must be playing up.

I tip down an empty seat next to the aisle. 'Is Mrs Hettie Brown around?' I ask a stout woman in a thick overcoat and wearing a wide black hat that must be a pain in the neck to sit behind.

'Mrs Brown,' she calls to her left.

Two women half a dozen seats away say 'Eh?' and 'Yes' in unison. The woman in the hat points at them, then jerks a thumb at me and says by way of introduction, 'In the red woolly cardy.'

The seat next door but one to Hettie is vacant so I stand again, shuffle crab-like in front of four pairs of shoes which are drawn back to permit my passage without treading on corns. I sit again.

'Mrs Brown?' I ask across a heavily scented woman between us, huge bosom highlighted by a silver antique brooch that pins a yellow shawl at her chest. 'I'm Phillip Todd, a friend of the late Mrs Lillian Sharpe's family. I believe you knew her?'

'Pardon?' says Hettie, pitching her frail upper body towards me.

'Mrs Sharpe? Why, yes,' says the middlewoman.

'We're trying to get in touch with her son from Australia.'

'Eh?' says Hettie, face a wrinkled puzzle.

'Mrs Sharpe's lad, the one we never knew she had,' booms the middlewoman.

'Well, don't ask me, I'm sure,' says Hettie vaguely.

For someone who, according to Harry Laven yesterday, was at death's door, she looks quite healthy, but, suspecting she is harder of hearing than Doc 'Say Again' Sam Walls, I direct my next question at her companion. 'Did he call last summer to see Mrs Sharpe?'

'Yes – but too late.'

Got Laven, the bastard, I think with overwhelming joy. 'Did your friend . . .' I nod across her at Hettie. '. . . see him?'

She turns to Hettie. 'Mrs Sharpe's lad. That coloured bloke from Australia. You talked to him, didn't you?'

'Yes,' says Hettie.

'When?'

Her middlewoman answers for her. 'In the summer, like you say.' Her chubby face swivels back again. 'Wasn't it?'

Hettie says Yes, but I can't be sure she's following so I spread my net. 'Did you see him, too?'

'Not to talk to,' replies the middlewoman. 'Only from a distance chatting to her.' Her head goes back to Hettie. 'But you talked to him, didn't you? Mrs Sharpe's lad. You talked to him?'

'Yes.'

81

'What did he want?' I inquire quietly.

The middlewoman, I assume, heard the story from Hettie immediately afterwards, and at more leisure, so much of what follows is not from Hettie's mouth, though she nods sagely and says 'That's right' here and there.

Arnie arrived unannounced at the Laven home when groups of residents were sitting on benches in the sunshine in the back paddock. He sought out and found Hettie Brown, said he already knew his mother was dead, but wanted to know if her last years were happy. 'It was a surprise to everybody, I can tell you. Who would believe it?' the middlewoman says.

I ask if he asked what had happened to the proceeds from the sale of Mrs Sharpe's house in Forest Town.

'Yes,' says the middlewoman, 'but she didn't know, so she directed him to Matron's office. We didn't see him come out. He never said goodbye or anything.' Hettie nods confirmation.

'Did Mrs Sharpe have other visitors – an official of her old union, Mr Grady, perhaps?'

Blank expressions tell me they have never heard of, much less seen, Steve Grady.

I try again. 'Other relatives, members of her family?'

'No,' says the middlewoman with a rather superior smirk. 'Not that we know of. She left what she had to the home.'

'Do many residents do that?'

'Oh, yes. Not me though. Or Mrs Brown here. We've close family, see.' The middlewoman preens a little as though wearing a badge of honour at being part of a family that hadn't totally abandoned her.

I double check. 'But Mrs Sharpe left all her money to the home?'

'It was all done proper.'

'How do you mean?'

'With a will and everything. Signed for. Like the jabs.'

This is a bonus and I cash in. 'What jabs?'

'The flu jabs. We're sure it was that, aren't we? Poor souls. It took a dozen or so of them, Mrs Sharpe included. Bless 'em.'

'What did?'

'The flu,' she replies, irritated with me.

'When?'

'Last winter. Going down like flies, weren't they? Three funerals a week for a month.'

'Did you have the jab?'

'Oh, no.' She shakes her head indignantly. 'Mrs Brown neither.

Did we? Good job, isn't it? It was supposed to stop you catching it. We reckon it gave them it, don't we?'

'Looks like that,' says Hettie musingly, not so sure.

I have to be. 'Why didn't you have the injection – it was an injection was it? . . .' Both nod solemnly. '. . . if it was going to stop you catching your death of cold?'

'That's what it gave them, isn't it?'

'So you were lucky?'

'Sensible more like.' She nudges Hettie. Both smile.

'Why?'

'We didn't sign up for it.'

'Why?'

'We sign nothing unless my son and her daughter have had a good look, do we, Mrs Brown?'

'No,' says Hettie, then for emphasis, 'Never.'

A bald-headed man sitting in front of us has been stirring in his seat for some time. He turns round, unable to resist joining in. 'They said it was Beijing flu.'

'Did you catch it?'

'I wouldn't be here now, if I had, now would I?'

The middlewoman nods.

My eyes stay on the man, noticing faint blackheads on his cheeks – a sure sign of a working life spent underground down the mines. 'Did you have the injection?'

The middlewoman answers for him, echoing his words. 'He wouldn't be here enjoying himself, if he had. None of us would. Good, isn't it?'

Smashing, I agree, before steering her back. 'So only those residents who had the injection got the flu and died?'

The frontman nods. 'And it was supposed to stop it. That's what they promised.'

'Who promised?'

'The makers.'

'When?'

'We were all called to a meeting . . .'

'In the lounge,' the middlewoman interjects.

'. . . and there was a man and Dr Walls . . .'

'. . . and Councillor Laven and Matron . . .' she helpfully butts in again.

'That's right,' the frontman confirms, 'and they told us it was new and safe and would stop us being ill in the winter.'

'But we'd have to sign up to take it,' Hettie adds.

My heart is reeling with all of this, these wonderful leads, coming from almost every direction. I feel knee deep in golden eggs. 'Did all the people who died sign consent forms?' I ask.

'You couldn't have it without agreeing,' says the middlewoman.

'And all of them died?'

'Yes.'

Oh, my God, what have I got here? I think, all joy vanishing. 'Where did this man who gave the talk come from?'

'Don't rightly recall. It was . . .'

The front man stops the middlewoman in mid-sentence. 'That new place. Don't know its name. At my old pit.'

'Where did you work?'

'Moorwood.'

Hedges Pharmaceuticals, I realise, childlike excitement racing through me again.

'Did Dr Walls give the injections?'

'Some of them,' says the frontman.

'Did all those people who caught the flu have close families like you?'

'None,' the middlewoman says, more pleased than regretful. 'There was hardly anyone at any of the funerals.' Her face saddens. 'Poor send-offs. Poor souls.'

'And, since they had no close family, did they all leave their money to the home?'

'Expect so.' Doubt crosses, then clears her plump features. 'Some, certainly.'

'Most, I reckon,' says the man in front.

'Were their wills witnessed by a solicitor?'

'Oh yes,' says the frontman. 'All done proper.'

'Do you know the name of any of the solicitors they used?'

'Coroner Jordan, mostly,' he replies straight away.

I can barely contain myself. 'You're absolutely sure?'

''Course I'm sure. Sat before 'im for three days when he took an inquest on a face man killed in a roof fall.' His eyes go over my right shoulder. Behind you, they are telling me.

I turn my head. Matron is standing in the aisle, flushed face like thunder.

'Enjoy the rest of the show,' I say, rising to pick my way carefully past the row of feet.

She almost blocks my exit. 'What are you doing?'

'Discussing the merits of the plot with my fellow thespians.' I smile pleasantly.

'You've no right.'

I decide on a bit of fun. Why not? It's a long time since I had any. Besides, I'm beginning to enjoy myself. I beckon her close with a flicked index finger. She lowers her head, turning an ear towards me. 'Don't let on, but Jack gets his inheritance and the ogre gets the chop. I do like happy endings, don't you?'

# 11

The acrid smell of fresh cigarette smoke escapes into the damp, dismal street as the front door is pushed open. Stupidly, I envisage Emma waiting for me in the dark.

A switch on the wall is found and flicked. Dunphy lights up. He is on the brown couch, legs stretched towards the half-empty Ladderex and the blank TV screen. Next to him, also sprawled out, partially hidden from view, is a more powerful figure. Oh, Jesus. The shotgun sidekick.

Heart and gut tight, I stand still, one hand glued to the switch, the other holding the Yale key. I restart my breathing, trying to steady it, too shocked to talk.

Dunphy leers over his left shoulder. 'Don't bother shutting the door.'

I back into it to close it, finishing the job with the sole of a shoe. 'Make yourself at home.' It gargles out, not my voice at all.

'We're not staying.' Dunphy's eyes scuttle away. 'We're not looking for trouble.'

Neither am I now I've second-glanced his mystery mate. He is not in black tonight. His red shirt is Nottingham Forest's home kit, motif of a white tree over the heart, sleeves rolled up. Broad bones are beneath blue tattoos on his forearms.

No weapon is being trained on me so I'll chance a mild protest. 'You'll find it, breaking into people's houses.'

'You've some need to talk,' says Dunphy, rather amiably.

I take a few, slow steps to a low chair at right angles to the Ladderex and look down on a deep green waxed jacket, three-quarter length, so heavily stained that camouflage patches seem to have been painted in black oil. 'Mind if I sit down in my own house?'

Dunphy pulls himself up, approaching upright. 'I said we're not stopping.'

'Don't let me keep you.' I pick up the jacket, furtively feeling, finding the outlines of a coil of thick twine and a folded-up knife, but no hand gun. I drop it on the fawn carpet, lowering myself in its place. 'I've had a busy day.'

'Don't I know it,' Dunphy grouses. His pale, podgy face glistens. He looks more than ill-at-ease. He looks ill.

The man in red lifts right black boot over left at the ankle and stares across at me. He's mid-twenties with close-cropped fair hair I never noticed last night. Maybe he'd worn headgear. Maybe I'd been too stunned by his shotgun to take it in. Either way, eight months out of action has left me badly out of practice.

I finally get round to what I should have done last night and start to size him up, noting that hairs, not his own, adhere to his black track-suit trousers. I look back at Dunphy, but nudge my head towards his partner. 'Who's he?'

'Ah.' He sits up properly, beaming. 'Meet Brucey Boy.'

'How do,' says Brucey Boy, nodding matily.

Now that I'm capable of listening properly I detect an accent straight out of the coalfields. His tanned, unpitted face results from the outdoors, not from working underground. 'And what do you do, apart from scaring people shitless?'

Dunphy answers for him. 'Gamekeeper.' Bruce smiles lazily. 'He came for the ride.'

He's here, I realise, because Dunphy knows that he's so badly out of condition he can't handle me on my own, even with a gammy leg. I'm not altogether sure I can handle Bruce, even on two good legs. At the band of his black bottoms his stomach is flat and hard. Beneath his red shirt a barrel chest breathes steadily. There's not an ounce of flab on him.

No gamekeeper, this, handed-down hunting instincts tell me. This is a poacher for commercial gain, not for his own pot. And if there's no game about he'll make a night out of it anyway by breaking into a few homes and clubbing anyone who gets in his way.

'Councillor Laven wants to see you.' Dunphy speaks the title and name reverently.

I am dying – wrong word, keen – to see him again, too. He's top of my list for tomorrow. I'm anxious to discover how anxious he is to see me. 'Why?'

'For a chat.'

'Can't it wait till tomorrow?'

'Too late,' says Dunphy, gravely ominous. Then, lightening up, 'You work quick . . .' A malicious smile spreads slowly over his face. '. . . for a lame duck.'

I sniff sharply. Hear a phrase like that after you've been limping around and you begin to understand how blacks must feel hearing their natural colour associated with extortion or bans. Temper is held in check. 'I'm new to this lark. I don't have your contact.'

'A lark?' Dunphy, face twisted, hasn't the same self-control. 'That what you think it is?'

'More fun than all the red tape in the police service, that's for sure,' I effuse.

'Fun?' He gasps, speaking oddly, as though he has his bottom set of false teeth out. 'Is that what you're having? Making a monkey of me in that Evergreen shop? Having me sitting in a car-park all afternoon after chatting up that red-haired bitch? Pissing off to the panto?'

So, I'm thinking, Matron missed Jack's return trip up the beanstalk to tip Laven who's phoned Dunphy and Brucey Boy to bring me in.

'All in a day's work for us gumshoes,' I smile.

Bruce unwraps his boots and plants them firmly on the carpet to pull himself up. He nods at his waxed jacket. 'Pass my coat.'

Smoke is curling up from a saucer on the couch between them. A cigarette, just one, has not been fully stubbed out. They hadn't been here long or Dunphy would have half filled it. I nod at it, making a bet with myself that they overtook the returning No. 63 bus after Matron phoned Laven and Laven dispatched them. 'A no-smoking zone, this place. Put that out.'

Without wetting his index finger, Bruce suffocates the smoke, as though squashing a bug.

Dunphy rummages in his pocket to find packet and lighter and ignites a new one, to show who's in charge.

While they were distracting each other, grandstanding, I've leaned forward, frisking the coat again. Some of the stains are dried blood. I hand it over as we all stand.

Ah, well, I tell myself, showing them out and trying the door, another fifteen quid coming up; thirty, if Laven's talkative. Let's hope his talk is just as careless.

There's been a leak from Jordan Associates.

*

87

Two lurchers breathe through a metal grille down my neck. Their rough coats smell damp and composty, the scent of a forest in winter. The grey one snarled, the brown yapped when I climbed in the back of a Nissan with a longer wheelbase than normal, like one of my old Special Ops trucks. Both were silenced by a shout from Bruce. 'Shut it.'

Now the brown is sitting, scratching his huge head. The grey, as lean as a greyhound, has stretched out on a blanket that's filthier than the outside of the vehicle, more mud visible than maroon paintwork.

Bruce has not bothered to belt up. He is driving so fast and erratically, through two lights at yellow already, that Dunphy has pleaded, 'Steady up. We don't want to be gonged.'

He's dropped his tab end in the foot well. If it's as dirty around his shoes as here in the back, with dog hairs, old newspapers, bills, hooks, even a caked shovel, it will make an insignificant addition to the squalor.

Brucey has slowed from fifty-five to forty miles an hour and we have a long way to go in a 30 mph zone yet. This trip is not going to take half as long as the forty minutes on the No. 63 so I begin to probe. 'What's Laven want with me?'

'Wait and see,' says Dunphy, gruffly.

'Ruffling a few feathers looking for Aussie Arnie, am I?'

'Shut it.' Bruce addresses me as though he has a third dog in the back.

A great start, I think, watching that hotel, flags still limp, go by. A mile or so further north, I begin again. 'Lunched with your old mate Armstrong today.'

'What makes you think he's my mate?' Dunphy is looking ahead.

'Thought you went back to cadet days on the coast.'

'He was a wanker then and he's a wanker now.'

'He speaks well of you, too.'

Dunphy's neck turns with curiosity, like a young bird out of a nest. 'What's he been saying?'

'Don't you two keep in touch?' A long shot aimed at confirming continued contact between them, so I'm not too disappointed when he doesn't reply. His silence compels me to answer his question. 'Warned me off associating with a bombed-out ex-bobby.'

He looks sideways at Bruce. 'I resigned.' Eyes front again. 'What did you say?'

'That I bumped into you night-watching at Laven Havens.'

Bruce guffaws loudly ahead of him.

'Baa . . .' Dunphy burps the rest. '. . . stard.'

'Let's hope we don't get pulled over for speeding. I don't want to be seen with you, Dunph. I want to protect my pension till discharge.'

It was a coded message to slow down. Bruce's response is to put his foot down. Even on main roads it's becoming a bumpy ride. Bruce glances over his shoulder. 'You that cop who almost bought it on the rail track?'

Like a drill instructor, Dunphy orders: 'Eyes front.'

'Fuck off,' says Bruce, but he obeys. 'Seen your picture in the *Post*. What you leaving for?'

I say nothing. He looks across his shoulder at Dunphy. 'That's right, innit? He's quitting?'

'So he says.' Dunphy belches loudly and automatically says, 'Excuse me.' No one does.

'Why?' Bruce is half turned again, so I'd best come up with an answer.

'Fifteen quid an hour, right, Dunph?'

'Jesus,' says Bruce, enviously.

Dunphy swivels round. 'Is that what Jordan Associates are offering you? After my contract, are you?'

I give him a bland smile. 'Did you sit there all day, by the way, or did Laven pull you out after you tipped off Armstrong where he could find me?'

His neck goes into his shoulders, not rising to any bait.

I stick to my lie. 'I was giving depositions on that railway line shooting . . .' I nod towards Bruce. '. . . to Michelle Fogan for my personal injuries case.'

He grunts. 'Screwing her, are you? Everyone else has.'

'You, too?' I ask flippantly. He turns back abruptly to face front. 'Like who?' I ask.

A low laugh ahead of him.

'Who?' I demand. 'Come on. I'm interested. I fancy her.' An uneasy suspicion dawns within that I may be telling him the truth for a change.

'You're wasting your time,' he tells the windscreen.

Unaccountably irked, I goad him. 'The way I heard it you were booted out of Jordan Associates.'

He turns towards the rear again, his face dark. 'You heard it wrong. Mission accomplished there, see. Useless, you'll be, in this game.' He shakes his head deliberately and repeats, 'Useless.'

'Never mind,' I say cruelly. 'If I'm ever out of work, I can always come to you for a job as night-watchman.'

Bruce laughs, enjoying the needle.

We skirt the Redhill roundabout at the bottom of Sherwood Forest in silence, which Bruce breaks as he takes the A60. 'So what's it like, getting shot?'

I sigh. 'Not to be recommended.'

'I've come close a time or two mesen.'

'You a poacher-turned-gamekeeper or the other way round?'

'Ask yourself where tonight's venison casserole came from.' Dunphy's short laugh at his own joke is interrupted by a longer belch.

'Laying heavy, is it?' I jest, expecting a torrent of abuse.

'Something is,' Dunphy replies distantly, thumping his chest twice with the rounded end of a clenched first.

'Seriously, though,' says Bruce seriously. 'What's it like?'

I recall a pain that burned so intensely that I'd wished he'd been a better shot and finished the job, to put me out of my agony. I say nothing.

Dunphy lights up again. Bruce tuts and winds down his window. He won't let the topic drop. 'Did you shoot back?'

I tell him we hadn't been issued with firearms.

'Would you have done?'

'Yes.' An honest reply. 'If it was him or me.'

'Ever shot a man?'

'No.'

'You, Dunph?'

'No.' Dunphy doesn't add that he was never weapon-trained.

'Wonder what it's like?' Bruce muses morbidly.

'Seen the result of it, though.' Like so many men who can't live with the knowledge that they have never really soldiered, Dunphy is about to give the impression of being in the thick of frontline action. I know he's about to tell a tale that's a legend in the force.

Only one serving marksman in the East Mids Combined has the dubious distinction of killing a man – Deputy Chief Brooks.

'Give then,' Bruce asks Dunphy eagerly. 'What happened?'

Dunphy spins out a yarn which starts back in the early eighties, before the mergers. The deputy was a chief inspector then, a trained marksman. Dunphy was a constable. A holiday-maker was almost cut in two by a blast from a .12 bore fired through the thin skin of a caravan from the outside.

'See him?' asks Bruce, interrupting the flow.

Dunphy nods and tells how the deputy was assigned to launch a hunt for an armed man seen fleeing from the seaside caravan site. From the description, Dunphy put up the name of a local man with convictions for petty crime.

They went round to see him to ask the usual 'Where were you at the time of the crime?' and 'Have you a shotgun?' He produced one from a shed, trained on them. So the deputy shot him dead through the chest. 'Went down like a felled tree,' Dunphy concludes.

'Jesus,' gasps Bruce, impressed. He turns his head towards the back. 'Could you have done that in your day?'

I suddenly feel past it, like an old man, and speak with a genuine touch of doubt. 'If I had to, I suppose.'

'Me, too.' A single nod ahead of him, as if he was trying to convince himself.

The smell of pine, damp tonight, not sharp, is being sucked into the truck through Bruce's window. Coming up to the left is Thieves Wood, to the right Harlow Wood.

'What was the motive?' I ask as casually as I can.

'Robbery,' replies Dunphy. 'Found some stuff from the caravan in the shed.'

'Was your mate Armstrong with you on that job?'

He shakes his head, still in the distant past. 'A sergeant by then, over here.'

'So how did it end up?' Bruce asks a question that everyone on the force knows the answer to.

Dunphy shrugs. 'Justifiable homicide.' Then he adds, as if justifying the coroner's verdict, 'Naturally.'

And Dunphy had one promotion and one transfer to Sherwood on amalgamation while By-the-Book Brooks went on and on and up and up to deputy.

'What did the gunman nick?' asks Bruce, professionally intrigued.

'A radio and bits and pieces,' Dunphy tells him.

'Shot dead for that!' says Bruce, professionally appalled. 'He'd have been better off poaching.'

'What's the going rate?' I ask in by-the-way fashion.

'Pound a pound.'

'What's one worth?'

'With head, hooves and guts taken, a fallow weighs in at sixty or seventy.'

Dunphy lapses into silence, breathing shallowly, shoulders heaving.

Just ahead of us, out of a wood to our right, glides a deer, no bigger than a Labrador dog, with small swept-back horns. It trots, almost ambling, across the road towards the wood opposite.

'Montjack,' Bruce declares delightedly. One hand comes off the wheel. Something clicks. From the roof an expanding cone of yellow lights up the road. In the wide, rounded end of it, the deer is caught, static and stranded, looking at us.

There is time and distance to brake or, with no traffic coming the other way, room to drive round.

He touches the accelerator slightly, tightens his grip on the wheel, hunches over it.

'For fu . . .' Dunphy protests.

From the front a soft bump.

A tan blur flies up and left into the dead bracken that fronts Thieves Wood.

Bruce laughs darkly to himself. Dunphy turns to view the road behind. 'Aren't you even going to collect it?'

'Ribs stoved. Ain't even dog meat,' says Bruce, grinning across his shoulder at the back of Dunphy's head.

Dunphy turns still further, facing me. He looks so ill that I doubt that a close-up of Bambi twitching in the bracken could be more deathly.


# 12


'Thank you for coming,' says Councillor Laven, with icy politeness, sitting at the absent Matron's desk.

He is wearing a double-breasted dinner jacket with narrow, shiny lapels, and a stubby black bow-tie. You don't dress in DJs for the panto, not even the dress circle, so I assume he's been dragged from some civic do. This must be important.

As with Armstrong who greeted me with more or less the same words, I decide against 'Not much option' and say nothing.

'What, tell me, are you playing at?' he demands, dropping all pretence of pleasantries.

Dunphy follows me in; not Bruce who'd dropped us off, with no exchange of goodnights, and noisily sped away. He stands with his back to the door, rubbing his chest vigorously.

I walk towards and sit uninvited on the typist's stool.

'Well?' demands Laven.

I swivel comfortable. 'I told all yesterday.'

'You didn't tell me you were working for Jordans.'

'Why are you two so paranoid about them?' I speak urgently and nod at Dunphy. 'He's obsessed with them.'

Laven repeats himself. 'Why didn't you tell me you were working for them?'

'I'm working – if that's what you want to call it – for a chum in Australia whose neighbours were taken for thirty grand by the missing Arnie Gillman. That's all there is to tell. What's the fuss?'

'Then why did you go to their office this morning?'

'I'm blue in the face from telling him . . .' I look at Dunphy who is purple in the face. '. . . that Jordans are handling my compensation claim over this.' I pat my right thigh. 'Nothing to do with Gillman.'

Disbelief is disfiguring his bronzed face.

I feign impatience. 'Don't you listen to *Afternoon Special* on the Beeb? My chum was on the programme from Sydney yesterday, appealing for info about Gillman. Check with the station. They're bound to have a tape.'

'I might,' he says, frowning.

'She didn't mention the missing thirty thou. Not on air. Naturally. She just asked listeners for sightings of him and gen about his mother, Mrs Lillian Sharpe.'

Sensing safe ground, I go on, 'There was one phone call and one letter from listeners, both concerning Lillian. I was asked to check on them.' For good measure, I reinforce the point. 'I can give you my lady friend's Sydney number, if you like. Check with her.'

He is smiling – just. 'A bit ungentlemanly, wasn't it, to gatecrash our night out at the panto?'

I am stony-faced. 'No more than you telling me Arnie never came here seeking his mother.'

Belatedly Laven plays with his words, the politician. 'What I said was that we had no record of it.'

A smart politician would have said that this morning but I let him off the hook. 'You mean, you didn't note the visit in your records.'

'Never do, unless it's a doctor.'

'Then he did come here?'

An unhappy nod. 'In the summer. Six months after his mother died. Like you said, he already knew from an old neighbour that she was dead.'

Confirmation of the leak to Laven from Jordan Associates. What I said here this morning was that Arnie got his info from an old workmate. What I typed at lunchtime was that his info came from a former neighbour. Again I act dumb. 'What did he want?'

'Money.' A grim smile. 'That's what all this is about, isn't it?'

'What did he get?'

Laven backtracks evasively. 'What he wanted was what he thought was due to him from the sale of her house.'

I persist. 'And what did he get?'

'I told him most of the proceeds had been spent on residential fees.' He's as slippery as a Cabinet minister on *Question Time.* 'I can show you the accounts. The residue had been absorbed by our charity trust in accordance with her last wishes. It's all in her will, perfectly legally.'

'How did he react?'

'Rather badly. Amazing, isn't it? Threatened a song and dance. And that after we'd looked after her while he was on the other side of the world. Then he pops up here, wanting to cash in or he'd go to the press.'

He grumbles on quite a bit about harmful media coverage, the way politicians do. 'Ill-informed comment. Always causes misunderstandings.'

I sum it up for him. 'A story about a fatal epidemic here would have been bad for business.'

'Inconvenient.' A slight shrug. 'No more. All the cases were natural and certified as such.'

I want him to know that my research has been thorough. 'So what was the outcome of your chat after Lil's friend Mrs Hettie Brown directed him to this office?'

He smooths a brown file that was before him on the desk when we walked in. 'We agreed an ex gratia payment.' He hurriedly heads off my next question. 'Three thousand pounds. He had come a long way at considerable expense.'

Involuntarily, my head jars back. Two possibilities spring into it. Either hush money was paid. Or Arnie was killed, like Bambi

94

on the A60, to keep him from exposing the mass deaths that occurred here last winter. I home in on the former to mask my darker suspicion. 'Terrific.'

Now he's too jolted to reply.

'My instructions from Harbour Heights are to recover what I can from any bank account over here.'

A hangdog expression. 'So you are working. It isn't a favour to a friend.'

I nod towards Dunphy, who is standing awkwardly as though a disc had slipped. 'Like I told him, I cop for ten per cent of anything recovered, but not until April when I officially leave the force; the next tax year.'

Laven smirks, knowing a tax dodge when he sees one.

'This three thou,' I continue, 'was it a cheque?'

His face blanks. 'Come now, Mr Todd.'

'It is important. A cheque means a bank account which can be traced. I could apply for a county court order to freeze anything left in it.'

He sits rock still. I push him. 'Did you tell the police this? They were, after all, making inquiries about Arnie.'

His face has turned full circle back to deepest suspicion. 'Are you here officially?'

An innocent smile. 'How can I be? I'm on sick leave and not going back.'

'Then how do you know?'

Dunphy speaks, rather croakily, for the first time in the office. 'Are you plugged into a gossipy pal at HQ – Heather Hann, for instance?'

'No,' I answer sharply. 'Nor am I likely to be. You and your contact put paid to the Old Pals Act getting yourself arrested.' Dunphy lapses back into smouldering silence.

I shake my head sadly. 'The tenants at Harbour Heights reported him missing to the police. My friend from Australia said so over the radio, for all the East Midlands to hear yesterday. You really ought to listen in yourself. It's no secret. You should be more trusting.'

Laven's expression registers relief again. Not so Dunphy who looks about to pass out.

'So did you tell the police?' I ask, doggedly

A longish pause. 'A policewoman was here, certainly, a couple of months ago,' Laven finally concedes. 'She mentioned nothing about Gillman being wanted for theft.'

Well, Heather Hann wouldn't, since I made it all up. See if he's making up the pay-off, I order myself. 'Did you mention the three thousand pounds?'

'It's a private matter.'

'Have you reported it to them?' I float a name. 'Superintendent Armstrong at division, for instance?' I study Dunphy. 'He's a pal of yours, isn't he?' His face is so pained that it's unreadable. I turn to Laven. 'Spoken to someone like him recently. Or Deputy Chief Brooks maybe?'

His face is watchful. One name or other has rung a warning bell. Having only one pair of eyes, I can't be sure which. 'Why should we?' he asks.

'Both Brooks and Armstrong are discreet operators. If it was a cheque, they could easily find out where it was banked.'

'Cash,' he's forced to answer at last. 'He wanted cash and that's what we paid.'

Time to firm up the questioning. 'Can you prove that?'

He opens the file, slipping out a sheet of paper. He stands and walks rather wearily towards me, handing it over.

On Laven Havens notepaper is typed: 'Received in cash in full and final settlement of late Mrs Lillian Sharpe's estate, £3000.' It was signed 'A. Gillman', witnessed by L. Dunphy, security consultant, and dated 2 July.

I don't hand it back. 'Can I have a copy?' He's dubious, so I add, 'It would look good in my final report. Shows I've not been sitting around, charging fifteen quid an hour.'

With raised eyebrows he signals to Dunphy who lumbers, dragging his feet, from the door, takes the receipt and retraces his heavy steps, disappearing into the corridor.

I nod after him. 'Is he all right?' Healthwise, I meant.

Laven walks back behind his desk and sits. 'He's past it, I'm afraid.'

'Got good contacts, though.'

He smiles invitingly. 'Perhaps we might be able to come to some arrangement. Having establishments in such isolated spots does pose security problems.'

'Perhaps,' I say, not thinking of poor old Dunphy being jocked off yet another job, other things in the forefront of my mind.

'A contract, perhaps?' Laven suggests.

Two days on the market and people are throwing work at me. What's all this about dole queues? I ask myself happily. 'Maybe.'

His face becomes serious. 'Don't think for one moment that I've accepted this business about not acting on behalf of Jordans in this matter. I know otherwise.'

Had he written, instead of spoken that last line, the 'know' would have come out in italics.

I know he knows. How? Who told him? Not Superintendent Armstrong. I flannelled my way round it with him. Someone within Jordan Associates, has to be. Coroner Jordan, his clerk Ogden, Dr Say Again Sam Walls. Not Michelle Fogan. Can't be. Or he'd know that the missing thirty grand was fiction.

Hearing Dunphy's heavy approach, we hurriedly and quietly agree to discuss the details of a possible contract later. Dunphy reappears, hands me my copy and places the original on Laven's desk.

Laven smiles hopefully. 'Case closed then.'

I smile benignly. 'I'll just follow my nose for a couple more days.'

'Why?' The smile fades. 'Where?'

'He had no car, did he?'

Laven nods.

'So I'll try taxi firms to see where they took him from here.'

He is shaking his head. 'Let me assure you that he was well and happy when he departed. You dropped him off, didn't you?'

'At the Savoy.' Dunphy names the big beflagged hotel that we passed on the road here.

'I'll go there then.'

'And afterwards?'

I haven't worked that out yet, so say nothing.

'Is this assignment of yours open-ended?' he wants to know.

'The retainer is for a couple of weeks' work,' I ad lib. 'Then I report back and they decide whether to fund further inquiries.'

'Once you have satisfied yourself he returned to his hotel and, presumably, have cross-checked his signature . . .' He nods at the copy I am holding. '. . . I'd rather hope that would be the end of the matter.'

'Oh, no. I'd press on. I could stick an advert in the *Post*. I'm on ten per cent of anything I recover.'

He ponders for a moment, eyes down. They come up. 'We can advance you ten per cent of our settlement to her son as a sign of our goodwill pending further negotiations.'

Christ, I think. First my inquiries panic him into confirming Gillman visited here – something he was denying this morning. Now, he's buying me off with a payment upfront and a contract to come. He's terrified of me. I'm close to something – something big. But what? And who else is in it with him?

Back on doorman's duty, Dunphy is too preoccupied exercising his left arm to notice his job is being negotiated away with a three hundred pounds advance.

'Cash,' I smile regretfully. 'The taxman, you know.'

'We don't carry that amount in petty cash. Security, you know. Tomorrow?' What with his council and charity work he can't see me before eight in the evening. He stands. 'And that will be that, I take it?'

I stand. 'No further inquiries about Arnie from Arnold, I promise.'

'Shall we shake on it?' Laven offers his hand, giving me little choice.

We do. Neither is masonic. 'You've been very helpful,' I say, meaning it.


# 13


'Accommodating bloke, your boss,' I say, sliding into the passenger seat, bad leg first.

'Belt up,' growls Dunphy, doing so behind the wheel of his Peugeot. It's not a road safety tip, but I follow suit. On full choke, he starts up and turns the heater full on. In silence, we travel up the rutted driveway.

Get him talking, I order myself. Get him to open up. He's the weak link.

Something sinister happened here. Something to do with those flu jabs? Some experiment for HP that went wrong? Killing off residents for their estates?

Someone inside Jordans has shopped me. There can be no other explanation for the absolute certainty of his knowledge about my role. What is my role? Find Arnie, if he's alive, certainly. Identify Dunphy's police mole, if I'm going to make a success of this new job.

It's gone beyond both now. They must be used as means to an end. What is the end? To find out what happened here last winter, simple as that. I owe it to old folk, like my Gran, who might one day have come into a place like this.

Work on him. Quickly. While you're on your own. Try bribery first.


The game plan decided, I use a gentle opening gambit. 'How long have you worked for him?'

'Since I quit, on and off.' Dunphy's reply judders out as if the potted driveway is rattling his voice-box as well as the car springs.

Going through the opened gateway, he asks moodily, 'Where to? The Savoy?' A frozen smile. 'A waste of time, you know.'

'Tomorrow will do,' I answer airily.

Almost eleven on the dashboard clock, too late to make the Burnt Stump, but there are afters to be supped in every town and every cop, past or present, knows where to find a late drink. 'Where do you live?'

'Above the shop.' He nods ahead through the windscreen towards Mansfield, its street lights reflecting an orange glow in the clouds. 'Nothing as swanky as your place, though.'

Must be soulless then, I commiserate privately. 'Fancy a drink there?'

An exhausted sigh. 'I'm knackered.' He looks it, too, his gaunt face discoloured.

I ask to be dropped off at my car at Arnold near Jordan Associates, which leads smoothly to the next question. 'How long did you freelance for them?'

'Eighteen months.'

My tactic has to be to hammer a wedge between Laven and Dunphy and I have only ten miles to do it in.

He is driving just as erratically as Bruce on the way up, in the centre of the road, on full beam, but slowly, as if it's a built-up area, instead of the heart of the country. Thankfully, no vehicles are coming the other way on the narrow lanes. 'He's offered me a job,' I say.

'He'll not get rid of me, ' he grunts, then, trying to convince himself, 'Daren't.'

I don't offer reassurance. 'You've got to admit your value's diminished with this court case hanging over you.'

'Told you. I'm in the clear.'

'Come on. You know as well as me that Special Branch don't bring a case unless there's a more than fifty per cent chance of a conviction.'

'No chance.' He is speaking with a confidence that isn't apparent on his face. 'OK, they know it wasn't Armstrong who phoned . . .'

'He was alibied at a symphony concert, wasn't he?'

Dunphy is so surprised by my knowledge that the car veers to the right as he turns to me. 'How did you know that?'

I put on a puzzled frown. 'Are we talking about last Guy Fawkes night?'

Dunphy repeats, louder, 'How the hell did you know?'

'Armstrong gave me his side over lunch at the Burnt Stump.'

Now he's more puzzled than stunned, thinking a problem through as he straightens up. 'I thought it was . . . the HQ local . . .' He adds in afterthought, '. . . where you saw him.'

'I never said that.'

'Got that impression, that's all.' Then, trying to sound casual, 'Anyone else there?'

'No. Why?'

He steers out of trouble. 'Just assumed, that's all.'

'Assumed what?'

'Forget it,' he growls.

I want to stay on this track. 'The crew who picked me up in the car-park near the Co-op were Armstrong's boys. They took me to division, not HQ. Didn't you recognise them?'

Distracted, he gabbles something about new fellows and being ten years out of touch.

I stick to the subject. 'Don't know what you've got against Armstrong. He's decent enough.'

'Used to be,' he agrees reluctantly. Before I can explore this, he returns to his pending court case. 'They can't prove it was me on the blower. And the target won't talk. Too much to lose.'

For a second I hold fire. Do I reveal I know Steve Grady, the Knitwear Workers' union rep, was his target? Not yet, I decide. 'What were you after?'

He fires back, angry. 'Sod off.'

'What I mean is . . .' I am having to take cover. '. . . why take the chance? It was a barmy thing . . .'

'Needed the info fast, all right?' He replies very indignantly, his competence questioned.

'But you were rumbled. You didn't get it.'

'It was just confirmation we wanted. We ran with what we'd got. Good enough, in the end.'

'For what?' Silence. 'Come on. Let's level with each other.'

'Fuck off,' he snaps to end the subject.

100

Silence for half a mile. The car is hotter now than an old folk's home, yet he shivers now and then. I'm going to have to dangle money. 'Fancy a partnership?'

He laughs derisively. 'Got one.'

'Who?'

'The deputy.'

My face fills with total shock, can't prevent it at the thought of By-the-Book Brooks being his sleeping partner.

A little laugh. 'Name of Lawrence. Used to be a pit deputy at Moorwood. That's what Brucey calls him. The deputy.' His tone hardens. 'An old woman.'

'Why work with him then?'

'He bought himself in,' Dunphy replies.

With his pay-off when his pit shut, I suspect, at a time Dunphy's business was in financial trouble. 'Seriously. I could buy in, too. Michelle Fogan reckons I'm good for fifty grand compo for this . . .' I pat my leg. 'Put a price on it.'

He is thinking, not laughing, now. Money has talked.

'We'd make a good team,' I enthuse. 'I'm experienced on surveillance and new tech. You've got a fink on the force.'

His smile is very sickly. 'A word of advice. When you get one of your own, don't introduce him to your client. Ever. You just get cut out.'

'Is that happening to you?'

'The bastard can't cut me out totally. I went into bat for him when the shit was flying.'

I can't work out what or who he is talking about and daren't ask point-blank.

We have reached the much busier A60 and he has to wait for a gap in fast-moving traffic to turn south. He dips his headlights as he negotiates the crossover.

I revert to reassurance. 'I can't see Laven cutting you out.'

'Daren't.' He takes his left hand off the wheel to tap the side of his nose conspiratorially. The car drifts right again to the centre of the road. He's signalling to me that he knows too much. My aim is to find out what.

A distant car flashes its lights. Dunphy utters an obscenity, flashes back but corrects his path.

'What's to know?' I proceed languidly. 'He's highly respected, just decorated . . .'

'For Other Buggers' Efforts . . .' It's a cynical term that's often applied to the Order of the British Empire in the New Year's

101

Honours List, especially in the police service. By-the-Book Brooks got one or something similar in a recent Queen's Birthday list.

I attempt to continue. '. . . does a lot for the old folk . . .'

He butts in again. 'And himself.'

'Really?' I try to sound surprised.

'Wise up, Sweeney.' He's coming the old soldier now. 'All his charity crap is to secure his political position.'

I look suitably shocked. 'You do surprise me.'

'You're in for a lot of surprises if you join him. He'll use any dirty trick to get any problem out of the way.'

'Is that why he paid off Arnie Gillman?'

'And you, you jammy bastard.' He burps. 'Small beer to him.'

I come the new boy. 'Naive of me, I suppose. When you look at his business empire.'

He flicks his head in the direction from which we've travelled. 'How did he raise the cash for places like that, you should be asking yourself.'

'Property development,' I venture, recalling Emma's briefing.

'Don't you read? The bottom's dropped out of the market.' He pauses to make sure he has got my attention, showing off his knowledge again. 'Hedges staked him, didn't they?'

It's working. He's talking, opening up. I double check as casually as I can. 'HP, the new drugs firm from Moorwood?' He nods laboriously. 'How did he pull that off?'

'Pulled his rank as the council's health chairman, I suppose. There's lots of government grants for firms moving into old pit villages.'

I need time to ponder this, and want other info anyway, so I let it pass with the comment, 'Big dosh, eh?' I look across him into Thieves Wood. 'That nutter Brucey Boy. Is he on your security staff?'

A harsh snort. 'God forbid. Laven buys game cheap from him at the back door. Keeps down catering costs.'

'They eat a lot of game then, the old folks?'

'Too much.' He belches again and the car is filled with a warm, gamey odour. You, too, I'm thinking. 'Laven sent him to make sure you came.'

We are beyond the spot where Bambi was mowed down and I condemn Bruce bitterly, concluding, 'He's a heartless sod, that's for sure. How could anybody do that?'

He mumbles, marbles in his mouth. 'Serve him right, eh, if one dark night one of his mates tripped over a tree root and blew him away with a shotgun. Justifiable homicide, eh?'

I energetically nod agreement. He's talking in more riddles, close to gobbledygook, but I have to humour him.

We travel a mile or so in silence which I end. 'So what about it then, Dunph? My up-to-date know-how and your long-established contact. Dunphy and Todd.'

He is biting his lip, not saying yes or no.

'Set a price and I'll get my lawyer to draw up an agreement.'

He breathes out heavily as though exuding smoke from a cigarette, which, oddly, he has not yet had on this trip. 'Not that Fogan bitch.'

'Why not? She's handling my claim. She seems a good operator . . .'

'She's OK, but . . .' His mind seems to drift.

'Well, then?'

'She's no love for me.'

'Why?'

'I screwed her.' I'm turned towards him, genuinely shocked, and it must be showing.

'Not like that, you prat,' he says out of the corner of his mouth, thin lips darkening. 'Over a case. And a lover. She hates me. Forget it . . . her . . .' He has spoken so urgently that he trails off, breathless.

'What happened?'

Now, he is shaking his head so violently that his shoulders are heaving up and down. The car veers right again.

Approaching headlamps, not all that distant, hit us full in the face, his so wet it reflects the pale yellow beam back through the windscreen. He stares ahead and makes no move to correct himself.

'Jesus, Dunph.' A shouted exclamation fails to raise him from some sort of torpor.

We are heading straight for a huge lorry which is not slowing down, demanding its right to its side of the road. Panic grips me, the sort I experienced when I faced death eight months ago.

I shoot my left hand across my chest to tug the wheel down, not too hard. My right hand yanks the gear stick, making the engine howl.

We come out of the path of an articulated trimmed round the edges with fairy lights. Horns blare as it passes so close that its draught rocks us perilously close to the nearside grass verge.

103

Buttocks raised out of the seat, I reach across Dunphy's chest to grab the wheel, two-handed.

Dunphy lets go. His chest drops downwards. I have to hold an elbow up and rigid to stop his upper body slumping on to the wheel. I'm driving now, like my grandpa used to steer my dodgem at Bakewell funfair, when I was small.

My head spins. My hands sweat. I am shouting, swearing and screaming at Dunphy. His head is lolling on my shoulder.

I release one hand to feel for and find the handbrake. Kangaroo jumping, we stall to a halt. 'Dunph.' I turn my head across my shoulder and shout into his ear, an inch away.

One final gasp, much deeper than Gran's last, and his head drops forward as far as it could go without falling off.

Dead. I know it, even before I feel for and fail to find a pulse in his grotesquely extended neck. Dead.


No use in press-downs on his chest, no point trying the kiss of life. Nothing will help, I know for certain when I open the driver's door and recheck his pulse.

You've as good as killed him, an inner voice rebukes, chasing him around all day, pressuring him. Oh, come on – another voice, just as reprimanding – Laven, not you, gave the orders. Blame him. Better still, accept it for what it is, natural; nobody's fault.

Knees bent, back arched, I pick him up. His head, arms and legs no longer belong to his body. They just follow gravity and dangle as I carry him to the near side and lower him into the passenger seat.

I walk back in front in the headlights. Cold rain seems to sizzle as it hits my hot face. The rest of me is icy cold and drained.

I climb behind the wheel, corpse beside me. We'd finished up – God knows how – half in a lay-by facing the way we were travelling.

I start up and drive very slowly, hands gripping the wheel to stop the shakes, towards the nearest hospital, to let doctors certify him DOA, do the formal ID and wait while they notify division who'll inform the coroner. Jordan will order a PM, of course, to confirm natural causes, ruling out an inquest.

All routine, really, but routine that involves me, it begins to dawn. Division and HQ will know within half an hour that a notorious ex-cop has suffered a fatal coronary while driving a still-serving officer around late at night.

Think what the upper echelon will read into it. Deputy Chief Brooks to Armstrong: 'Were they working together, Todd moonlighting while on sick pay?' Armstrong: 'I told him only at lunchtime to stay away from Dunphy.' The deputy: 'Unless he's got a good explanation, we'll suspend him.'

I've got a good explanation all right, but I'm not prepared to give it to either yet.

Think on, I order myself. Who can put me with Dunphy tonight? Brucey and, more recently, Laven. He'll hear that Dunphy's dropped dead. Will he come forward? Why should he? There'll be no appeal for witnesses over a natural death.

He won't keep our meeting secret. No need. What will he tell anyone who cares to ask? 'We were discussing Todd's possible recruitment to our security staff when he finally gets his discharge. All perfectly above board. They left together.'

Instinctively, the decision comes, without a further single thought, hardly a life or death one anyway.

Sorry, Sligopath, this might sound selfish but you're dead and I'm still alive with a job to do.

At the Redhill roundabout, I complete a full circle and head north again, just a few hundred yards.

In front of the pumping station with the high square tower, I pull in, stall the engine to a stop and switch the lights to beam. Using my left knee on the driving seat for purchase, I lift Dunphy's dead weight back into it. His head flops towards the wheel.

I take his black A–Z contacts book out of his inside pocket and slip it into mine.

At this time of night, no motorist will stop for a driver who looks as though he's having a kip at the wheel. When someone, a police patrol most likely, does find him, they'll conclude he felt ill and pulled in.

And if Laven or Bruce do link him to me, I'll say, 'He dropped me off at my car. He was a bit breathless, come to think of it.'

I start to walk. I have escaped death again. I feel very much alive and, God, it's good.

# 14

'Hi. It's me.'

'Errrr.' I have forgotten our script.

'You did ask me to call early,' says Emma defensively.

'Mmmmmm.' I moisten my tongue, pull down my jaw to open glued eyes and focus on the radio clock; so early that she's ahead of the AA traffic check even after I'd finally remembered to put back the alarm by an hour.

'Still asleep?' A hint of anxiety now. 'Were you up that late? Nice night?'

I repeat the happy-ending line, all I can manage, and she laughs lightly. She was always better than me first thing; this morning more so. My leg is sore and stiffer than usual after a three-mile hike from Dunphy's car to mine.

God, I wish she was lying by my side, just to talk to, to hammer out some of the thoughts that went through my mind in a restless night. Were they too wild? Too dark? She'd have listened and helped forge them into some sort of shape.

'Peregrine Cummins,' she says, businesslike. 'His only registered interest is Hedges Pharmaceuticals. He gets paid by them – a consultancy fee.'

'For doing what?' I ask, more or less awake.

'Normally nothing.' Another playful laugh. 'He's supposed to keep an eye open for stuff coming up, new legislation and the like, that will affect the drugs trade and lobby for or against accordingly.'

'Isn't that corrupt?'

'Oh yes. Unions do it, too. They sponsor MPs' campaigns – i.e. foot the bill – and expect them to dance to their tune.'

It's too early for a debate about what's wrong with British democracy, so I don't respond.

Cummins is at home, she goes on. She'd phoned him for a quote on the run-down of the coal industry. Having some constituents caught up in the fall-out, she knew he'd be wise enough not to volunteer his views. She gives directions how to get there. 'Are you still interested in Councillor Laven?' she goes on.

'Marginally. Why?'

'Only that there's a press release in about him and all other Tory Euro candidates being available to the media tomorrow at some boring working breakfast in London.'

Any good? she asks. Not really, I reply honestly.

I'm tempted to inquire if the police have released anything about a motorist found dead in his car, but don't.

She wants to know if we're still on for Mozart tomorrow night and I tell her I'm looking forward to it. She says she'll let me get back to sleep and we wrap up, friendly, but not overly affectionate.

Sleep is impossible, so soon I am lying in a green-tinted Radox bath, easing my leg, thinking, like Archimedes, an idea vaguely beginning to stir.

Overnight, that good-to-be-alive feeling has disappeared. Dunphy's death is a major blow, I recognise. He was the weak link, a way in that's now a dead end. To avoid the blow changing from major to mortal, I replan a day with lots to do. The foam's smell of damp pine finally shapes the idea into some kind of form, something extra to do.

The local radio headlines are digested with breakfast – two whisked eggs scrambled in fried butter. There's nothing about any motorist dead in his car outside the pumping station on the A60. He'd have been found by now, I'm sure of it, but natural death is seldom news.

No newsboy calls at this place with a morning paper, not got round to placing a regular order yet. The postman seldom drops anything through the letterbox.

With nothing better to read, Dunphy's contacts book is studied over strong, instant coffee. Under A is Armstrong's ex-directory home number. Proves nothing. He handed it to me over lunchtime drinks yesterday. It's in my pen pocket.

Under B, no Brooks is listed. Proves nothing either. I disguise that phone credit card as a mythical extension to Jacko Jackson's home phone number.

The downstairs phone is used to call the Savoy Hotel, introducing myself as a research assistant from Jordan Associates, solicitors, seeking the dates of the stay of A. Gillman from Sydney, NSW, last summer. 'Write in,' a receptionist suggests, guardedly but politely, 'and the manager will consider your request.'

Apart from Mum, I've written to no one since I left Emma's word processor behind at home, not even Christmas cards.

Some time or other, just to go through the motions, I'll drop by the Savoy and slap my not-quite-expired warrant card on the reception desk. Not just yet, though; more important things to do.

Nearly nine, which means By-the-Book Brooks will be in his office at HQ. His secretary takes my next call.

On the advice of my solicitor who is threatening publicity I'm anxious to avoid, I ask for an urgent meeting to discuss my uncertain future. She slots me in for ten past three.

My timetable is fixed now. It's going to be a twelve-hour day minimum. Which is what? Fifteen an hour times ten, then add times two. A hundred and fifty quid, plus thirty.

If I get some juicy low-down on those HP flu jabs, I'll trade it in for Michelle Fogan to use in her separate lawsuit against the company tomorrow. She might offer double pay. What's that?

Three hundred and sixty. In a day!

Strewth, I could get used to this job.


Apart from shortening Peregrine to Perry, Cummins' contribution to the classless society had been to add the word 'Farm' to 'West Bank Manor' in black letters on the top bar of a five-bar white gate, making it sound a place of toil rather than the retreat of an absentee landowner.

It still looks like a manor, standing in isolation well back from a narrow lane a mile or so from the nearest village.

The house is three-storey, mature red brick, flaking here and there. On a windless day thick smoke curls lazily from a tall chimney in the steep, blue slate roof. White paint gleams on windows and front door.

At the lane end of the driveway, a small red post box is fixed on a telegraph post. It advertises twice-a-day collections – for his exclusive use, I suspect, as there are no other houses within view.

The tyre tracks on the long approach are neat lines of newly laid flagstones. Exhaust fumes have scorched the grass between them shorter than the front lawn which has a thick, uneven coat.

Behind a line of naked poplars, a riverside field looks more like a flood plain after the rains, home from home to a flock of seagulls paddling in it. The sky is grey, the clouds high; no rain yet this cold morning.

Behind the house the driveway opens out into a Tarmac yard, once a crew yard. The hay barns and livestock pens have gone. All that remains of its agricultural past is a long, empty greenhouse, glass panes caked with dirt, at the entrance to an orchard of bare, straggly trees and a row of half a dozen dilapidated stables; all signs of the home of a townie trying to look countrified.

I park up, but don't lock up, and walk by unpruned roses next to the side of the house.

A fair-haired woman in blue, thirty-something, spots me as I pass a window. She has opened the front door by the time I've reached it.

My warrant card is produced for the first time in eight months. My rank precedes my name and request to see Mr Cummins. 'Come in,' she says with a duty smile on a pale face that bears only the faintest touches of make-up.

She leads me, soundless in spotless cream trainers, across a light hall with a pine staircase running up from it. Her blonde hair reaches down to the shoulder blades on a denim shirt. A shapely backside is encased in pale jeans.

I'm pointed to a room and told to make myself at home, which would be easy to do. There are three-, two- and one-seaters, all deep brown, grouped around a black grate in which logs burn slowly, not enough heat for a sizeable lounge. The longest seat has newspapers scattered about the cushions. More are in a pile alongside a cream telephone on a small round antique table by a maroon and cream Regency striped wall.

She does not follow me in, but continues down the hall. I remain standing behind the three-seater facing the fire. I glance down on an unopened broadsheet paper. Staid though it normally is, it has the government's latest sex scandal on the front page, thinly disguised as a serious piece on the effects of all the adverse personal publicity MPs are getting on the Conservative party's Euro election chances.

I've noticed before – but only because Emma pointed it out – how holier-than-thou quality papers castigate the tabloids for running gutter press scandals, then find some highbrow reason for retelling the same story.

Next to the paper is a well-thumbed document with typed capitals on the title sheet: 'VOLUNTARY EUTHANASIA'. With one eye on the opened door, the other takes in: 'Submissions to the Medical Ethics Committee of the House of Lords'.

Cummins walks in. Like nearly all new Tory MPs, he's fortyish, dark and handsome, but only five feet ten, as tall as me. He, too, is in denim shirt and jeans, his pressed to a crease. It's either a symbol of their togetherness amid the domestic disharmony of their party or he's failed to declare Wrangler in the Commons register of interests. 'Hope nothing's amiss, Inspector.' He smiles as he demotes me.

'Matter of fact, it isn't a police matter.'

His smile is fixed into place now and doesn't alter as I tell him of my injury and how I got it. I put on a peevish face. 'The event drew a certain amount of flak from the opposition benches during some debate about civilian deaths arising out of police actions.'

He nods vigorously, though I don't recall seeing him in the TV snatch from the almost deserted Commons. 'Astonishing, aren't they, when it comes to law and order?'

Either because he's concerned about my wound or he's pegged a political ally, he finally spreads his arms in an invitation to sit. I take the one-seater by the fire, he the three-seater at right angles to me.

Tidying up the papers, he admits he wasn't in the chamber at the time the railway line death got its public airing. Next time he'll say something in defence of the police service generally and me in particular to put the record in Hansard straight.

I shake my head. 'Thanks, but not on my behalf. I want out of it. The reason I'm here is to seek your help in expediting my medical discharge.'

'They're not letting you go, surely?' He launches into a pep talk. Wrong time to lose experienced men with the government gearing up for a crackdown on crime etc. 'You'll want to be a part of that, won't you?'

Nothing would please me more, I respond, but all that's on offer is admin with prospects of future advancement frozen and I've better things to do.

'Are you a constituent?' he asks pointedly. Emma had fore-warned me of this. MPs won't poach other members' cases. It's not that they respect each other's territorial rights. They don't like to waste their time with protest letters and phone calls if, at the end of all their hard work, there's no vote in it for them.

I incline my head in the direction of the village I'd recced on the way here. 'Just put in a bid for that white cottage for sale on the main street. Hope to sign the contract when my compensation is settled.'

His smile is such a permanent feature that it's impossible to tell if he knows the property. What he does know is that there might be a vote in me. 'In what way can I help?'

'HQ are shilly-shallying,' I complain, 'and, unless she gets

110

satisfaction and soon, my lawyer is going public.' I drop the first in a series of names I'm going to try out on him. 'Michelle Fogan of Jordan Associates. Know her?'

He nods, the smile gone. 'A firebrand, or so I gather.'

I hot the pace up a bit. 'She's had a fair amount of success with personal injury and medical neglect cases recently, I'm told.'

He laughs awkwardly. 'Not too much, I hope. She's against us tomorrow.'

I look surprised. 'You still practising law, then?'

'Oh, no, no.' He closes his eyes briefly but tightly. 'Just an action concerning a company I advise.'

Hedges Pharmaceuticals, I know, but don't say. Instead: 'I don't want more publicity . . .'

'Instruct the Fogan lady accordingly, then,' Cummins suggests, crisply professional.

'On the other hand, I want a quick clean break so I can take up a job offer, well paid, too, with Dunphy and Lawrence, the certified bailiffs . . .' It sounds less sleazy than private detectives, like a *Sun* reporter posing as a *Times* man.

I wait for some sign of recognition, but his head stays still, forcing me to continue. 'They do a lot of security work as well for Councillor Laven's charities.'

Recognition now. 'Does wonders for the old folk. Just got a New Years honour, richly deserved.'

I nod, wondering who recommended him for it. 'When he interviewed me, about a security contract that is, he wasn't, well, very confident that he'll soon be the North Mids MEP.'

Cummins pulls a face. 'Afraid he could be right . . .' He pats the folded front page beside him with its love scandal headline. '. . . unless we get our act together soon on these sorts of shenanigans.'

His hand moves on to the Voluntary Euthanasia document. 'Specially when there are so many important things to discuss.'

I flick my head towards it. 'You raised a fair bit of flak for yourself over that.'

He cocks his, more pleased than suspicious. 'You're well informed.'

'You were in the news around the time my bit of trouble . . .' I pat my thigh. '. . . was getting a mention in the Commons. Plenty of time to read and I was taking an unusually keen interest in Parliamentary affairs.'

'Bloody nonsense, wasn't it? Mischief-making, tying it into a review of the social security budget the way the media did.'

His face becomes very animated as he gives me a longish lecture on his position on mercy killing, concluding, 'Movement towards permitting doctors to help end the life of a patient dying in pain, distress and without dignity is gathering a head of steam.'

To encourage more, I tell him of an aged cancer victim who shared my grandmother's ward, unable to speak or move.

'Exactly,' he beams.

'But what happens,' I query, 'if, say, I had wanted to get rid of my dear old gran for her estate?'

He fingers off his reply. 'One, the patient must be in pain and/or distress. Two, condition terminal which no treatment can change. Three, the request must be approved by more than one doctor. Four, it must be in writing and withdrawable at any time.'

I double check. 'The written consent of the patient, you mean?'

He is nodding vigorously again.


The written consent of the patient, I muse. Like the forms those old folk at Laven's signed before being injected with jabs that spread, rather than checked, an epidemic.

Chilling thoughts curl like damp smoke into question marks within me. Could they have been signing their own death warrants? Were they really pro flu jabs?

Cummins gabbles on about 'the humane option'. I am studying him, not really listening.

Here is a man seeking power and position, someone who views controlling the ever-mounting social security budget as the way to achieving that ambition; who advocates euthanasia while praising Laven's care for old folk; who advises a drugs firm with access to those same old folk via Laven.

For what purpose? For trials. Of what? On a lethal jab which will put to sleep old people like old dogs.

Debate rages within me. Unthinkable. So was what the Nazis did, but they did it. But this is a civilised and democratic society. With politicians and civil servants prepared to see innocent men go to jail to cover up a secret switch in foreign policy. With doctors who get backhanders from drugs firms to push their products. Hand on heart, would you trust either profession with your own life?

Well, put like that . . .

Cummins is now questioning the way medical science is prolonging life without matching advances in maintaining its quality. I have been silent for so long that he asks, 'What do you think?'

I play safe and reply, 'It's a dreadful dilemma.'

So dreadful it hardly bears thinking about, but think I must. Not about how I would have acted had Gran suffered senility for years, instead of lying on her death-bed, warm and comfortable, bright as a button to the end.

Not about Grandpa if that stroke at the age of fifty-six had been paralysing, not fatal, condemning him to years of being unable to do the most basic things for himself, even signing consent for lasting relief from such misery.

Ethical questions like these are too deep, too painful, right now. I must concentrate on finding out exactly what things happened at the Laven home last winter.

Now Cummins is pessimistically predicting that the Parliamentary committee will not go the whole hog, but compromise by allowing doctors to withdraw treatment once they have exhausted their duty to try to save life.

I tell him of the deaths of my grandparents and add that, had their final days been different, I doubt whether I could have found the courage to commend mercy killing.

He wants to know if I have parents and I tell him of my mother, still comparatively young. 'In later and different circumstances, you might find within you that courage.'

To emphasise that he's claimed the final word in this one-sided discussion, he asks, 'In what way can I help with your more immediate problem, Mr Todd?', prematurely civilianising me.

'By raising it with the Home Office. One call from them to HQ is often enough for the deputy chief to take some action.'

He is frowning. 'Are we talking about Mr Brooks?'

I nod, not too energetically.

'That doesn't sound like him.'

I don't tell him that at HQ By-the-Book is regarded as being i/c 3D – discipline, dogma and discharges. Instead I backtrack. 'He's dragging his feet on my case.'

'Why?'

On the one hand, I answer, he doesn't want me to go. On the other he's offering no incentive to stay.

'Always struck me as very sound,' Cummins chips in.

'Oh, he is,' I say, adding for emphasis, 'As a pound, but Dunphy and Lawrence won't keep the job open long.'

Again the names don't appear to register. Let's see if this one does. 'The prospects are limitless. There's talk of a major security contract at Hedges Pharmaceuticals.'

He is frowning again. 'I'd beware Messrs Dunphy and Lawrence, if I were you.'

'You know them?' I ask, suitably surprised.

He shakes his head. 'Who are they?'

I choose present tense very carefully. 'Dunphy's an ex-colleague on the force, a former sergeant. Lawrence was...' I can't very well say 'redundant pit deputy', not very sexy in private eye terms, so I make him 'ex-National Coal Board security'. I pause. 'You have reservations?'

'Security in multinationals is somewhat more high-powered than those two sound. We're dealing here with drug developments worth millions, computer hacking, all manner of high tech matters.'

'We?' I query, very quietly.

'I'm just a Parliamentary adviser to them, you understand.'

I nod my understanding.

'A new head of security is about to be announced once all the details have been finalised. A high profile appointment.'

A hopeful face gets no name, so I'm forced to continue, 'He might, of course, contract out some duties.'

'He might, but not until he's in place, I wouldn't have thought.' He shrugs, uncertain. 'All I'm saying is don't give up your career until you've made absolutely sure you have something better to go to.'

After thanking him for his time and advice I'm led out. 'Good day to you, Chief Inspector,' he bids, finally and fully acknowledging my rank.

Even as I pass the sitting-room window I can see he's already on the cream phone.

## 15

The shop above which Sligo Dunphy lived is on the corner of two terraced streets on the hilly east side of Mansfield.

The window that fronts the busier street displays coloured photos of the partners in black frames on either side of a plastic easel with a stiff white placard that lists their specialities in block capitals: 'CERTIFIED BAILIFFS, DEBT RECOVERY, PROCESS SERVING, SECURITY CONSULTANTS, TRACE INQUIRIES.' In upper and lower case, giving the impression of an out of alphabetical order afterthought, is: 'All confidential legal services.'

John Lawrence's strong, serious face is fair, lined and jowly, brownish bags under distant brown eyes, hair brushed forward, unparted and receding, Dunphy's age.

Behind the display, fawn vertical blinds have not been drawn tightly enough to block a snatched view of a burly, bespectacled man standing over a sitting woman.

Just gone noon, I see on a wall clock behind them. I push open the duck-egg blue street door, stiff from either a swollen frame or under-use, and step inside and up to a grey formica counter.

The man is Lawrence, standing behind the woman who has her head down over a thick cash book. He doesn't look as good in the flesh as in his photo. The bags beneath tired eyes are browner and bigger, magnified by steel-framed bifocals half-way down a pitted nose. He finger-prods them up as he looks up, rather annoyed at being disturbed.

The woman at a well-filled desk is mid-fifties, brightly dressed, not in mourning. Her neat, shortish hair has a blonde tint. 'Yes?' she says, barely withholding a sigh.

I fix a beam on Lawrence. 'You must be Johnny Lawrence.' I stick out my hand across the counter. 'Heard about you.'

He straightens his back and walks, not at all nimbly. This gives me time to take in three more desks, one with a word processor and printer like Laven's, one empty, grey filing cabinets next to clean magnolia walls, a potted palm in front of window blinds free from dust. Not Jordan Associates, but not the flea pit I'd expected either.

He reaches the counter to take my hand. 'Phil Todd,' I say. 'How do.' I grip his hand tightly, shake firmly and hold on, looking over his shoulder. 'Dunph not about?'

'No.' He eyes me cautiously.

'Oh.' I let go of his hand.

'Can I help?'

'He told me to pop in around noon.'

'About what, Mr Todd?'

I try a baffled expression. 'Didn't he mention me?'

He shakes his head.

'Oh.' I switch my features to disappointed.

'Haven't you heard?' He pauses, gathering himself. 'He's collapsed . . .' I let my face fall. '. . . and died.'

I groan softly. 'Jesus. What a shocker.' Chin is lowered towards chest. In the way people do when they get bad news, 'What a shock. Jesus,' is repeated.

'Mmm ,' he says, giving nothing away.

'I was with him last night. At Laven's. He dropped me off in Arnold.'

He seeks the time of the trip. Not wanting to be too specific, I pause for a moment's thought and tell him, 'Around eleven.'

Did he seem all right? he wants to know. A touch of indigestion, I answer.

'Got his bang on the way back,' he mumbles.

'Bang?' I query, genuinely concerned at the prospect of his death being treated as a road crash which would require an inquest.

He throws his right hand across a grey shirt and taps his heart. 'Coronary.' I try not to show relief. 'Pulled off the road and died.'

I sigh sadly. 'Well, that's it then. Well . . .' I look from him to the woman and back again. '. . . Dunph and me . . . er . . .' I take my time. '. . . well, we discussed a bit of business last night . . .'

Sombreness loses out to interest on his face.

'He was quite keen,' I continue, 'but said a decision was out of the question without you being in on it.'

His thin lips are just holding back a smile. 'What on?'

'You won't want to even think about it now with all this worry.'

'Think about . . .'

'Unless, of course, you've time for a quick one.' No response. I press on, 'You look as though you need it. I know I do after news like that. Jesus. What a shock.'

He turns from the counter to another busy desk next to where the woman is sitting and picks up a thick, blue jacket from a high-backed chair.

He pulls it on before opening a flap in the counter. As he turns to lower it, he speaks across his shoulder to the woman. 'Mind the shop, Maggie.'


It's no strain on a sore leg to keep in step with Lawrence who walks quite slowly, breathing noticeably laboured.

The high cloud is breaking up, allowing a pale sun to make its first appearance of the week, somewhat shyly, a long-absent friend uncertain of its reception.

He talks as he walks. Sherwood division had called him just gone one. A patrol crew had found Dunphy soon after midnight. The national vehicle computer came up with Dunphy and Lawrence as the registered owners of the Peugeot.

As Dunph was twice-divorced, with no children, his next of kin being a married sister in Galway, Lawrence went to the City Hospital to do the formal identification.

There'd have to be a post-mortem because he hadn't seen a doctor lately but, the police hinted, the result was a foregone conclusion. He'd phoned his sister who was flying across to fix the funeral when the coroner issued his certificate.

He hadn't known until I'd told him where Dunphy was last night because, each having their own speciality, they sometimes went days without seeing each other. I mention he was accompanied by Brucey Boy. He says, face disapproving, that he sees him even less than his partner.

Having tutted here and there, where appropriate, I give him my rank and length of service. The limp provides an excuse to tell him of the wound and impending medical discharge. 'Known Dunph from our days up here in the '84 coal strike.'

This, in turn, gives Lawrence the opportunity to gripe, as miners do, about the year-long dispute. He was a member and branch official, not of any union, national or breakaway, but of the association of colliery overseers and deputies, sort of underground foremen. It explains why Dunphy and Brucey called him the deputy.

He moans quite a lot, not without justification. Having helped to keep the home fires burning to win the dispute, suffering abuse and at risk from militant pickets, and having contracted bronchitis in his years underground, he was declared redundant when his pit, Moorwood, was shut in the late eighties.

I suspect he sunk a fair chunk of his hard-earned pay-off into Dunphy's business.

From collier to debt collector is not the quantum leap it sounds. Their image of hard-drinking wife beaters with coal in the bath went out with his namesake – D.H. Many live middle-class lives, which the national union's out-of-date, out-of-touch leaders failed to comprehend when they tried to turn them into socialist storm-troopers.

What the day-to-day danger of their job gives them is the resilience to rise to the occasion. Several ex-miners are special constables, weekend bobbies doing their bit for law and order, and a few have become bailiffs, serving injunctions and feeling the collars of those who disobey their judges.

We have walked some distance downhill, passing several smart pubs and the theatre in its little cultural oasis.

Stretched out ahead are the orange, lemon and cream canopies on the wooden frames of stalls in a market-place packed with shoppers.

We thread our way through. At an ornate statue, pink stone greened by algae and whitened by pigeons here and there, we veer away from the pillared town hall towards a pub with a curved, white-clad front and black shop-style windows.

I guess he is taking me to his local for a longish session. I'm going to lead the way in, get to the bar first, suggest a double scotch, make sure he's seated before I place the order which will be ginger ale for me. I'm going to do all the buying, get him well pissed and talking.


First through the door, my step is slowed by the sight of Brucey among a small, but rather loud, drinking school. He detaches himself and ambles, loose-limbed, up to us, half-empty pint glass in hand. His face is flushed. Not his first of the day, I detect.

His red Forest shirt advertises an ale alongside the Major Oak motif on his chest which is not the brand of beer on the labelled pumps behind the U-shaped counter. 'What yer want?'

Lawrence looks at me, not him. 'I'm getting these.' Without waiting for a reply, he turns to the barmaid. 'Tomato juice, please.'

'Make it two,' I pipe from behind him.

An amused smile dances across Bruce's wide mouth.

Lawrence looks beyond the barmaid to cold food displayed in transparent cases next to the till. 'An egg and cress and ...' He turns to me.

'Beef salad.'

Bruce downs the rest of his drink in one go and holds the empty glass to the tree over his heart. Lawrence still ignores him as he settles up with a tenner.

Only when it becomes plain that he hasn't included Bruce in the round does he speak to him. 'Some bad news, I'm afraid.'

'Heard,' says Brucey, pre-emptively. 'From Laven this morning.' He looks from him to me, a glare. 'What happened?'

I tell him what I'd told Lawrence; he what the police told him.

'Fuck me,' says Brucey, sadly.

'It's what you get when you don't take care of yourself,' says Lawrence, pocketing his change.

'I take care of myself,' Bruce replies, the tree expanding on his chest.

'As long as you know,' says Lawrence, turning away, glass in one hand, plate in the other. I pick up mine and follow over the tiled floor to an empty table.

As we sit side by side on a dark leather wall bench, Bruce returns alone to the bar. His gang standing before a dart board in a square blackboard begins to break up. He is proffering his empty glass to the barmaid.

Lawrence, I guess, has made this longish walk to ensure that Bruce knows about Dunphy's death. His duty done, he doesn't want to drink with him.

He sits upright, as if taking the chair at some union meeting. Even before biting into his sandwich, he becomes very official. 'What bit of business did you have with Dunph?'

I bump up the expected proceeds from both injury compensation and Gran's house sale and tell him we'd discussed my buying in as a junior partner, but any decision had been put on hold until Lawrence had been consulted.

He is eating, only manages a Mmm, so I go on to anticipate that he won't want to make any quick commitments in view of the overnight developments.

'Are you leaving with a decent testimonial?' he asks, bluntly. I give him my puzzled expression. 'No black marks, I mean.'

'No.' Pause for a surprised look. 'Of course not.'

'Reckon you could get certification as a bailiff from the county court?'

I reckon so, but ask why.

'Dunphy, the pillock, had ours withdrawn because of his arrest over that computer hacking.'

I tell him what I've heard about that case in some detail and put on a hurt expression. 'He told me he was in the clear.'

'The bubble went in,' he says.

A puzzling statement this. Bubble is an oft-used police term for complaint or tip-off. I guess that Lawrence picked up the slang of

119

the service working with an ex-cop. I guess, too, that he means someone complained or tipped off someone about Dunphy hacking into the computer. I'm not going to burst this particular bubble with too many questions too early.

Certification is important, he is explaining, because solicitors used authorised bailiffs for lots of legal work like process serving and repossessions.

I flick my head towards the bar and Bruce. 'Is he in the business, too?'

'Dunph used him on spec. The heavy at evictions.' I wonder how many lorry-loads of repossessed property got lost on the way to auction. 'He's a . . . er . . .' He was going to say something nasty about Bruce, but tones it down to '. . . unreliable.'

I am sensing a fractured working relationship here and still don't pry.

Naturally, I insist, I'd want an accountant to look at the books before investing. He shrugs OK. Naturally, he counters, he'd want me to apply for and get a bailiff's certificate before negotiations could commence. I nod OK.

He asks what I was doing bumping into Dunphy and Bruce at Laven's and I tell him of my moonlighting missing person inquiry, not naming names.

'Success?' he asks.

'Some,' I reply modestly. 'Still a couple of loose ends.'

Now I do try a name. 'My solicitor is Michelle Fogan.' I am watching his face which gives nothing away as he munches. 'She's handling my compo claim and house sale. I'd want her in on an agreement.'

Straight away he shrugs to say: No problem.

I finger a crumb from the corner of my mouth. 'Dunph thought there might be trouble with her.'

Completely out of context, he demands, 'How well did you know him?'

I exaggerate our relationship, ending with a smiling, 'He was quite a case.'

'He was a total shit,' he says, smiling back, 'and, if we're going to do business, we're going to have to be honest with each other.'


Not speaking ill of the dead is a maxim that gets minimum mileage over two more tomato juices, both on Lawrence who continues to ignore Bruce, drinking quite rapidly alone at the bar.

120

Dunphy conned him out of half his redundancy buying into a business that turned out to be going bust, Lawrence complains. Only negotiating skills learned in his shop steward days won the contracts to refloat it. 'Idle, useless on admin,' he declares, disgustedly.

I start dishing the dirt on Dunphy's enforced departure from the police service ten years earlier.

Lawrence cuts me short. 'Strong Arm told me.'

A breakthrough, so I sing Armstrong's praises for a sentence or two, then ask, very casually, how he got to know him.

'From the strike. Used to co-operate on ways of getting the workers through the picket lines without causing a riot.'

We swap a few picket line tales, then I report, 'Saw him this time yesterday.'

'Wish I'd checked with him before going into business with Dunphy,' he says, deeply disgruntled.

Time for a spot of fishing. 'Dunph was telling me he owed Armstrong from some escapade in their young days.'

'Wouldn't surprise me. People were always having to dig him out of trouble.'

'Did he mention it?'

'Not interested,' he replies between bites.

Another cast is tried. 'How about some fatal shooting involving Deputy Chief Brooks?'

His tired eyes are guarded, distrustful. 'Full of crap, he was. Always getting Bruce...' He flicked his head at the bar. '... pissed and giving him the great-I-am.' Then, aggressively: 'Why?'

'Retaining his police contact will be useful to both of us if we go into business. Know who he was?' I ask, very quietly.

His determined headshake is a bitter disappointment. His bored reply, 'Maybe his contact book will show it,' is a major worry. How long before they find it's missing? I fret.

'Let's lay our cards on the table,' I urge, impatient to get on with it. 'If, say, we do reach a deal, what sort of work will you expect me to continue from his caseload?'

'Councillor Laven was his biggest single client. Meet him last night, did you?' I nod. 'Another shithouse.' Another nod.

Gently, I probe how well Lawrence knows Laven. Hardly at all, he claims. Dunphy regarded him as his private assignment.

I float another name. 'Was Perry Cummins, the Tory MP, also a customer of Dunph?' Before he can ask his usual, cautious 'Why?' I speed into, 'He's got some tie-in with Hedge Pharmaceuticals at your old pit.' A lie now. 'Dunph mentioned last night a possible security contract there.'

'Bullshit.' Dismissive.

'That's what he said,' I maintain evenly.

'He was always full of deals that never came off. He was bulling you. To make the business look good, a multinational on the books.' He shoots a pitying look. 'Haven't you heard?'

I shake my head.

'They're signing up a security director. That's what Strong Arm told me. Forty thou a year.'

I don't want to sit here looking dumbstruck, so I whistle enviously. 'Should have applied for it myself.'

'There's no way, is there, that any half-decent security director will give major security sub-contracts to a man with Dunphy's track record? It's blarney.'

'Pity,' I say sadly. 'Is Armstrong in for the job?'

He looks doubtful, says nothing.

I try again. 'If you're an old pal of his – and I know him well myself – do you think we could use him, like . . .'

Brusquely he cuts me off. 'No chance.'

'I mean, on the QT. Now that . . . with Dunph dead . . . we're short of a police mole . . .'

'Too straight.'

'So he wasn't Dunph's contact then?'

He laughs derisively. 'They loathed each other.'

I go straight in. 'Was Brooks his mole then?'

'Don't know. Honest.' His expression looks more suspicious than honest; not without reason. Some of my questions must seem odd from someone who's merely exploring the possibility of buying into a business.

All I can do is re-emphasise the value to our potential partnership of good, quick information from official channels, then retreat to an old subject. 'If Michelle Fogan handles any agreement, do you think we might get her firm's contract back? I get on quite well with her. And I'm doing a decent job on her missing person case.'

'Might.' He sounds and looks doubtful.

'What went wrong?'

He's suspicious again.

'If I'm going to try to sweet-talk her back into using our firm,' I point out, 'I need to know.'

He picks his words carefully. 'Serving two masters at the same time, was Dunph. Always a mistake.'

I don't follow and say so.

'While Dunph was working for Jordan Associates, he came across something very useful to Laven. And since he was his main client, well . . .' He dries up, looking at me intently.

I sense I can't push this and sigh with genuine frustration. I'm more or less satisfied he never knew Dunph's police contact and fear the secret may have died with him. He has no inside info from Laven Havens; another dead end.

He is looking at me, so I revert to the third string in my bow. 'Better get back to my missing person inquiry.'

'Much to do?' he asks, just to keep the conversation going.

'A hotel to check out and a union bod to see tomorrow.' I add, almost a throwaway, 'Steve Grady.'

His features sharpen. His eyes narrow. His body sways towards me, crowding me. 'What's your game, mate?'

Such is my surprise I can think of nothing to say, just frown deeply.

'You an undercover cop or something?'

I shake my head vigorously. 'Christ,' I gasp it. 'No.'

'Well, you'll not implicate me in any of Dunphy's shitty doings.'

I put on an expression of shocked innocence. 'What are you talking about?'

'All these questions, names. Laven. Michelle Fogan. Now Steve Grady.'

'But . . .'

'But what?' He snorts. 'All this let's be honest crap.'

'I am being honest.' And I take him honestly down the long road I have travelled these last forty-eight hours, naming names – Arnie Gillman, Harbour Heights Residents Association, Dennis McCarthy on *Afternoon Special*, Laven Havens and Mrs Warminski who mentioned Grady and the legacy due to their union.

All the time distrust lessens on his face.

'I just want to ask Grady if Arnie had been in touch about his mum's estate,' I conclude. 'That's all.'

Suspicion has finally been replaced with the shadow of sorrow. 'Sorry.' He mumbles something about having no faith in ex-cops after his bitter experience with Dunphy.

I say nothing, letting him stew in the shame of jumping to the wrong conclusion.

His upper body has pulled away. He is looking away. 'It's just that, er . . . well, he and your solicitor were an item.'

I can hear the juice from my mouth travel noisily over my Adam's apple. 'Michelle's kiddie, you mean?'

He looks taken totally aback.

'She makes no secret of it.' I laugh another lie, back in my stride. 'She even wanted me to baby-sit.'

'What . . .' low, slow, '. . . is secret is . . . the father . . . on whom Dunphy was double checking on the police computer and got caught.'

I sit back and look ahead of me, not daring to look at him. I have lied so often on this assignment that they are coming out automatically. 'Dunph told me most of it last night.' I give my head a puzzled shake. 'But not that.'

He smiles secretively. 'What he can't have told you – because he didn't know – was that I put the bubble in.'

I turn sharply. 'To the police?'

A headshake. 'To Steve.'

I look hard at him to ask an unspoken Why?

'A decent bloke. Married, two kids. He was the only official from the regional trades council who'd even talk to us rebels during the strike. Got to look after your mates, haven't you?'

I feel like a stiff drink and a bit of time to think. Going to the bar and buying another round would have given me both, but Lawrence declines. I excuse myself to go to the toilets instead.

I do a lot of my thinking, even note-taking, in toilets these days. Let's hope Vice isn't running a purge on cottage queens hereabouts. My conduct would take some explaining.


It lasts longer than three small bottles merit but I have much to mull.

So Steve Grady is the father of Michelle Fogan's baby.

Dunphy must have discovered this when he was working regularly at Jordan Associates. Who from? His gossipy old mate Ogden, the coroner's clerk? What's the connection between Ogden and Dunphy? Worry about that later.

Dunphy tipped off Laven about Grady. About what? That he's the father of a love child? Who gives a shit? He's a provincial union leader, not a national politician, not a Tory anyway.

Dunphy comes unstuck seeking confirmation from the HQ computer. Confirmation of what? Why?

Could it be that Grady was making waves over the grand donation due to his union from Lillian Sharpe's estate? Could be. Confirmation of something detrimental on Grady in Special Branch files would buy him off or frighten him off. Must be.

Sharing the same office, Lawrence rumbles what Dunphy's up to. Out of loyalty born in the adversity of the coal strike, he tips Steve Grady about what's going on.

What was going on? Can't be the kid. This is the Labour party, not a Tory shiredom. These are the secular Notts coalfields, not the chapel-going Welsh valleys.

OK, I've worked some of it out, but by no means all.

Bruce has taken my place on the wall bench, and doesn't stand as I approach. Lawrence does, anxious about getting to the airport to meet Dunphy's sister off her plane.

'When's the funeral?' asks Bruce, whose accent is broader and thicker after his solo wake at the bar.

'Up to her,' Lawrence replies curtly.

Bruce tries a conciliatory smile. 'Laven's offered me a job.'

'Dead man's shoes,' rasps Lawrence, turning, motioning me towards the door. 'All you're fit for.'

'What about him?' Bruce slurs after us, truculent in drink.

Good question, I concede, but neither of us bothers with a reply.

# 16

In the bright, bustling market-place, I announce I have a couple of quick calls to make. Lawrence, fussily friendly again, keen to make amends, offers the use of his office phone.

For a second I am tempted to walk back with him. Countless questions race round my head, bursting to emerge, notably: What dirt was Dunphy trying to dig out on Steve Grady? What use was Laven intending to make of it?

Now is not the time to ask them, I reason. To do so would entail levelling with Lawrence about the flu epidemic and HP's jabs. I rate him, but don't know him well enough to trust.

To squeeze more out of him without giving him that trust risks another flare-up and, more importantly, prompting him into tipping off his union mate Grady that I'm asking questions. I need to get to him first – and fast.

No one must overhear what I have to say. Maggie, minding the shop, is the least of my worries. What concerns me most is the phone call Perry Cummins was making before I was even off his premises.

A chain of calls would have followed, I am sure of it. From now on in, no one can be sure who'll be listening into whom.

We walk quite briskly across the cobbled square. I realise with relief his rush to leave the pub has more to do with keeping his airport appointment than snubbing Bruce. I hope he's no spare time to call Grady.

Frowning, I flick my head back at the pub. 'Who is he – Brucey Boy?'

'Some thug Dunph hired, a relative or friend of a mate; otherwise unemployable except as a night-club bouncer.'

'And a poacher,' I add. I tell him about the deer he mowed down.

Lawrence gives Bruce's surname as Smith, too common to mean anything to either of us. Dunph paid him cash in hand.

Moonlighting, I think. Dodging the Inland Revenue. But then on this job I, too, am technically part of the black economy, the only economy that's doing much these days.

At the entrance to the street leading up to the theatre we part with a handshake and a promise to talk again after Dunphy's financial affairs have been unravelled and a price can be put on a partnership.


A phone box is vacant in a block of four on a pedestrianised street beyond a row of bargain clothes stalls.

I feed in a fifty-pence piece before tapping a number I've called once already today.

'East Mids Combined,' says the switchboard woman. I request the Missing Persons Unit.

'Sergeant Hann,' says a second woman.

'Sweeney,' I say.

'Oh.' Surprise in her tone.

'I've got a meet at HQ with Deputy Brooks at three ten.'

'Where will it be?' she asks.

'The usual spot,' I reply. 'Where will they be?'

'The usual places.'

We hang up without the usual banter, even a thank you and goodbye. No one will be able to trace that call. It was all so brief that I could have got away with ten pence.


Two numbers I can never remember are necessary for the next call. The contacts book, which I've carried since being caught short for change on Tuesday, is thumbed open at J to find them. The 100 operator takes down both.

Only the last four numbers are repeated back to me by the man who answers. 'Sweeney,' I say, brightly, then make the mistake of asking, 'How's it going?'

'Terrible.'

The last eight months have been terrible for Jacko Jackson, my partner on the day I was wounded. He retired soon afterwards to write crime books based on his thirty years in CID. At his New Year party, the only festivity I attended, he complained loudly and increasingly drunkenly that his first manuscript had been rejected by ten pisspot little publishers. Now the count has gone up to a dozen pisspots.

'What are you up to?' he finally asks.

I tell him briefly but honestly, no time for cock and bull.

'Holy Moses,' he sighs dreamily. 'What a story.'

It is astounding the change that has come over him. Life is no longer good v. evil, right v. wrong, but stories to tell and sell.

I ask him if he's heard the latest about Dunphy and he complains, exaggerating a little, that he hears nothing from nobody these days. He grumbles on about phoning HQ to refresh his memory on one of his own cases he wants to draw on and getting the bum's rush.

When I tell him the clampdown on info is down to Dunphy's failed attempt to hack into the HQ computer, he denounces him as a bastard. And when I reveal the latest on Dunphy is that he is dead, he doesn't retract, merely passes the worried comment that he's about the same age.

I want to know if they ever worked the same patch since both were on the east side before amalgamation.

No, he says, Dunphy was coast, he was city-based. He knows, of course, that he quit after Brooks busted him from sergeant to constable for stronging up a confession for some picket line GBH. 'Most people would have been blown out, their pensions down the pan.'

127

He knows By-the-Book Brooks much better, having often been carpeted by him. They went back to his early days. 'He was a mid-seventies version of you, Special Ops, weapon-trained, tear-arsing all over the place, getting shot at, or in his case . . .' His voice tails off.

I complete it for him. 'Shooting dead an armed burglar on the coast. Was Dunphy with him on that?'

He can't recall and, in view of the current climate of paranoia at HQ, neither of us can cross-check, in the circumstances, he points out.

I float Armstrong, but he knows no more than me – that he started out on the coast so he may or may not have worked with Dunphy, that he did a good job in the coal strike and has been resting on his laurels ever since.

All of this is deeply disappointing and I tell him so, not in so many words. 'Some fucking use you are. Isn't there anyone outside of HQ you can ask?'

'I've an old mate who was coastal command DCI for years,' he offers without enthusiasm.

'Tap him up then,' I urge.

'On one condition.' I can hear the catch coming in his voice.

Oh, shit, I'm thinking. 'And what's that?'

'If it works, you give me the full story.'

'Never.' I'm appalled.

'Yes, you will,' he says urgently.

'I can't write,' I protest.

'Neither can I, but that's not stopping me.' A sadder tone. 'Maybe I need to change my main character. You could be it.'

'Out of the question,' I maintain firmly.

'All you have to do is spit it out into a tape machine. I'd even provide the blanks. Tomorrow night at . . .'

I am pointlessly shaking my head. 'Got a date tomorrow.'

'Who?'

'Emma.'

'Good.' He is very fond of Emma, genuinely upset at our split, but he's too wrapped up in the prospects of a fresh plot to repeat his usual Dutch uncle lecture about give and take in any relation-ship. He continues, 'I'll knock it into some sort of shape and . . .' He switches his flat local accent to awful Hollywood. '. . . change the names to protect the innocent.' It's a line from TV crime movies and he laughs at it.

'I don't know.' I do know I'm weakening.

He uses blatant blackmail. 'If I get first option, I make that phone call. Yes or no?'

I am running short of time, give up. 'Make another one, too, and it's a deal.' I give him the name and address of Hedges Pharmaceuticals, explain the query and, irked at being used, ask him if he's capable of looking up the number.

'That', he says, gravely, 'is no way to address a literary lion.'

We laugh and hang up.


Grady's bungalow is on the outskirts of Arnold, but gives the impression of being in the heart of the country.

It is one of only half a dozen dotted along an unmade hillside lane; at first glance, the cheapest – boxy and smaller than the rest, no double glazing, woodwork in need of a lick of fresh paint. A Ford Escort, left-wing red, E-reg, stands in the car-port, no garage.

A spotty youth answers my tap on the frosted glass of the front door. 'Come in.' He doesn't ask who I am. 'He's just on the phone.'

Hope it's not Lawrence, I think.

The hallway is sparkling magnolia. The lounge through which I'm led has a low, dark green leather three-piece, then an archway to lightly stained steps running down to a well-furnished dining-room. Beyond that is a conservatory where I'm pointed to a cane chair. 'Dad'll be right with you.' He climbs, light-footed, back up the stairs.

What looked like a modest abode from the front takes on a different appearance from here. The centrally heated conservatory is not prefabricated, but part brick, the glass framed in dark, hard wood. Some of the long sloping rear garden was lost when it and the dining-room were added to the bungalow.

Heavier footsteps on the wooden stairs and now I study a man, scruffy in brown cords and tartan shirt, coming through the dining-room.

My first reaction is puzzled envy. How could Grady – mid-forties, thinning fair hair, face pale and drawn – pull a cracker like Michelle Fogan?

'Want me?' he asks. His flat local accent has nothing to commend it either.

'Sorry to bother you when you're off. Phil Todd.' Rising, I stick out a hand which is taken in a weak grip. 'A member of yours, Mrs Warminski, suggested you might be able to help.'

'What about?' He doesn't make a move to sit.

'Over the past couple of days I've been making inquiries about a missing man whose late mother was also a member of your union.'

'Who?' Curt.

'Mrs Lillian Sharpe.' His brown eyes switch to alert. 'I gather you may also have made inquiries about her and her son.'

'Who told you that?' Sharper still.

'Mrs Warminski.'

His brisk questioning must make a change from the normal long-winded advocacy at industrial tribunals, where all petty little union officials think they're Perry Mason, but is off-putting one-on-one. A long answer might slow the pace a bit. 'As I understand it, your union's widows' and orphans' . . .'

He breaks in, shaking his head. 'Why are you making inquiries?'

'I'm seeking the whereabouts of her son.'

'On whose behalf?'

'His former employers.'

'Who?'

'Harbour Heights Residents Association in Sydney, where he worked as . . .'

'Why?'

'They want to trace him.'

'Why?'

'He went missing on a cricketing trip to England last summer and they are concerned about his safety.'

'Have they contacted the authorities?'

'The police, yes.' His face tenses, then lightens a touch when I add, 'They drew a complete blank.'

'Don't see how I can help.' It's the first thing he's said that doesn't have a question mark after it.

I go on, 'Well, it might be possible to trace him through his bank account.'

'So?' Back in the old routine.

'If he inherited something from his late mother's estate it might have gone into that account.'

Not even a So? this time, just a glare.

'Was Mrs Sharpe's estate settled after her death without difficulty or delay?' I continue.

'How should I know?'

'Wasn't your union due to receive a thousand pounds she willed to you?'

His features set firm. 'I'm not at liberty to discuss union finances. Or the private affairs of a late member.'

'But . . .'

He is shaking his head severely. 'My duty is to employees, not employers on the other side of the world.'

I repeat some of what I've said about the concern of his employers, but he stops me with, 'You're going round in rings.'


Too bloody true, I grumble privately. Not a bad phrase, though.

What am I on, after all? A fishing expedition. All through I've used missing Arnie and his late mum as the bait.

There are two circles of corruption at work here and I force myself to see them as separate rings on the surface of fish-rich waters. Two rings only.

Forget Michelle Fogan. Don't allow her and her child to muddy the waters. Whether Grady was her lover, is the father, has nothing to do with anything.

Concentrate on those two separate rings.

One revolves round Dunphy and his police mole – Brooks or Armstrong and now into that tight circle has stepped Sergeant Clarrie Ogden, Coroner Jordan's clerk.

Causing much bigger ripples is the ring that centres on the old folk's home and what happened there last winter.

Inside the ring for certain are Hedges Pharmaceuticals and Laven. Involved, too, could be Jordan himself in his capacity as a solicitor who drew up some wills and Dr Sam Walls in a medical role, or both in their capacities within the coroner's department where they failed to act on the mounting number of deaths.

The rings merge where Dunphy broke surface. He's used some info he obtained from either his mole and/or his work at Jordan Associates to aid Laven and HP in a cover-up. And he was trying to get more from Special Branch files when he got himself hooked.

Something to the detriment of Grady, some past secret that's nothing to do with adultery.


'Harbour Heights Residents are clients of Jordan Associates for whom I act . . .' As I resume, his eyes widen a little. '. . . having succeeded Mr Liam Dunphy in the post of their inquiry agent.' Wider still. 'I gather you knew him.'

He has to clear his throat before he can ask, 'Why do you ask?'

'Because I regret to have to tell you he has died suddenly.'

'Well, er, yes. Hmm. I'm sorry to hear that.' He looks more shocked than sorry. At least I know that Lawrence has not been on to him to warn him to expect a visit from me. 'Met him, hardly knew him,' he mumbles.

'I've taken over the inquiry from him. Have you ever spoken to him in connection with Mrs Sharpe's son?'

'No.'

'Have you spoken to Councillor Laven about Mrs Sharpe's estate?'

'Why should I?'

'Because she died at one of his old folk's homes.'

No response.

I'm going to have to slander the dead. 'I have reason to believe that monies due to Mrs Sharpe's son may have been . . .' I can think of nothing other than '. . . purloined.'

'By Mr Dunphy?' he asks.

I shrug.

'Does Councillor Laven know?'

I still stay silent.

'Well . . . er . . . no, no . . . We had no trouble. A bit of a delay. But no trouble. We got what we were due to. It's in the bank. I'm not prepared to say how much. So, er, we've no complaints. So, I, er, don't think we can help you.'

A cod question now. 'Was Dunphy involved in any way in obtaining the settlement?'

A headshake. 'We dealt direct.'

'Were the services of Jordan Associates used in any way in the transaction?'

'If you represent them you should know that,' he replies very drily.

I smile, non-committal.

'No,' he's compelled to say, 'it was dealt with directly between Councillor Laven and me.' He laughs uneasily. 'No point, is there, in running up legal fees?'

I'm going to harden up the questions. 'Have you had any dealings of any sort with Dunphy?'

'I don't see . . .'

Harder still. 'You see, my information is that he was caught by the police trying to break into their files for information about you.'

'That's *subjudice*,' he huffs, barrack-lawyer style.

132

'Not now he's dead, it's not.' The big one now. 'Was he blackmailing you?'

'Now see here . . .'

We are almost standing toe-to-toe. 'Was he?'

'Are you?'

'In a sense . . .'

'You're no better than Dunphy.'

'. . . but only to get information.'

'Drop dead, too.'

'Come on, Steve.'

'Get your information elsewhere. And get out.' He jerks his thumb in the direction of the steps.

I stand firm. 'Did you report this blackmail to the police?' He takes my arm at the elbow. 'If not, why not?'

I allow myself to be guided out of the conservatory. 'I shall certainly be reporting this,' he says lowly.

On the stairs he drops a couple of steps behind me, so I have to speak over my shoulder. 'Yes, but who to?'

In the hallway he slides between me and the magnolia wall to open the door as I reach it. He actually puts a hand flat to my back to push me through it.

On the doorstep I stand, smiling, and wondering how many private detectives get thrown out like this.

It would never have happened in the old days, my police days.


# 17


I am five minutes early for Brooks. He is his usual ten minutes late for me, an old ploy.

He likes to keep you waiting, wondering, worrying, especially before disciplinary inquiries which he chairs.

Twice I've appeared before him at formal hearings, rapped knuckles on both occasions for being rude to more senior officers.

Last month I was back for a less formal, much shorter interview in which he told me what would be on offer on my return from sick leave.

Standing in his secretary's office, looking out of the window, I recall the open-mouthed astonishment on his face when I told him to stick it and the job and limped out.

The first-floor view from here is of row upon row of parked cars between this lovely mellowed red building and the noisy A46. Mine, though, is not in sight. That's tucked away where I always used to park – in a bay with evergreens on three sides, so the bosses never knew whether I was in or out.

A soft cough behind me, his silvery-haired secretary, super efficient, attracts my attention. 'Right, Mr Todd.'

The phone on her desk hasn't rung. Her computer screen shows cartoon fish swimming which means it's on idle. No footsteps have come across the corridor. She knows without being told that the statutory ten minutes' torture is up.

She rises and leads me over the cord-carpeted corridor, opening a heavy door marked 'Deputy Chief Constable'. She waves me, hand beckoning to shoulder, like a traffic cop, but doesn't announce me.

The office has the floor space of Gran's living- and sitting-rooms, kitchen and hallway rolled into one. It's a fair walk on thick brown carpet to his large desk where he sits in a brilliant white shirt and black tie.

His head is down over papers so I get a good view of his hair, thick and black, just greying above neat, high sideboards. It will not come up until I have stood here for a while, alongside a chair facing him, deliberately placed just off centre. It's another old routine, the squaddie before his CO; a boss's technique he mistakenly thinks is unique.

I fill in time by looking out of the long window behind him on a far better view than his secretary's. A low sun is casting dark green spidery shadows from a host of native trees, bare but beautiful, across the paler green fairways of a golf course that surrounds HQ, once a country manor, since despoiled by ill-matching flat-roofed extensions.

Brooks must be a slow reader because the letter on top of a thick file is fairly short. He picks up a gold fountain pen from a blotting pad, ponders, adds his name, blots it. He replaces the pen, picks up the file and drops it in a tray to his right. Out of a tray to his left my file is lifted. He places it carefully before him.

Finally his deep brown eyes come up to meet mine. He nods me into the chair. 'It is, perhaps, fortuitous . . .' He likes words like that. '. . . that you asked for this appointment,' he says, eyes down again, 'otherwise, I would have sent for you.' He looks up belligerently. 'Why do you wish to see me?'

'To discuss my future.'

'We discussed that last month.'

I say nothing.

'Are you sure you have one?' he asks aggressively.

Silence is maintained.

He eases one buttock off his executive chair, throws the back of his head against the padded rest and rocks away from me. 'Why are you undertaking a private work inquiry whilst on fully paid sick leave?'

'I'm not,' I reply, very politely, asking myself: Who's put the bubble in – Superintendent Armstrong or Laven?

He shakes his head. 'Not my information.'

I shake my head, that's all.

'Are you denying that you have made inquiries about...' He rocks forward, over some notes. '... a missing man called Arnold Gillman on behalf of Jordan Associates?'

Well, well, well. It's worked. 'Yes.'

He realises he has committed a mistake often heard in courts of lumping two strands together in one question. Annoyance flitting across his swarthy face, he splits them up. 'Are you denying you have made inquiries about Gillman?'

I'm going to stand by my story, let him prove otherwise. 'No, I'm not, but not on behalf of Jordans.' I cross right leg over left, trying to look at ease.

'That, I repeat, is not my information.'

I'm not going to ask where his information comes from. Had it been an internal source – Armstrong – he would have volunteered it by now. It has to be Laven and he'll not admit association with him. Or is it someone within Jordans?

I'm going to stick to steadfast denials. 'I don't know who's put the bubble in but he's got his wires crossed. Jordans are handling my compensation claim against you.' I mean the police authority, but deliberately personalise it. 'Nothing to do with Gillman.'

Nonplussed, needing to cross-check his information, he has to fall back on the loyalty to the service line. 'It's out of order, in my view, to be poking your nose into the affairs of the Missing Persons Unit.'

'If I get a positive lead, Sergeant Hann will be the first to know,' I say, pleasantly.

'On whose behalf are you acting?' His tone is not quite so pleasant.

'It's a favour to a friend with whom I stayed on a trip to Australia.'

135

He's completely stumped, can't confront me with his informant. 'Do I have your word on that?' he asks lamely.

I suggest he asks his secretary to dig out the tape of Tuesday's *Afternoon Special* if he wants to check. 'I can't pretend that once I quit I won't be working for Jordans or indeed other law firms.'

'Is that your post-service plan?' he asks, mixing pomposity with disapproval, fixing me with an unsteady look.

I'm going to goad him. 'We all have to job hunt when our time comes, don't we? It's got to be better than security.' His eyes dart away. 'My plan was to go in with Dunphy.'

His eyes stay away. 'This may come as a shock but . . .'

I save time. 'Know about it. I was told when I lunched with his partner. It was a shock.'

It's no shock that Brooks knows. OK, there are scores of non-suspicious fatals every day on a patch this size. Only an exceptional case, a VIP say, would wind up on a deputy's desk. An ex-member of his force, particularly one so nefarious, is such an exception. I'll not read anything into that remark.

My right leg is stiffening. I change to left over right, still trying to look casual. 'You knew him, too, he told me.'

'Didn't everybody?' His tone is extremely edgy.

He shuffles his papers to signify the end of the subject but I want to dwell. 'Mr Armstrong cautioned me against doing business with Dunphy . . .'

'Wise advice,' he tells his file.

'. . . when I lunched with him yesterday.'

'You have an active social life,' he muses, refusing to be drawn. 'Now.' He braces himself. 'Why have you been going outside the force with your complaints?'

I frown. 'Sorry?'

'It's a straightforward question.' His voice is so jumpy that the sentence judders out. 'Why have you been complaining to an MP?'

My, my. His phone has been busy. 'I asked him to use his good offices in Whitehall to expedite my discharge.'

'To embarrass me, you mean . . .' I only manage a protesting No as he lets off steam. 'You know damn well these things take time. There's medical reports, insurers.'

I just about get out the point that it's a month since I made my application to leave, but he isn't listening.

'The offer on the table is only provisional.' Now he acts hurt. 'Such disloyalty after, what – twenty years?' Sixteen, actually, but

I don't correct him. 'No one has ever suggested we wanted rid of you.'

'It's what's known in industrial tribunals as constructive dismissal,' I say bitterly.

'It's entirely your own volition. You mentioned nothing about leaving when I visited you in hospital.'

'I had other things on my mind,' I say with an acidic smile, 'like amputation.'

A puzzled frown. 'What I can't grasp is why you want to leave now you're virtually recovered.'

'We went through this sitting here last month.'

'It was an excellent posting . . .' Brooks looks uncertain. '. . . in the situation you find yourself.'

The posting he offered was collator in the Major Crime Squad, the present incumbent, a sergeant, about to retire. 'Admin. A sergeant's job,' I say dismissively.

'Only because he was always too busy to get round to promotion exams,' says Brooks, true enough. 'I'm upgrading the position twice. It's the only upcoming vacancy, the CID chief assures me, in her department.'

'I'll be stuck there for ever.'

'Only until there's a suitable post at superintendent rank.' He is sorting through papers. 'You won't be ready for operational duties for another six months, the doctors say. That's Chief Superintendent Malloy's clearly stated view, too.'

I am fighting a losing battle here and need to open up another front. 'It's a dead-end job, a belittling offer and you know it.'

'For God's sake. What's behind it?'

That's a question I can't answer, so I say nothing.

'It can't only be that.' He wears an appeasing expression. 'Come on, man. Out with it.'

Far from working, I suddenly find myself in a tighter corner and scratch at my brain for a way out, finding one that fills me with guilt, but needs must. 'You know I can't work under Miss Malloy again.'

'Why ever not!' Shock. 'I thought you two were close.'

'Were,' I echo sullenly.

'What's gone wrong?'

'Work it out for yourself.'

He shakes his head, lost.

My left leg is too heavy for my right. I uncross it and smack the exposed trouser knee. 'This went wrong. She knew we were lying in wait for an armed killer, someone who had shot his victim in the back . . .'

'She thought he'd got rid of his weapon,' he breaks in, stoutly loyal to his CID chief Carole Malloy.

I'm working up a nice paddy. 'She could afford to think that, running things from afar. I was frontline, unarmed, and I got this. I could have got him. There was no need for it.' I slap my knee so hard it stings.

'Phillip.' It's the first time he's ever used my first name. He is waving down with both hands, seeking to calm me. 'That's easily said.' I know he is talking about pulling the trigger, the only man on the force qualified to do so. 'It's a great burden to carry through life.'

'Not if it's justified.' I can see the pain of memory in his eyes. 'And on the railway line it would have been.'

The outcome was unfortunate . . .'

'Unfortunate!'

'. . . tragic, but, operationally, the decision was right.'

I hang my head.

'What's brought this on? It's not like you. Is everything all right at home?'

I mumble something about problems, head still hanging.

Aggression having failed, he's all compassion now, offering me a counsellor for my personal troubles and a uniform posting for my professional problems to get me away from Chief Superintendent Malloy's command. He urges me to postpone my comeback for another couple of months.

By the time we end his next appointment is running twenty minutes late. He is desperate to talk me out of leaving.

Not because he wants to keep me, that I'm certain of, but to stop me poking around Laven and HP in an independent role, like every other person I've encountered these last three days.

'The force can't afford to let you go,' he smiles patronisingly as I rise.

You can't, you mean, I think. I promise to re-examine the whole situation, a promise I intend to keep.

An orange sun hangs in a stunning sky of pinks and crimsons, blues and purples. Suddenly I hate sunsets. They remind me of Emma and Koh Samui and the way it used to be.

I pull into a deserted lay-by, get out, making sure every door is locked. Inside an old red phone box, back to the sunset, I pass the two numbers under J to the operator, don't wait for the last four to come back. Without introduction, I ask, 'Any joy?'

'Just put down the phone on Hedges for the second time,' Jacko reports. 'Nothing first time. Said I was from the Police Federation and wanted to invite an ex-colleague, Howard Armstrong, to a reunion. They'd never heard of him.'

'And the second time?'

'Put on my American accent,' he says, proudly. He hears my groan. 'Well, they're multinational, aren't they? Told them I was London office of *Secure World* – good title that, eh? – and was lining up a series of articles about private enterprise head-hunting top cops for their expertise in security matters. "Try again in a few months' time," they said. "We're about to recruit just the man for you."'

'Get his name?'

'Embargoed until the formal announcement.'

Brooks, I am thinking; has to be, but all I express is the hope that his mate on the coast was of more use.

'Gold dust,' he replies.

Armstrong and Dunphy had worked together as young detectives on one *cause célèbre*, a right cock-up. A girl in a seaside village had been indecently assaulted, a bad attack, just short of rape. They arrested a near neighbour, the village idiot, got a confession, the only real evidence against him. An incompetent defence lawyer didn't dispute it, much less query a black eye and cut lip.

Two years on, a rapist was caught on the job up north. He asked for a score of attacks to be taken into consideration, including the one on the coast for which the near neighbour was serving time. 'Big internal inquiry, of course.'

'What was the result?'

'Hush money in damages. A promise to tighten up procedures, have a social worker, solicitor or relative present at future interviews, the usual crap,' says Jacko, cynically.

'What happened with Armstrong and Dunphy?'

'Got away with it. Insisted they only took down what the neighbour told them word for word and his facial injuries resulted when he resisted arrest.'

'What was your mate's feeling?'

'The old noble cause corruption.' This is the in-phrase for cops who have a hunch who did a crime, can't prove it, so they bend

139

the evidence to make a charge stick; for praise and promotion, not for backhanders. They kid themselves they are making the streets safer. What they are really doing is perverting justice. 'He thinks Dunphy manufactured the confession. Armstrong turned a blind eye, and kept his mouth shut. That's hindsight, by the way, based on the fact that Dunphy was caught in the coal strike in a repeat performance.'

So, I'm thinking, Dunphy owed Armstrong, not the other way round. He couldn't have been twisting Strong Arm's arm for confidential info; no leverage.

'Was By-the-Book on that job?'

'Dealt with locally.'

'Did he handle the subsequent internal inquiry?'

'An outside force.'

Disappointed, I ask, 'What about that fatal shooting?'

'Holiday-maker dead in a caravan. Blasted in his bunk. Holes in front of caravan indicated the shot was fired from the outside, went straight through.' He is telling it like a paperback blurb.

'Dunphy was first on scene. Witnesses describe fleeing man with shotgun. Brooks shows up an hour later, tooled up because it was an armed manhunt. Dunphy tells him the description fits a local poacher.'

He's still talking staccato. 'They go to his smallholding. "In all night," he claims. "Got a .12 bore?" they ask. He leads them to a shed, goes in ahead of them, snatches his gun from a corner, is about to train it on them and Brooks opens fire. One shot to the chest. He's as dead as the holiday-maker.'

'Anything out of the ordinary?'

'One barrel had been fired. The other was loaded. Forensics had no doubt it was the murder weapon. There were bits and pieces from the caravan, a gold pen, for certain, in the shed. The jury at the inquest brought in unlawful killing, robbery as the motive, on the holiday-maker and justifiable homicide on the gunman.'

'What's your mate's feeling on that?'

'Well, the poacher had no record of petty theft. No one was ever quite sure why he shot blind from outside the caravan.'

'Any theories?'

'The accepted thinking was that the holiday-maker heard him approaching, about to stage a hold-up. He looked out of the window and may have been able to recognise him.'

'Was Armstrong involved in any way?'

'He'd made sergeant and been transferred by then.'

140

'Was Doc Say Again called to the scene?'

'Never was police surgeon on the coast, always Sherwood.'

'Jesus, Jacko.' I'm going off him. 'Isn't there anything odd about it at all?'

'Only that there had been a spate of caravan burglaries and they didn't stop with the gunman's death.'

I vent my frustration. 'This info's not worth two seconds of tape for your bloody research. You're useless, Jacko. The deal's off.'

'You're the one who's useless, matey.'

'Get on with it,' I grunt.

'You asked a good question about the sex case clanger, but forgot it over the shooting.'

I wrack my brains, shaking nothing loose. 'What was that?'

'Who handled the inquiry?'

'Who?'

'With bodies all over the place, and no one to charge, who do you think?'

I am quite cross now. 'Stop pissing me about.'

'Come on. Try. It's not going to wind up in crown court. There's no one to put in the dock. So . . .'

Finally, I see what he's driving at. 'Coroner's court. Who was the coroner on the coast in those days?'

'Some old buffer, long since dead. Not Jordan. He's always been Sherwood-based, too. But you're getting warm.'

I try again. 'Who was the coroner's officer on the case?'

'At last,' he sighs. 'Constable Clarrie Ogden. Odd, isn't it, that soon after Brooks was promoted, so, too, were Dunphy and Ogden. Odd, too, isn't it, that years later when Brooks should have bounced Dunphy over that phoney coal strike confession he merely busted him, so he could keep his pension.'

So, I theorise, Brooks had been settling old debts.

'Is the deal back on?' Jacko wants to know.

Not quite, I think. 'One more favour. I'm going to phone you in, what, half an hour from Jordan Associates.'

'I've told you all I know.'

'I need an excuse to go in there, use their phone. Just waffle about anything. You usually do.'

The receiver goes down on a string of amiable obscenities.

# 18

Clarrie Ogden is hanging on to the phone, not talking, when I pop my head round the door marked 'Coroner's Dept'.

I step inside, press clenched fist lightly to left ear and make a dialling motion with my right index finger. He nods to the empty desk. I sit and tap Jacko's number from doubly refreshed memory. 'What shall we talk about now?' he asks.

'Anything,' I say, upbeat, making it sound like a question. Picking out a sheet of plain paper from the top drawer, I finally get to listen to him urging me to kiss and make up with Emma, not that it's any of his business.

I take out my ballpoint, interspersing a few yes's, OKs and reallys and making the occasional note and doodle. 'What's HP's number, by the way?' I ask suddenly.

Cruelly, he grumbles about not being my legman, but gives it to me. I write at his dictation.

'What do they do exactly?' I ask, feeling Ogden's eyes on me.

'What do you think they do, you lame brain?' Jacko sounds shocked. 'They make drugs and loadsamoney, don't they?'

'Like flu jabs, you mean?'

Jacko supposes so, and guesses at half a dozen other common ailments, one of them sexually transmitted, to which I add out loud bronchitis, writing it down in a list.

Frowning, Ogden hangs up and, soon afterwards, so do I with a sincere 'Thanks a lot.'

He is looking at me, gravely, and speaks formally. 'Have you heard about Dunphy?'

I nod solemnly. He confirms where he was found and when. I trot out a 'What a shocker,' then ask, 'Are you involved?'

He spreads his hands over papers on his desk. 'Just about to issue a certificate. Sister's picking it up tomorrow.' He jolts his head to his replaced phone. 'That was the pathologist. Massive heart attack.'

'Want a statement from me?' We eye each other, he cautiously. 'He dropped me off at Arnold. Must have had it on the way home.'

He shakes his head. 'No inquest.'

I put on a funereal face. 'Will you be going to the funeral?'

He hesitates, as if he hasn't thought about it until now.

'Wasn't he an old mate?' I go on.

'He popped into the office now and then,' he concedes, guardedly, almost grudgingly.

I feign surprise. 'But you go back a bit, don't you?'

He can't disguise his. 'How do you know that?'

The clock on the wall shows five past five. Brooks has the reputation of starting and knocking off early. It will soon be too late for Ogden to cross-check with him anything I'm about to say. 'Just come from a By-the-Book bollocking session. Someone bubbled me for moonlighting while on sick leave . . .'

'Wasn't me,' he interjects, alarmed.

I heave my shoulders, easygoing. 'I know who it was. No problem, anyway. He accepted my explanation.' I pause. 'We yarned a bit about Dunph. Said all three of you were together on that seaside shooting.'

'He said that? His face registers sheer disbelief.

'Just in passing,' I smile.

He sighs. 'I went along later. To do the . . .' He looks down at his papers. '. . . the normal, you know.' He is thinking.

'Wonder if Brooks will go?' I ask, looking away in thought.

'Doubtful.' He sounds it.

My eyes return to him. 'But you were all in the shit together, weren't you?' He is looking ready for a coronary himself. 'Looking down the wrong end of a gun, I mean. Believe me, I know the feeling.'

Ogden is at flustering pains to emphasise that he was not present when Brooks fired the fatal shot, only turned up later to do the preliminary inquiries for the coroner.

'Must get on.' Bald head down, he signs something, then starts to gather up his papers.

I have to keep him talking for a while, so he doesn't make that check call to Brooks. 'Saw Dunph's partner this lunchtime.' I nod north towards Mansfield. 'And a sidekick called Bruce Smith. He tells me Councillor Laven has offered him a security job.'

Ogden, confirming nothing, breaks off from clearing up for a little rightist rant about long-term unemployed not really being interested in finding work of which there is plenty if they bothered to look.

True, I agree, outlining some of the offers that have come my way merely by putting myself about. We have a lengthy grumble about social security scroungers and tax-evaders.

Gone half-past now; safe, I calculate, to make a move. 'Is Miss Fogan in?'

'Busy.'

I screw up the sheet of paper and toss it in the bin. I pocket my pen. 'I'll just tap on her door.' I stand. 'Fancy an early drink at the Burnt Stump?'

'Busy,' he says, making a conspicuous show of looking it.


Michelle Fogan, in a black blouse with thin yellow stripes, almost Man United's away strip, looks up from a file-strewn desk when I stretch my neck round her door after one tap.

No smile welcomes me. Her pale face is drooping like Eric Cantona's collar towards the end of a goalless wet Wednesday at Wimbledon when he's been marked out of the game, bogged down, well hacked off.

I won't ask if she's busy. 'We need to talk.' I step one pace in, then one back into the door, clicking it shut.

'I'm rather tied up,' she says, hardly moving her lips.

'Dunphy . . .' I begin.

'I know.' She sucks in her cheeks impatiently.

'How long was he legging for you?'

'Look . . .' Exhausted eyes behind granny glasses invite me to view her stacked-up desk. 'I've got . . .'

'Around eighteen months. Right?' I nod at her files, assuming she's swotting up the Hedges Pharmaceuticals case-papers for tomorrow's hearing. 'When did you get the brief on that?'

She sighs wearily, placing her pen on the file. 'I'm sorry but I'm up to my eyes and I've already had one interruption.' She nods at the phone. 'Stephen Grady.'

'You his lawyer?' I ask with a smile.

She shakes her head determinedly.

'Good. Then you can tell me what he said.'

'He was whingeing about your visit.'

'Wanted me off the Arnie Gillman inquiry, did he?'

'In a word, yes.'

'And what did you tell him?'

'That you were making inquiries authorised by me – and that, by the sounds of things, you were doing a thorough job.'

She's letting him stew, not entirely for professional reasons, I assume, chuffed. 'Thanks.'

She smiles for the first time, just a slight one. 'What's it all about?'

'I'll tell you. But first...' I nod at the papers. 'Those and Dunphy arrived here at the same time?'

'Thereabouts.' A petulant tone again.

'Doesn't that strike you as strange?'

She motions me closer, frowning.

I reach her desk. 'I suspect he infiltrated this firm to monitor your progress on your action against HP.'

'I don't believe it.' She speaks rapidly. 'I can't believe it.' She flops back, believing it now. 'Bastard.' She nods heavily. 'Dear God.' She closes her eyes. 'All this bloody work and all the time...' She stops, opens her eyes, seeking confirmation. 'He was leaking everything to Hedges?'

'Via Harry Laven.'

'You know...' She shakes her head, still finding it hard to believe. '... I could never understand it.'

She tells me a bit about tomorrow's case now. It's ten years old, transferred to her from Wales by an old law school chum. 'He sticks mainly to crime and he knows I like medical matters. Besides, the hearing had been scheduled for Nottingham.'

A widow is suing Hedges over the death of her young collier husband, she explains. He'd come to this coalfield as a striking picket, collapsed and died, a long way from home. In silver foil in his pocket had been found revolutionary new Hedges pills for bronchitis from which he suffered.

There was no evidence that he'd consulted a local doctor or on how he'd got hold of the pills. The company was defending the action on the grounds of unauthorised use of a drug, subsequently withdrawn.

What she could never understand was why, every time she got a breakthrough, a medical expert to give a specific statement on one aspect, they trumped it with another casting doubt on the testimony.

Her hands wave over her papers. 'All this bloody work.' She rocks forward. 'Right. I'll ask for an adjourn...'

Silent for some time, I leap in. 'Hang on.'

Her exhausted eyes narrow, not used to being interrupted by a hired hand, and she completes the word, '... ment.'

145

I pat thin air one-handed, slowly and gently. 'Just hang on. Let's work out what's gone on here.'

She wants to call in Ogden from his office down the corridor to cross-check when Dunphy started work for Jordans as a casual inquiry agent. 'He recommended him to the Old Man.'

My fast talking to talk her out of the idea only rouses a festering suspicion. 'Do you think Ogden's in on it, too?'

I must shuffle this away. 'It was just the police Old Pals Act in operation.'

She looks at me unsurely and I know she's wondering, not without justification, if she can really trust me. She's going to have to wait for the answer to that.

'Did Dunphy do any research on the HP case?' I ask.

Her long complicated reply is quite kindly phrased but the message is cruel – that the case is too scientific for any thick ex-cop.

I look around her filing cabinets, all neatly labelled, and caustically reply that what thick ex-cops lack in medical know-how they can make up for with expertise in burglary.

She rewards me with another faint smile, soon switched off. 'And he was working for Laven?'

'All the time,' I confirm, 'and Laven's financially tied into HP.'

She asks how. For the time being, anyway, I just tell her that, as chairman of the council's health committee, he smoothed the path to the old colliery site at Moorwood for HP and all the government grants that went with it.

'Ss,' she hisses, not completing the obscenity, 'and here was me thinking . . .' She trails off, not wanting to share her thoughts.

I need them. I nod at the files. 'In building your case against HP have you picked Dr Walls' brains? He's a police surgeon, after all, and he's always around.'

'No.' A single shake. 'I've used experts in the field – chest, drugs. Sam's not been in on it.'

'Mr Jordan?'

Her eyes narrow.

'Is he in on it in any way?' To head off a Why? I speed on, 'He seemed supportive of you yesterday.'

Another headshake. 'The old captain of the team bit. For your consumption, I suppose. Letting you know who's skipper here. He's quite cross with me for hiring you.'

'Why did you?'

'Why not? That letter from Sydney had been sitting in the

pending tray for a week while he'd gone off for a Christmas cruise. I was the holiday duty partner, so I actioned it.' A tantalising smile. 'You don't regret it, do you?'

'Oh, no,' I gush. 'I'm enjoying it.' Pause. 'So Jordan's not involved in that?' I nod down at the HP files.

'Outside of his inquests his specialities are probate and property. I've not consulted him. Nor has he seen the papers.'

'And Sergeant Ogden?'

'Not his department.' Suspicion rekindles on her face. 'What are you driving at?'

'It's what's known in my old trade as elimination. It only leaves Dunphy. Why was he fired from here?'

No response, lips pursed, clamming up.

'You hinted, talking to Mr Jordan in front of me yesterday, that it was personal.'

'It is.' Crisp.

'To do with your child?'

Her face is icier than when I walked in.

'You make no secret of it. Neither did my own mum.' I smile at her, hoping she's got the message that I'm a love child, too.

She seems to; at least she smiles back, quite warmly. 'May I remind you that I engaged you solely for four days' work on the missing Arnold Gillman.'

'What am I supposed to do, report back to you on Arnie alone and forget everything else I've learned?'

The frost on her face returns, not quite so sharp. 'I don't see what my personal life has got to do with you.'

'Absolutely nothing, except Dunphy discovered who the father is and Laven turned that knowledge to his commercial advantage.'

'Tell me more,' she says, with a frigid expression that tells me she doesn't really want to listen.

'This fella of yours . . .'

'Ex-fella.'

I nod at her phone. 'I can hazard a guess at a name if you like.'

'No need.'

'Do you want to hear this or not?' I ask testily.

She shrugs, to tell me that's up to me.

'This ex-fella of yours is a star of the left, a union official . . .' She's paying attention now. 'Dunphy finds out about you and him and child, but Laven tells him it's not enough.'

'Enough for what?'

I have to speculate here. 'To stop him making inquiries at the

147

Laven home about Arnie's late mum and a thousand pounds due to his union under her will.'

She smiles thinly, knows I'm talking about Steve Grady. Why we don't both just come out with his name, I don't know, but if this is the way she wants to play it I must go along.

I continue, 'So Dunphy tries to plug into my old HQ's files to find out what he can on him, gets caught in the process. Dunphy's partner Johnny Lawrence rumbles his game and tips your ex-fella off.'

'Why?'

'A union favour from ten years back.'

'You're wrong.' Her face is set stern. 'He has a wife and two children. In the end he couldn't face leaving them.'

If that's what Grady told her and that's what she wants to believe, the girlie romantic, let her.

There is no confirmation of what I suspect and that's this: Grady co-operated with Johnny Lawrence and Howard Armstrong during the coal strike. Don't ask me why. Yet.

But if that came out he'd be branded in trade union circles as a state informer. Far, far more damaging in his left-wing world than any secret affairs with wealthy professional women or any number of love children; both vote winners down at the working man's club, I'd gamble.

Why spoil her illusion that she was dumped for family duty if it makes her feel better?

And why, smartarse, spoil your own illusion that you've come up with an answer? Aren't you forgetting something? Dunphy was caught *before* he got any low-down on Grady from police records. So there has to be another reason why Grady is running scared of me. What?

Irritating questions these, but I sit back, trying to look as relaxed as in the bath when an idea rose with the scent of its pine. 'That's Dunphy taken care of. How about Laven?'

She looks down on her papers. 'HP's my immediate problem, not him. Lord . . .' She closes her eyes as if in earnest prayer. 'I do so want this one.'

She describes the hardships the widow, her client, has suffered, displaying a passion for justice in a profession whose members sometimes strike me as jockeys happy to be retained to ride any horse that's running in the race as long as there's a decent fee and half a chance.

'And now you come in here and blithely tell me that they know

148

all the arguments we'll make tomorrow.' She hangs her head, red hair falling forward.

It's time to level with her, a bit anyway. 'Get Laven and we may get HP.'

Her weary eyes come up.

I am torn between suspicions of mass murder for Laven's own financial gain and an HP pilot scheme to test for Cummins, their paid Parliamentary mouthpiece, his embryonic theory for reducing the ever-increasing expense to the state of the ageing population.

Sitting here, before a sharp lawyer without a shred of proof on either, both seem so far-fetched that I fear I'm about to make a complete conspiracist idiot of myself.

I go for compromise, always a safer line. 'I think he uses his residents for clinical tests.' I tell her briefly what I learned on my outing to the panto. 'He gets them to sign consent forms they're too confused to understand. Something went badly wrong last winter. I think it was an HP trial.'

'Why?' she demands yet again, eagerly this time.

I tell her I saw HP after the names of several late residents when I looked over Dunphy's shoulder on to the computer screen in Laven's office on Tuesday night.

'God, if we could only prove that,' she says, almost entranced.

'Maybe we can.'

'How?'

'By doing what thick ex-cops are good at.' I go on to explain in some detail.

'If only you could,' she sighs, eyes shut for a second.

'For fifteen pounds an hour?'

A saucy laugh. 'And a big bonus.' She comes out of her reverie. 'You can't.'

'Why not? Dunphy was doing it to you.'

She stops, thinks, then chuckles, very sexily. 'As your solicitor I'll have to claim I didn't hear that.' She looks down at her papers. 'Can't concentrate now.' She glances at a gold wrist-watch. 'Fancy a drink across the road?'

I'd welcome the chance to get to know her socially so a hint of regret is injected into my reply. 'I've two calls further up the road. Tomorrow lunchtime still on?'

She nods, confirms the time and place, and keeps her head down to write something on a small black leather-bound pad, tearing off the top sheet. 'My home number.'

I stand to take it from her across the desk. 'Ring me with anything. Anything at all. Any time.'

I turn and head back to the door. 'And don't get caught,' she calls after me with the thinness of tension in her voice.

# 19

There's only a couple of answers needed from Howard Armstrong. I've been in the Burnt Stump almost an hour, bored witless, and still haven't had the chance to put the questions.

Armstrong, blue-suited tonight, hailed me to join his half-dozen cronies, all veterans, a couple I know, standing at the bar. Once more I've told the tale of my shooting, evasively non-committal about my future.

To background music – Whitney Houston, but, mercifully, not too loud – Dunphy's death has been raked through, me not letting on I was with him last night. It's stale news now, the time for false expression of sorrow long gone. Not much regret is voiced, particularly by Armstrong.

Three fizzy ginger ales are extending my bladder. Excusing myself, I head for the nearby loo.

I like to concentrate on this task, feet well apart, the 'at ease' position, don't look over my shoulder when the second of two sprung doors is pushed, then snaps back in its frame.

'Well?' A voice to my left.

I'm delighted Armstrong has joined me, but frown all the same. 'Well, what?'

'What have you decided?'

I take a detour. 'Saw Brooks this afternoon.'

He groans with relief that's nothing to do with anything I've said. Then he sort of sighs out, squeezing his words, preoccupied, 'Don't trust him.'

'Why not?' I ask, looking down, not a pretty sight. I'm finished, but hear quite distinctly that Armstrong, who's been on pints, has some way to go, so I stand my ground.

'Thought he was leaving you to me,' he grumbles.

I shake something, not my head. 'How do you mean?'

'He phoned yesterday, told me to have a stiff word with you.'

Without asking, I've got one answer I came here seeking;

astonishing what blokey confidences and gossip are sometimes shared in the privacy of the privy. 'About what?'

'You running around with Dunphy.'

'How did he know?'

'Don't ask me,' he says guardedly.

'What did he say, exactly?'

He is shaking his now. 'That he'd had a call, saying you were keeping bad company.'

I zip up and zip my mouth, turn away, take a few steps behind his back to the basin. Hands under running water, I say over my shoulder, 'Did Brooks tell you where to dispatch your crew to find me?'

He walks up behind me. 'Yep.'

I turn away and punch the automatic drier into action. 'Only Dunphy knew I was at Jordan Associates.'

He takes my place at the basin. 'That's not the way I heard it.'

No, I reason, but that's the way Dunphy heard it. That's why he was so surprised last night when I told him I'd been here, lunching with Armstrong. He gave Laven my location and Laven told Brooks. Dunphy had expected me to have been whisked to HQ to see Brooks. I've got collusion now.

Above the drone of the drier, Armstrong is lecturing me about the risky game I'm playing, the beer talking. I need it to talk on. He is shaking his hands, waiting to put them under the drier.

I make him wait a little longer, rubbing mine. 'So when we were talking in there yesterday . . .' I incline my head towards the bar. '. . . you were firing his bullets?'

A step back finally gives him access to the hot air. 'Only trying to help.' He is rubbing his hands as though there's blood on them.

'Why did Brooks get you to deliver his lecture?'

'You were trampling around on this patch. "Down to you," he said.'

A stranger walks in and heads towards a cubicle, a sit-down job. I lead the way out through one door, but stop in the carpeted lobby short of the door back into the bar. A flick of my head draws him closer. 'I don't trust Brooks. I think he wants me to drop litigation, then he'll give me some dead-end job.' A straight look in his eyes. 'Like he screwed you.'

His drop.

'Seen for myself the way you're wasted,' I go on sympathetically. 'You had a terrific record in the coal strike. Everyone says so. Terrific.'

He preens a little, the right chord struck.

'What went wrong?' I ask.

'Dunphy.' He is facing me, my back to the wall. 'I worked with him, you know. On the coast.' He sighs mournfully. 'A long time ago.' He dries up.

'Come on, Strong Arm,' I appeal. 'I've upset Brooks in some way and can't work out why. I need to understand the politics before I can make a decision.'

'I got too close to Dunphy.' He looks down, going further back in time. 'He thumped a suspect.'

I can't prompt him with what I know, so: 'And?'

'Manufactured his confession.' He is wearing a confessional face.

'Did he land you in it?'

'What do you think?'

I don't know what to think yet, so, 'How did it turn out?'

'The poor little sod was innocent, so when the real offender coughed, there was hell to pay.'

'Where did that leave you? With dirty hands?'

'They weren't exactly clean.' He tones his involvement down a bit, the way all cops do in a case gone wrong. 'I was a bit wet behind the ears.'

'You stood by him at the inquiry?'

A reluctant nod. 'Told him afterwards, though. "Never again. Next time you're on your own."'

'And was there a next time? In the coal strike?'

'He stitched up some poor little picket for GBH on a strike-breaker. And I do mean little.' He brings a hand up. Fingers outstretched and stiff, he taps his collar bone.

'So small,' he goes on, 'that I remembered him; black-haired Yorkshire youth. Next day I was in court with one of my own pinches. Saw him in the dock. At the time he was supposed to be hitting someone with half a brick I'd personally seen him in a peaceful demo. Yet he'd given a full confession to Dunphy. Work it out yourself.'

There's no need to. Armstrong would either have to blow the whistle on Dunphy or stand idly by while another innocent man went to jail – for a considerable length of time in that hysterical climate of opinion in which judges and magistrates, to their ever-lasting shame, were also caught up.

'Like a fool,' he continues, unhappily, 'I tipped off his union's lawyer via a trades council contact.'

'Steve Grady?'

'Yer. We traded info now and then.'

'Quite right,' I agree.

He is not encouraged by my support. 'Thought it was on the QT.'

'And someone bubbled you?'

'The lawyer, not Grady. Raised hell and, when Brooks backed Dunphy, he said, "Right, we'll call a senior officer to prove it." He didn't name me, but Brooks didn't have to be a genius to work out it was me. It left him with no alternative but to take disciplinary action against Dunphy.'

I put on a puzzled face. 'It's surprising that Brooks just demoted Dunph . . .'

'Stress of the job was the defence.'

'. . . but didn't sack him.'

'They go back, don't they?' he smirks.

'Where to?'

'That fatal shooting.'

'Heard the folklore, of course, but it was before my time. Did something go wrong on it?'

'I was transferred by then.'

I press him. 'Did Dunphy cover for Brooks on that shooting in the same way you covered for him?'

'Honestly don't know.' His honest look becomes puzzled. 'Why?'

I have pushed too far. 'To judge how far I can trust Brooks, believe what he's offering. Can I?'

'Look what happened to me.' He looks forlorn. 'Nothing. That's what happened. That's the bitch of it. I was rapped for not going through channels. I wasn't demoted or promoted, just transferred to admin and left to rot.'

The ice box, they call it. They don't sack you. They try to freeze you out.

'Ever demand to see Brooks, have it out with him?' I ask.

A solemn headshake.

'Why not?'

'Because I suspect he knows about me going into bat for Dunphy at that inquiry. Why reopen that can of worms with my pension round the corner?'

The man who went into the cubicle comes out, eyes us aggressively, suspecting a spot of importuning, and we go quiet.

I look down at my dirty brown shoes on the patterned carpet.

153

I'd like to tell him his troubles with Brooks will be over soon – that he's departing, either to be security director at Hedges, or, better still, to jail for corruption.

I long to share confidences with him, tell the truth to get the whole truth about what went on in the coal strike between him and his union pals, Johnny Lawrence and Steve Grady, something that Dunphy tried and failed to discover for Laven.

I can't, daren't. Once he was a good cop. Now he's a pisshead and gossip. It would be round the bar in five minutes.

My feet have gone cold. I drag them over the carpet to catch the door before it springs all the way back and follow him out, feeling suddenly sad and tired and lonely and anxious.

I know I'm going to have to go through with it on my own.


Just off the Redhill roundabout is one of those roadhouses, standard design, standard menu, where I drop in for a standard beefburger with a glass of milk over the *Evening Post*. Dunphy hasn't made it. I don't read the sport, too much on my mind.

Face it, I order myself. Right now, you're all you've got. Talk it through; a team talk for one.

Well then, what's the match plan? Putting myself about, covering a lot of ground, dropping a word in this ear and a different word in that to see whose mouth they later come out of. What's achieved? Go on, list them. Like a team sheet.

Lawrence, you can forget. Armstrong, too. Brooks just used him yesterday to put some space between him and me. You've used them. Now drop them.

Either Brooks or Ogden was Dunphy's informant. One or other owed him for something connected with that seaside shooting, but catching the mole, you've already decided, is the smaller ring on the water's surface.

Concentrate tonight on the bigger circle of corruption. Is the tactic working establishing what happened at the Laven home?

Partially. It's frightened Steve Grady into contacting Michelle and Laven, and Laven into contacting Brooks. Perry Cummins MP, too. He reported me to Brooks.

I pay up at the till, actually remember, a bit late in the assignment, to stow the receipt in my pen pocket.

I drive half-way round the roundabout and head north again up the A60, beyond the pumping station. No vehicles are parked on the grass verge where Dunphy stiffened up.

Beyond the turn for the Burnt Stump, where Armstrong will still be drinking and gossiping, I worry that I should have gone for that extra question.

I should have said, 'Was Grady the source of your hot info on flying pickets in the coal strike? Will his help be recorded in Special Branch files? Is that why Dunphy tried to break into the computer?'

Too late now. Even if he'd answered, would it have mattered? Whatever's on record Dunphy didn't get to. There's something else about Grady you haven't scratched the surface of yet.

Concentrate on Laven, your target for tonight.

On the wooded approach to Mansfield, there's no glance right at the hospital entrance where that fateful decision was made. For an hour, Emma hasn't entered my mind; wonderful what solace you find in work.

All the women who made this assignment possible, this curing breath of fresh air, flit into my thoughts. Michelle Fogan dwells there the longest. Bright. Beautiful. Bossy. Bad news, I fear. She flits out again.

Concentrate.

A glance left to where the mown-down deer in its bed of curled bracken will be stiffer than Dunphy in the morgue. Well, Bambi, I think, if there's any justice, let's hope last night's venison casserole at the Laven home did for Dunph. Did me a favour. With him gone, tonight there's only Brucey Boy and Laven to worry about.

Worry about Laven.

Tonight, you must listen to him more closely than wildlife for the approach of an enemy, all he has to say and then work out who told him what, the classic way to prove conspiracy.

Grady, for sure, has been on to him. He'll hit me hard with questions about that thousand due from Mrs Sharpe to his union. Will he drop Cummins in it, too?

You must listen and watch tonight, like an owl in a tree, then swoop and make your kill.


Turning off the A60, the dashboard clock shows almost thirty minutes to spare; time not to be wasted.

Two return trips and I know the way through the maze of country lanes to the home well enough to find the phone box where I ended up lost forty-eight hours ago.

I pull on to caked sand in front of the kiosk's door, get out, lock up, open the boot, exchange brown slip-ons for black wellington boots and take Gran's heavy black torch out of a Sainsbury's bag.

The sky is cloudless, the stars bright. Cold air nips at my face and hands.

The light from the phone kiosk cuts a widening cone of yellow for twenty yards into the gap between the regimented rows of pines, ninety feet high.

The grass beneath my boots is short and fine, very wet still, but not squelchy. The light from the phone box fades into deep shadows cast by the dark canopy of fir high above, closing out the starlight. I switch on Gran's flash.

From my right comes a scampering sound – squirrels among the pine needles and twigs that litter the forest floor.

Another twenty yards and my eyes eventually accept that I need not be walking on the grass. Each side of me run two lines of rolled limestone, the width of two wheels apart.

What on cursory inspection on Tuesday, hanging on to the phone for directions, had looked like a fire break between the trees now appears to be a lane for logging trucks with tracks to prevent their heavy loads compacting and eroding the sandy soil. I take the right side track.

The deeper into the forest, the stiller and warmer the air. Nostrils seek the bathtime scent of pine, but find instead the fruity smell of rotting vegetation.

Ahead, the hiss of distant traffic – from the A60 a few miles to the east. From much closer comes the bark of a fox, more of a yap really, like a small dog's, irritating.

There are no clouds to hold the reflected neon lights of the more distant Mansfield. My eyes are so focused now that I do not need a torch to see the tracks begin to bend a hundred yards ahead of me.

I thumb it off. A mistake. My left toe-cap catches something. Shit, I curse, as my body pitches forward, right leg bearing my full weight for a second, stabbing, hurting, but holding up, till my left catches up.

I stop, turn and switch on the light. A root, as long as its parent tree is tall, has snaked out of the plantation in its search for moisture and cut diagonally beneath the ride, patches of it eroded and exposed by the lumberjacks' lorries.

Had Gran's torch been a shotgun, with the safety catch off, it could easily have gone off. What did Dunphy say last night?

Something about tripping up and being blasted? Was that some sort of death throes confession?

For two hundred yards I take shorter, careful steps and see that several other roots have criss-crossed the tracks. Every step I think of Dunphy, unable to make sense of what he said.

The flash is switched off again when the side of the home comes into ghostly view like an L drawn in thick, black crayon. The old building to the left wears its steep triangular roof as a witch wears her hat. Two lights shining on the ground floor are yellow eyes. The sloping roofed extension to the right is her long nose.

It's two hundred yards ahead with the forest as cover for half that distance. The final hundred yards is a clearing of rough grass with a thick boundary hedge of trimmed conifers. The chalkstone tracks run as far as I can see in this light.

I stop for a minute or so, getting my bearings, then turn and walk back. Next time, I'll ride up this ride as far as I can, tooled up with the implements of my trade.

# 20

'Ah.' Seated at Matron's desk, Laven eyes me intently, quite welcoming, as I walk in, dead on eight.

With fumes of ale hanging over the office and a mud-splattered Nissan outside, parked alongside Laven's silver Scorpio, it's no surprise to find Brucey Boy here, too.

He is on the typist's chair which, on previous calls, had been my berth. His face is so flushed, skin shiny and tight, eyes heavy, that I wonder how many more pubs he's hit since lunchtime.

Laven rocks himself back in his chair. 'Good.' I amble up and stand before him.

'I'm just about London-bound.' He's wearing a light grey suit and bow-tie, hardly my idea of travelling comfortably. I remember tomorrow's early morning photo call for his party's Euro candidates that Emma mentioned. 'Haven't got a lot of time,' he adds.

'Neither have I,' I lie, desperate for every second I can keep him talking. 'I'll give you a lift to the train.'

Without a thank-you-but, a brisk headshake is declining my offer. 'Everything all right at the Savoy?'

He tugs each end of the narrow bow-tie, maroon with black polka dots, tightening the knot, not a clip-on. He works his jaw. Puffed cheeks rise towards his owlish eyes, dragging his mouth into a U. The result is hardly a smile.

No point in telling him that I've not got round yet to a final check at hotel reception. 'Fine.'

'Satisfied?'

A satisfied nod.

He stiffens rather than straightens his languid posture, beams. 'Good.'

I drop an eye sideways on Brucey Boy. He is sitting tight, not making room for me, so I half turn and lower my left buttock on the desk giving me a strategic overview of both of them. 'Sorry to hear about Dunph.'

It gives him the chance to accuse me of bad-mouthing Dunphy to Steve Grady. Instead, disappointingly: 'Sad. Yes.'

He leans forward, opens a stiff desk drawer. Head down, he addresses the inside of it. 'Three hundred, I believe.'

I hold my breath until his eyes come up and his right hand emerges clutching brown banknotes. He starts counting out fifties. The drawer remains open, its other contents alarmingly out of sight.

Instead of paying me off, I'd expected him to accuse me of breaking last night's agreement to drop further inquiries about Arnie Gillman and confront me with what I'd said to Grady.

'You sure I've earned this?' I ask, giving him a second chance.

'An agreement's an agreement,' he says pleasantly. He pushes the notes across the desk, followed by an undated receipt which says: 'For security services.'

I make no move to accept either and nod towards Bruce. 'He tells me you have him lined up as Dunph's replacement.' Bruce blinks, embarrassed by my breach of confidence. 'It must have been an awful shock when . . .'

Any topic will do, even this tedious one, so I gush out the abridged version of last night's trip, one eye on Laven, the other on the uncurtained window behind him.

All I can see in the glossy black glass are reflections of his fawn chair and his trimmed brown hair, not even the front trees of the forest.

This room is one of the ground-floor lights noted on my recce, the other the kitchen further along the corridor from which came the sickly sweet smell of hot milk as I walked in.

158

The window is sashed, one white frame above the other, both shut against the cold night air. They are fastened together by a copper knob on the top edge of the bottom frame that slides into a metal bracket on the bottom strut of the top frame. They are not gunged up with paint.

I'm volubly into how I got the shock news from Dunphy's partner Johnny Lawrence at lunchtime, Laven looking decidedly uninterested.

Now and then I glance at Bruce, trying to get him to join in the chat about our meeting. He seems to have drunk himself speechless.

Laven's face is registering the boredom that I am feeling as I conclude, 'When did you hear?'

He flicks his head towards Bruce without looking at him. 'First thing.'

I cock a quizzical look at Bruce. 'Err.' Pause. 'A police pal.' His first words are badly slurred.

Both fall into a moody silence. This is all they're going to volunteer. A police pal? What sort of policeman would make a pal of him? Who the hell is Brucey Boy anyway? What did Lawrence say? Family or friend of Dunphy who hired him. But Dunph had no family around here.

No time to think it through further, the silence lengthening, and I babble about the option to buy Dunphy's half of his business.

My eyes concentrate on the word processor, its screen greyish-black, switched off. It's an earlier version of Emma's at home, overtaken several times by ever-advancing chipnology. I note the dust-covered grey cable running behind to a plug on the wall and familiar disc drive below the screen.

Just one more thing to suss, but Laven stops the survey. 'In which case we can do more business.'

'How?'

'If you're going into security work full time, we have a vacancy that wasn't there last night when we discussed future openings, don't we?'

'As what?'

'Security chief.'

'But I thought . . .' I look at Bruce who is looking rather peevishly at me.

Laven looks at him. 'Perhaps you'd take him on the grand tour tomorrow.' Then at me: 'Familiarise yourself with our set-up.'

This is not at all the way I was anticipating this session to go. 'How much?' I ask bluntly.

'Fifteen pounds an hour, didn't you say?'

I shake my head.

'Isn't that what you said?'

'I'm tied up tomorrow. Have to see my solicitor.'

He smiles in silence.

Come on, I privately urge him. Say something like, 'Haven't you seen her today?' Then I'll know Clarrie Ogden's involved.

Instead, he says, 'All day?'

Blast, I curse. It's not working. Involuntarily, so wrong-footed, I blurt the truth. 'Lunchtime.'

'Take a couple of hours off then. It will be nice to know the organisation's in safe hands while I'm away.'

Glancing down at the receipt, I reiterate that nothing can be paid to me until after the new tax year, except cash.

'I've told my client,' I continue, not letting on whether I'm talking about Jordan Associates or Harbour Heights Residents Association, 'that Arnie Gillman was alive and well when he left our patch. It's been taken out of my hands.'

'What will she do now?'

There's only marginal interest in his expression but a thrill courses through me. He must know I was assigned by Michelle Fogan, not Jordan or any other partner.

'Dunno,' I reply honestly, and speculate dishonestly that she might hand the inquiry over to a London agency who charge a lot because they pay out a lot to bank contacts for peeks at private accounts. 'She could trace his subsequent movements that way.'

Now, surely, he must tackle me about some of the things I said to Grady about Arnie. Astonishingly, a slow, unconcerned nod indicates that he is totally untroubled about his whereabouts or fate.

My eyes go to the shelf above Bruce's head where the transparent box of discs still sits, key in the lock.

Laven turns to Bruce. 'Meet here at nine then? Take him on the tour and to wherever he wants to go at lunchtime.' He nods at the money and receipt. 'Sign, if you will. Put down any date you like.'

'Ought we to discuss hours, terms . . .'

'When I get back.' He beams. 'Get a feel for the job first.'

Someone, I'm certain, has been on and told him: 'Todd is on to us. Buy him off.'

I enter 6 April on the receipt, sign it, push it back across the desk towards him and pick up the notes, thinking: He's throwing money at me to involve and compromise me and, above all, to stop me from working for Michelle Fogan. Especially tomorrow.

The drawer squeaks shut on its stiff runners as I slide my backside off the desk top and slip the notes in my back pocket, not feeling in the least bought off.

# 21

*Friday, 7 January*
My head pops through the neck of a black track-suit top that's aired on the kitchen radiator for three hours while I dozed.

Know what's worrying me? my sinister reflection in the lounge mirror is asked.

You look like the Black Panther. Remember how he was caught and disarmed?

I was at university, twenty years ago, when his reign of kidnap and murder ended a couple of miles from Forest Town. They still teach the tale in training of two bobbies on patrol one cold winter's night like this. They thought he looked a bit odd, that's all, and decided on a stop and search.

Never thought I'd dread a chance encounter with a couple of uniformed coppers doing their jobs. With Excalibur, that Round Table half-marathon letter opener, and metal pliers in the thigh pocket and the other equipment they'd find searching the car, they'd feel your collar, bound to.

Soundless in black trainers, I climb the stairs, tugging at the collar to lift the top back over my head. In the small bedroom, I feel through drawers to find an old goalie's sweater, dark green, good camouflage in a forest.

Reinspection in the mirror above the dresser only convinces me that I'd still look suspicious driving at this time of night up the A60 by the very spot where that patrol took no time at all to find Dunphy dead in his car. What if that same keen crew, on the look-out for a Panther of their own, are on duty again?

I yank open an ill-fitting door to the wardrobe and take out an encased, expensive Pro Kennex that's not hit a black ball in eight months.

I'll leave it in view on the passenger seat, tell 'em I'm on my way back from an inter-club tournament. Still not good enough. I'll be driving away from where I live.

A few steps to the bedside table, and I pick up my warrant card which joins the tools of burglary at my thigh.

If any young patrolmen out to make names for themselves pull me over, I'll flash it, tell them they're interfering with a senior officer on a special op. One word to anyone, I'll warn 'em, and they'll be clerking for By-the-Book Brooks for the rest of their service. That should do it.

Need anything else? A disc, certainly, to copy anything interesting. We each had our own, never used each other's. I left mine behind. No point in bringing it here without a word processor. I wonder if Emma ever brings it up on to the screen to read my stuff – letters to mates and Mum, mainly. All she'd find is written proof of how much I loved her. Hope she has, know she won't.

Forget this. Forget her. Concentrate.

You daren't operate the printer, a clattering daisy wheel, at gone midnight, so just copy over one of their spares.

Forgotten anything? Gloves. I go back to the dresser. The brown leather pair with press-stud fasteners Gran bought me are still in the Christmas wrapping she never lived to see me open. Too precious.

The grey woolly ones I used for goalkeeping are too bulky. Think. Think. 'Keeping. 'Keeping. The skin-thin chamois I used under my stumpers' gloves for cricket. Just the job. I rummage till I find them in a tight, dry ball and stuff them in the thigh pocket which I pat.

I'm as ready as I ever will be.


My head is cold. Forgot that peaked blue golf cap, I chide myself.

Always the same, isn't it? Take care not to look like a burglar and you don't even see a patrol car on a fifteen-mile trip, not too fast, not too slow, to avoid attracting attention. All that worrying had been a waste, needlessly expended adrenalin.

I enter the ride by the phone box, kill the lights and drive at a crawl further up the twin chalkstone tracks than I'd walked earlier.

Not as easy or as smooth as anticipated. Having no headlamps is not the problem. The crystal-clear sky lights the clearing like a projector cutting a path over the heads of a dark, still audience in a cinema.

The trouble is that all the audience seems to be smoking. Grey mist is rising from the forest floor to knee height. Once or twice

162

the car bumps gently over unseen tree roots, and, a couple of times, lurches to tell me I have wandered off the tracks on to grass. Getting out, locking up, I can't see what tell-tale tyre marks are left behind.

I head across the wide grass verge and duck beneath the lower branches in the first row of pines. A damp, fusty smell surrounds me. Just a yard or two inside the forest it's so dark that I fumble to find Gran's torch.

Its widening beam of light melts into the fog around my feet. I hinge my wrist for horizonal, then vertical views. The trees inside the forest, starved of life-giving light, have no lower branches, just a few bare ones towards the top, close to thick, spreading crowns that block out the star-filled sky.

I follow the second row, short steps, trainers hardly making a sound, quiet as a mouse. Loud enough, though, to alert a tawny owl which whoo-whoos at the prospect of supper on the forest floor.

Wings flap and I crane my neck to see its silhouette on a bare branch near the top. Further away, a deer calls, more of a belch than a bark.

I emerge one row back from the edge of the plantation. Through the lower branches the L shape of the home looms.

The torch is doused. Another light disturbs me; not on the ground floor, one up. Watch and wait for a while, I decide, putting a hand on a tree trunk to take the weight off my leg. My palm comes away wet from rain that has taken more than a day to find its way in riverlets down ninety feet of cracked, grey bark. I fish out my chamois gloves, looking up from the task of pulling them on every second or so to find the light still shining.

Both feet and legs feel surprisingly warm, but my head is now so chilled that I am cursing myself again for forgetting a cap. I try to work out the sudden change in the weather, and remember what Grandpa taught me about radiation frost when the cold air seeks to warm itself on the earth and only causes consternation.

Condensation, I correct myself.

No, consternation, I admit, heart tightening, breathing shallow. Fog frightens me. Never did. Does now.

True, it's nothing like a spring fog, one of which settled over the railway line where I could hear, but not see, that killer marching Jacko at gunpoint towards me.

Dawn then, not one in the morning. Disorientated birds chirping all round, drowning the muffled voices, getting closer.

163

Hardly able to see a hand in front of you then. Now I can see, if not my warm feet, at least a lit window a hundred yards away.

Nothing like conditions then, I comfort myself. Unless danger creeps up on you like a snake on its belly, you will see it coming. Relax. My heart obeys.

The faint sound of running water floats towards me, strange on sandstone where few streams flow. The light goes off. The sound now of a cistern being filled so noisily that it travels a hundred yards through the clear, thin air, nothing to compete against, except the pounding of my heart. A pensioner with a prostate, I decide, and, for no real reason, think of Jacko and smile.

Silently, out of the forest, my right foot steps unseen into the fog.


One leg is stiff, one rubbery as I canter, crouching, through damp, ankle-deep grass; an easy pace, but I'm breathless by the end of the hedge. My heart blames lack of fitness. My brain knows it's fear.

At the corner of the extension, I don't stop to look about me, simply turn off the grass on to a concrete path and jog its length on tiptoe, thirty to forty yards, to reach the original, old house.

By the first window, I do stop. Hands cupped, nose pressed to a pane, I peer into a kitchen with steel hot-plates; wrong room.

A few shuffling side-steps to the next window. Hands form a porthole misting the glass, but I can see the back of the chair where Laven sat, the word processor on its desk behind, disc safe on the shelf above; right room.

Excalibur comes from the thigh pocket. Head tilted, hair touching a lower pane, I poke it into the gap between the frames; a tight fit. Just its tip appears on the other side of the glass. Paint flakes fall in a small flurry like snow as it slides a few inches to the copper catch.

A sharp upward jab. More of the blade comes into close view on the other side of the glass.

Out with the pliers. Three sharp taps knock Excalibur sideways. Metallic thunder seems to roll away over the paddock into the forest at my back.

In a contorted position, I stay still for several seconds, not daring to look around. The thunder dies in the trees. I do look now. The catch has shifted, just a fraction of an inch away from freeing itself from the bracket that traps it.

164

One more strike and the catch will have been moved 45 degrees. Holding my breath, I tap it, deafening myself. Muscles, breathing, heart immobilised, I wait. No lights turn on.

Excalibur is pulled free and pocketed with the pliers.

An upwards push on the strut of the bottom frame now. Agonisingly slowly, squealing like a mouse about to fall prey to an owl, it rises.

Right leg is lifted over the sill. Thermal long Johns cruelly tighten at the groin. My foot touches down on the carpet inside.


Ears ring to the din from the word processor warming up. Scores of times I've started up ours, never before realising just how much noise they make when you listen, have to listen.

Fingers feeling like bunches of bananas, I've already lifted down the disc box from the shelf, no need for Gran's torch in the starlight.

The screen goes from matt black to creamy white. The disc slot swallows the 'Deceased' file to find what Dunphy wouldn't let me see. Matt black goes to glossy black with white lines tumbling down; the familiar process of loading, all so unfamiliarly slow. Now the screen is ticking and sounding like a ship's fog horn, not distant enough.

A small square red light below the disc drive flickers on and off, illuminating the tips of the chamois gloves.

Suddenly the printer I have no intention of using connects itself, springing with a loud crank into frightening life.

I curse myself for not disconnecting it. After a minute or so, a long drag, time standing still, names come up in columns before me.

Across and down the cursor until a white block fits over Sharpe, L. HP. E for edit is entered.

Her file gives date of admission. The signing of her will came only six months before her death. Jordan told the truth about not drawing it up. Another solicitor did.

There's just one named beneficiary, not, naturally enough, Arnie Gillman, the son she never knew. Mrs Warminski had been right. A thousand pounds was earmarked to go to her old union's dependants' fund; the residue, when all outstanding accounts were settled, to the Evergreen Trust.

There are dates at infrequent intervals on which Mrs Sharpe saw a doctor, her long-time GP, I assume, for her last medical appointment, just a week before she died, was with a different medic – Dr Walls, Say Again Sam, the police surgeon.

Back to the menu to highlight a woman's name, any name, with HP after it. Say Again Sam was again her last medical appointment. This time Jordan did draw up a will leaving everything to Evergreen.

Three more names with the same suffix are picked at random. Three more times Say Again appears, twice Jordan. All left everything to the trust.

Phew. I'm actually shaking, shivering, not from the cold that comes through the half-opened window, from excitement, from fear.

I sit transfixed looking at the menu, not knowing what I'm looking for, decide on a flick through the disc box. 'Current', 'Finances', 'General' are thumbed back to reach H but there's no file beginning with that, just 'Politics' and 'Welfare' further on.

Five discs capable of holding thousands of words each means that letters to Hedges could be buried in them anywhere. Think. Think. What would you file Hedges under?

'Deceased' is ejected, 'Welfare' fed in. A new menu lists two columns of letters, none of them naming Hedges.

The routine is repeated with 'General'. Hedges appears six times with figures, some single, some double, and numbers in the eighties and nineties. Month and year, I guess. Date order, I order myself.

The first, dated two Christmases ago, is to the company secretary. 'Councillor Grady and I are delighted to accept your kind invitation to the opening of the new plant at Moorwood's new industrial estate.'

Must look up Grady on the main menu, I remind myself.

The second to the same addressee offers advice on a government relocation grant that's overdue. That has a signature block that gives Laven's position as chairman of the council's health committee.

The third is addressed to the medical director, agreeing in principle to an unspecified suggestion, subject to insurance cover.

The fourth begins, 'I have now obtained the necessary consents and have arranged for Dr Walls, our usual locus, to carry out the injections in accordance with the attached programme.' Sheet two gives the dates of appointments at various homes.

166

The fifth has 'Private' above the medical director's address block. Below it: 'Thank you for informing me by phone today of the results of your laboratory tests. It is indeed deeply regrettable that difficulties with the batch were not discovered before dispatch.

'Since none of the recipients have immediate family and Dr Walls is also engaged in the coroner's department, I anticipate no awkward questions from outside quarters.

'The outcome remains, however, that we have lost some twenty-five residents, all long term, and the income to accrue until the vacancies are filled.'

Twenty-five, I note, heart hardening.

'I write seeking confirmation that such losses will be covered by the indemnity agreed between us in November.'

November, in the autumn before the epidemic that swept through Laven's homes last winter.

I have to read it again, more slowly, to put it into context with what I already know.

What it means is that Laven offered twenty-five of his residents as guinea pigs to Hedges. They picked only old folk with no close relatives. He, sometimes aided by Jordan, got them to sign over all their worldly goods to him.

He took the precaution of getting them to sign consent forms to the HP jabs, administered by Dr Walls, so there'd be no comeback, if anything went wrong.

It did go wrong, disastrously and fatally wrong twenty-five times over. They were given anti-flu jabs from a faulty batch.

OK, it wasn't mass murder, euthanasia for gain or some ghastly social experiment, but almost as bad.

They had gone down, all of them, with flu and died because of a bum batch of serum. And Laven and HP had got clean away with it because they had a tame doctor and maybe a coroner in their pockets.

No, not clean away, not if I get away with this evidence.

The last letter acknowledges with thanks receipt of thirty thousand pounds. What's he charge? Three hundred a week. On top of all he'd copped out of his dead residents' estates, he'd stung HP for twenty-five empty places for a whole month. And they'd paid up without a murmur, cheap at half the price in the cut-throat world of drug manufacture for keeping a lethal mistake secret.

Mother of God, I must get away with this.

Exiting to the main menu, I look up 'Grady, S.'. He appears three times with numbers one to three after the name.

No. 1 is very formal. 'Re yesterday's letter. I have to inform you that the entire estate of the late Mrs L. Sharpe was disposed of in accordance with her witnessed wishes.' It was sent in the autumn about the time Grady saw Mrs Warminski.

No. 2 is much stiffer. 'In response to your further query, I must register my disquiet at having the caring service we provide here questioned by someone with the personal experience to understand the needs of medical research.'

Personal experience? What does that mean?

No. 3 is dated only a couple of months ago and is a complete climb-down. 'Enclosed is settlement of £2000 . . .' No chance of misreading it, because in brackets afterwards comes,' (two thousand pounds) agreed in our phone call. Sorry for any delay.'

Jesus, Laven had doubled the donation. Half of it, I'm convinced, wouldn't have ended up in the widows' and orphans' fund, but Grady's own account.

Now I know what it is about Mrs Sharpe that made Laven reach for his chequebook every time. Three thou to Arnie, two to Grady, three hundred to me.

Questions, that's what. He had to stop questions being asked, things coming out about those HP jabs.

Two big questions remain unanswered: Would a paltry two grand (half of which was due to his union) stop Grady blowing the whistle? Or has Laven got something else that silenced him?

Returning to the menu, I go back into the disc box and take out the first my fingers find. 'Politics' will have to do. I tap the key to copy a disc.

The screen brings up a warning note in a central block: 'If you continue, then all files on the destination disc will be permanently destroyed!'

'Politics' is about to be wiped. No bad thing. I press the key to proceed.

Copying takes an age, a tedious rigmarole, repeatedly switching the discs, the drive snapping its jaws at each transfer, the machine flashing and ticking loudly most of the time, fog-horning now and then.

I breathe rapidly through it all, willing it to end. My thermals are sticking to me. I can smell my own sweat. At long last, the screen invites me to return to disc manager. I enter, eject the copy disc, put it in the thigh pocket, switch off and replace the remaining discs in the box which I return to its shelf.

Standing behind Laven's desk, cold air at my back, I survey the office. Apart from the now missing and rewritten 'Politics' disc, there's no sign I have been here.

I crouch and throw my right leg out of the window. Back bent, I duck beneath the double frame, looking down into the mist, waist-high now, that covers the concrete path.

From within the fog, out of sight, comes a hissing movement. Leaping up towards the bridge of my nose is what I take in the total stupidity of total surprise to be a silver-headed snake with a narrow dark triangular neck and a round black body.

Just time to drop my chin, so that the contact occurs high on the forehead, an explosion of cold metal on thick bone; the last bone left in the whole of my body. All and any rigidity leaves me, vanishes.

My last sense is a feeling of uncontrollable floppiness, a gutted catch being thrown head first into a caldron of steaming water coming to boil.


# 22


Voices out of thick fog float across my wet face. Not that same dream, that old nightmare. Different.

A black snake slithers on the surface of a stagnant, steaming pool, getting closer and closer to a small, blond boy paddling in the shallows. Get out, son. Quick. Quickly.

He hears me and turns towards me. The boy is me, face panic-stricken. Out. Get out, Phil. Quickly.

He can't. I can't. His right leg, mine, is stuck. Held fast by quicksands.

'Deep shit, here.' A man's voice, agitated. 'Come round.'

\*

Grandpa. Please. Help me. Save me. Don't let it bite my leg. They'll chop it off. To cut out the poison. Don't let them cut it off, Grandpa.

I can stand no more, refuse to watch, drift away into the fog.

'. . . only a bit of a tap.' That same agitated voice.

'He'll live.' A new voice, calm. 'Unfortunately.'

A sword rises like a periscope out of a fog-shrouded lake. A man in a black uniform with three white stripes on each arm wades in to retrieve it.

Good old Grandpa. He's going to kill the snake, slice it in two, save me. 'Unfortunately,' he says ahead of him.

He turns to face me.

Ogden.

It's Sergeant Ogden, hate in his eyes.

My leg. He's going to cut it off. I grab it and tug on it frantically. 'You're not going to cut it off,' I scream at him. Ogden is smiling wickedly.

I close my eyes, unable to watch any more.

'. . . not fatal.' Ogden again, sternly. 'If I don't know what's likely to be fucking fatal, who does?'

I open pained eyes on to skirting board so close it's muzzy, can't make out the colour.

'You swan off to London and leave Bruce here . . .'

I close my eyes. A swan, neck outstretched, maddened, flaps across the water towards me. I draw my gun, stand my ground. Orange feet facing me, the swan skids to an emergency stop on the surface. Get your gun.

'Of course, he knows.' Ogden talking. 'Heard him on the phone, saw what he wrote. Flu. Bronchitis. HP's number. I've got the note.'

Oh, shit. Too clever by half. That's my trouble, I think through a series of yes's and mmm's.

'He's going to have to be,' Ogden resumes, voice quieter.

Play dead, a boy's voice within commands. I keep my eyes shut.

'. . . one disc on . . .' My forehead or heart, can't say which, thumps so loudly I don't hear the rest. My face is smeared in what feels like sump oil.

'. . . different system.' Ogden's voice aims in a different direction. 'Can you work that?' A mumble I can't decipher. 'Neither of us can. But Bruce saw him operating it. He's been into it. What's on it?'

My right leg is twisted beneath me.

'Oh, shit,' moans Ogden.

I moan.

'He's coming round. Come on. It's your decision.'

My left shoulder rolls against a wall, to find some purchase, relieving some of this unbearable weight.

The fog is beginning to lift. Everything is coming into sharper focus.

'Don't worry, Councillor. Go to bed and wait for the police to call. Act as though it's the first you've heard all night.'

The hollow sound, plastic on plastic, of a receiver returning to its base.

'What's he want us to do?' The first voice, tight.

'To make it look like an accident.' Ogden again. 'Can't be in here, he says. They'll search the place, find the files.'

'What's in 'em that's so sodding special?'

'Don't you know?'

No response.

'A flu jab programme that fouled up. He was on to it, asking questions at our place. We shuffled away the statistics so it didn't get out.'

'Got well paid, I hope.' A nervous laugh.

'How the fuck do you think you got this job?' Ogden, furious.

A silence seems to crackle on the cold air.

'How far's his car away?' Ogden asks.

'Back into the ride. Fifty yards.'

Silence for ten or a dozen long throbs in my head and thumps in my heart. Muffled footfall getting louder, closer. A toe end probes my kidneys, making me flinch, shock, not pain. 'He's coming to.' I can smell ale fumes, sense Bruce above me.

'Don't do that.' Ogden, sharply. 'There must be no more marks on him.'

'What about his face?' asks Bruce.

Ogden pauses. 'Let me think.' Another pause. 'It's got to pass every test.' Silence. 'In the ride, you say?' No audible response. 'Can you carry him there?'

'Easy.'

Another silence. 'Out there, in the woods, like, are there roots running from trees that you might trip on?'

'Loads.'

A longer silence apart from deep breathing. 'Right then.' Ogden again. 'Get him back to his car, put him in the driving seat. You've heard noises. Suspect poachers. You're going out to investigate. Take your shotgun.' Doubt tinges his tone. 'Are you up to this?'

'For ten thou, I'll do it,' says Bruce, all too eagerly.

'Has to be done.' Ogden is still doing most of the talking. 'Think what he'll tell 'em when he comes to. That I was Dunph's contact. End of pension, civvy job and jail. End of Laven, too. It's got to be done.'

Silence again.

'Stick to the facts,' Ogden resumes. 'It's your first night on solo duty. You want no cock-ups. You've seen a man loitering in the woods, heard strange sounds. Nothing suspicious enough to dial 999. But worrying. You call me for advice. A natural thing to do. We're right close. Got that? A close-knit family. I drive out like any close relative with a bit of experience would. We check the premises. Nothing. We come back in here.'

A soft shuffle across the carpet. 'Looking out the window you see a torchlight in the woods. Not a headlamp. Got that? Poachers, you think. "You're jumpy, seeing things," I say. You go out on your own, taking your shotgun with you. Right?'

'Right.'

'Pick him up then. Give me the gun.'


My left shoulder is pulled back. I give out a loud groan, rolling on my back. My face is filled to not far short of gagging with beer fumes.

A fist, then an arm is pushed beneath my crooked knees. A hand slides under my shoulder blades. My body jerks upwards.

Only my feet stay in touch with the carpet. A knee prods the small of my back. All of me is airborne now. My head swims as I'm turned 180 degrees.

A voice next to my ear, Bruce's. 'What about this blood?'

Bumpy forward motion now, then turn at 45 degrees, then stop. A lock snaps shut at the crown of my head.

Cold air hits me.

Heavy feet crunch on pea pebbles.


'Right . . .' Ogden is beyond my feet. 'You come out here and head for the woods. See the car. You load and cock, to fire a warning shot in case there's a gang of them, to scare them. That's all you intended. Remember that.'

It's proving a rough ride, head pounding, across the uneven paddock in Bruce's strong arms.

'As you approach the car, you trip on a root. The gun comes down and goes off. Make sure you get him in the head. We've got to blow away that butt mark.'

In his arms, I can feel Bruce's heart racing.

'Run back to tell me. I'll have heard the shot and will meet you half-way. I'll take a look. I must do that to explain my footprints at the scene.'

We stop.

'All right?' Ogden inquires.

A grunt in my ear. A knee at the small of my back lifts me higher in Bruce's arms. He is carrying his load more slowly, tiring. 'I don't like it,' he says unhappily.

Nothing comes from either in several swishing paces through the long paddock grass.

'It means a messy inquest,' Ogden reluctantly agrees, 'and, when they find out he was one of us . . .' He lapses into silence.

We travel lots of silent yards, impossible to estimate how many.

Ogden resumes urgently, 'Got another gun?'

'In the truck.'

'Good.' Ogden, sounding satisfied. 'Do it with this. Then run through the ride, back to your truck. Drive up north a few miles. Slowly, mind. Don't get nabbed. Get rid of the gun. Lob it into a lake. Anywhere deep. Then come back. The police should be here by then.'

'What do I tell 'em?'

'You went into the woods to investigate the light. You heard a flash and a bang and saw a fleeing figure. You gave chase to a strange vehicle by the phone box. Insist it was parked on the hard road. No tyre marks, see. Give a model and some, but not all, of an index number. You lost it after a few miles. Managing?'

'Yer.' An exhausted sigh, as Bruce heaves up my slipping dead weight from somewhere near his stomach closer to his chest. His heart is beating fast.

'I'll have heard the shot and found the driver dead in his car. I don't recognise him with his face blown away. I'll have called the police by the time you return 'cos I was worried about you being missing, wounded, perhaps, in the forest.'

Bruce clasps me still closer to his chest. 'But what was he doing there?'

'Keeping watch. Snooping. Waiting to break in.'

'There was lots of dosh about last night when he came.'

'Good. He came back for more. He's dressed for burglary. Another bent ex-cop on the make.' A laugh. 'Like it better?'

Ogden answers his own question. 'Much better, this.'

They go through it all again, me listening to a coroner's court specialist in death, giving a young kinsman a lesson on how to commit murder and get away with it, coaching him, answering all his questions.

Not a bad plan, either, I have to admit.

Ogden, first policeman on the scene, an expert at that, will be in on the CID team talks from the beginning.

He'll tell of chats he's had with me at Jordan Associates, of an invalid, embittered by experience, feeling disowned, depressed and desperately worried about his financial future. Laven and Bruce would do their bit by exaggerating the amount of cash in the office six hours earlier.

The investigation team would get a picture of a disaffected cop gone bad, a burglar being tragically but accidentally gunned down by an unknown poacher who stumbled on a tree root, fired his shotgun into a parked car, then fled in panic, chased by brave Bruce.

It was a version, I suspect, of what really happened in that caravan shooting. A rerun of what that poacher told Brooks and Dunphy when they arrived at his smallholding. He was claiming the shooting was all a tragic accident. When he tried to turn in his gun, trigger-happy Brooks reacted too fast and fatally.

Ogden had come along later, to tie up the loose ends and make it look good for a chief inspector at the inquest. His reward had been promotion then and a civvy job for life coming up. Dunphy's reward had been promotion and saving his pension when he should have been fired.

Brooks had never been Dunphy's mole. He was too high-powered for that. He'd been Laven's middleman and was about to cash in with a forty grand a year retirement job.

Ogden was Dunphy's way into police records and, in return, Dunphy had given him maybe money and certainly a job to an unemployable member of his family.

In the middle of the night, in the middle of a forest, I have finally made out the trees from the wood.

I make no move – just groan and fidget now and then. I'm outnumbered two to one, I'm unarmed, a loaded shotgun feet away. I'll bide my time. I'll make my move at the car.


Even with eyelids shut tight, I sense it getting darker, guess we are close to, if not in, the pines.

'Will it work?' asks Bruce, anxiously.

'Has before now.' A low laugh, confirmation of my suspicions. 'No problem if Brooks takes charge. And he might since Toddy's an ex-officer. And if Doc Walls does the prelim medical, well . . .' An easygoing laugh. 'Let's get the forensics right.'

'But will they buy it?'

'Brooks won't, but he'll do bugger all about it. Daren't. Doc Walls neither.' Pause. 'Is his car locked?'

We stop. A hand goes into my thigh pocket. Keys tinkle together on a ring.

'Keep your nerve,' says Ogden, encouragingly.

Mine is holding up.

Just.


## 23


'Careful,' Ogden cautions. 'Mind his head.'

A hand gently cups the back of my head as I'm lowered. A raised knee prevents me dropping further. Two arms still hold me, so the hand must be Ogden's.

I'm rolled out of Bruce's arms on to what has to be the driver's seat of my car. Strong fingers gripping the track-suit at my right shoulder stop me rolling on and across the passenger seat where I left the squash racket.

Ogden has done what policemen do when they are taking in a suspect – protected my head against the door frame. Every time I see it on TV I give a cynical smile. They do it so their suspect doesn't get a crack on the head which his lawyer can then claim was brutality in the cell to obtain a confession.

These two bastards are putting me into a position to shoot to kill and make it look like an accident. Ogden, with the knowledge of a thousand inquests behind him, doesn't want a mark on the back of my head as well as the front because it might show up in the post-mortem. I'll save my cynical laugh.

'Want the window down?' Bruce asks in my right ear.

'Gives you an uninterrupted shot,' says Ogden expertly.

The window is swiftly ratcheted down. The door slams shut, rocking the car and me. The smell of Bruce recedes. My head drops forward on to the steering wheel.

'Pull it back,' Ogden commands.

My head is yanked back by a tuft of hair which tugs at its roots. My cheek comes to rest against the cold rim of the empty window frame in the car door.

'Round a bit,' Ogden orders. My hair is pulled, neck twisted right. 'His forehead facing you?'

'Yer.'

'A clear view of the back of the house through the windscreen?'

Foul breath returns to my nose. 'Yer.'

'Right,' Ogden declares. 'Take the gun and walk slowly towards the trees. Find a root. Feel with your feet.'

The sound of departing steps, the rustle of stiff grass and snapping dried twigs. The owl hears it, too, and whoo-whoos at the prospect of a late supper.

'Here.' Bruce from some distance away. 'A big one.'

'Go the far side and give it a good kick.'

A dull crack.

'Just the job, eh?' Bruce returning, sounding pleased. His heavy footsteps are getting closer. 'What's up?' Bruce again, worried.

'That. Your shirt. There. Blood on it.'

'Shit,' Bruce sighs miserably. 'Must have got it on when I was carrying him.'

'Got anything else in the truck?'

'A sweater.'

'Any other footwear?'

'Boots.'

'When you're finished here, go to the truck, change into them and get rid of what you're wearing and the gun. Then the lab boys will find nothing here to link with you.'

They go through it all again, adding refinements here and there.

'His tools,' says Ogden. 'They didn't drop out his pocket or anything? They still on him?'

A hand slides down my chest, stomach and thigh and enters the pocket where Excalibur and the pliers clang tinnily together. 'Yer,' replies Bruce with a blast of bad breath.

'They'll match the tools to the window. He might have had a nose bleed. Or he might have stumbled and cracked his head on the window frame. He's got a gammy leg. He could have been scared he'd made too much noise and staggered back to his car to rest up or keep watch and have another go if no lights came on.'

'Explains his blood on the office carpet,' says Bruce approvingly.

Worryingly they debate the necessity of Ogden returning to the house, pondering whether he should stay and witness the deed. Thankfully, they decide he must, to move the box of discs into his car where the police won't look.

He repeats one last time what he's now enthusiastically calling the scenario sounding like a director on a film set. 'Walk fast and lose your balance. Pitch forward a few yards. Leave plenty of footprints. Go to the truck, change, dump all the evidence, drive around, come back with that story of the fleeing figure and the chase.'

'Can't fail,' Bruce pronounces, confidently.


I've kept my nerve for five more motionless minutes.

Ogden has gone. Bruce shuffles heavily on the grass now and then but I can't pinpoint his precise whereabouts.

From the trees comes the distinctive belching bark of a deer. Somewhere between that and me grass is being disturbed.

I open my right eye. Bruce is twenty yards away, facing me but his head is turned, earmarking a future game target.

Arms extended, the gun is held horizontally across the waistband of tight, light jeans. He is wearing his red Forest long-sleeved shirt. I can't see my blood on it from this distance, just the white motif of the tree.

Nor can I see his footwear. A grey mist covers the forest floor to knee height, thicker than when I parked here. Above it everything, the wide ride, trees beyond, is almost as clear as day under the starlet sky.

His face comes back, but I don't close my right eye. My left lid remains tightly down in an extended wink.

I feign a groan, more of a gargle really. He stands still, making no move towards me. I smack my lips and waggle my head, ever so slightly. He sways from one foot to another.

I belch, just a burp really. He seems to look over the car roof. I belch again, louder and longer.

From the trees my love call is returned. He swings his head round, taking his upper body, shoulders, arms and hands with it. For a second or two the barrel of his gun will be pointing away.

Now, I decide.

My left eye opens. My feet hit the wall of the well beyond the pedals. My knees bend, pulling my backside lower into the seat.

I know my head will be out of sight.

My gloved hands shoot out beneath the dashboard panel. Fingers find the gun and tighten around it. Feet push to straighten my legs. A tearing sound fills the car as a .38 Special comes away from the tapes which Heather Hann had used to attach it to its usual place.

I close my eyes and raise my head just above the window frame. I twitch it and groan loudly to try to mask movement and sound. I clasp gun to groin.

I reopen my right eye.

Bruce brings his shotgun round in a horizontal arc until it is pointing at me, butt nipped to his side by his right elbow. Left leg is slightly in front of right, about to shoot.

This is it then. The moment of truth. And I'm still not properly prepared.

He stands rock still, just his chest heaving.

I'm even stiller, only my right pupil active, taking in what could be the last sight it will ever record – a barrel of a gun.

I wait for it, for the yellowish-red flash in the grey mist and the pain and the panic I've known before, eight months ago, an eternity ago now.

Time stands stiller than me.

Nothing happens. Not a thing.

The moment that felt like another eternity passes.

*

Three strips of tape have come away to the accompaniment of a grunt, a groan and a gurgle. The .38 is between my hands pressed into my upper, inner thighs, barrel directed at my knees.

Bruce lets his left hand fall away from the gun. First two fingers inside the guard, he hinges his right elbow. The weapon rises slowly, vertical to his upper arm, a John Wayne pose.

Right, poser, I say. Now.

I bring my legs up as far as they'll come, till the calves touch the front edge of the car seat. I plant my feet firmly on rubber matting.

I press off the safety catch, one thumb on top of the other. Its click explodes in the air as I push down with both feet.

My backside comes away from the seat. My upper body swivels before my buttocks land. The gun goes up and away from my groin, barrel horizontal, sweeping towards, then out of the window, arms following until they're fully extended.

'*Armed police*,' I yell.

Live trees shout my words back to me.

'*Don't move.*'

Every creature of the night seems to be awake in the scattering, scratching, stirring forest, a big chorus of small, strange noises all round me.

'Do as I say.'

He is frozen.

I have the white tree in the sight of my right eye. 'I have a loaded weapon pointed at your heart.'

He is melting, sagging.

'*Don't move.*'

He stiffens.

'You have a choice, Brucey boy,' I call, quieter. 'You can empty the barrel into the air. Or take your chance.'

'Er . . .' A thin croak.

'What's it to be?'

'I, er . . .'

'It's your decision.'

He pauses, then, in a quaver, 'You're not a cop no more.' Another pause. 'It had better be loaded.'

'Lower that gun one inch and you'll find out.'

'You haven't got the fucking bottle.' Stronger, more confident.

'Try me,' I say, just loud enough for him to hear.

\*

Thunder bounces through the trees. Lightning tinges the mist a reddish yellow.

# 24

'It's me. Swee . . . Phil Todd.'

'Oh.' Michelle Fogan sounds sleepy. 'You're up early.'

All night, in fact, during which I was whisked up to hospital, then down to Sherwood divisional HQ.

All the time, apart from going into X-ray, Chief Superintendent Carole Malloy and Sergeant Heather Hann remained at my side, taking my long statement, the last part over a fry-up in the police canteen. They drove me back to this place via Jordan Associates where I dropped off a small padded bag.

The sky had been darkened by banks of black cloud coming up from the south, the whiteness of frosts on the verges and rooftops washed away by steady rain, hard, ice in it.

'What time is it?' Michelle asks.

'Just gone seven thirty.' It doesn't sound as early as a truthful 'just before'. 'Ready for the fray?'

'I suppose so.' Michelle is clearly not looking forward to her day in court.

'In which case,' I say as casually as I can, 'you ought to know that, over and above that pill which killed your client, HP produced a faulty batch of anti-flu jabs that killed twenty-five old folk in five of Laven's homes.'

'What?' Her exclamation is so deafening that my ear jerks away from the phone. 'Can you prove that?'

'It's on a disc in your office letterbox. You'll find what you need under Hedges.'

'Tell me all,' she demands, bossily.

I tell her most, not all. The rest can come later.

'Want to come along when I hit their solicitors with it?' she says, invitingly.

'I want to sleep,' I answer truthfully.

'Don't sleep past lunch,' she chuckles, rather seductively. 'See you then.'

*

180

'Hi. It's me. Busy?' I ask Emma, anything but myself, in bed, after a long Radox bath which, frankly, would have been more relaxing without its smell of pine.

'Hi. Quiet,' she replies, quietly.

'May have something for you. A shooting in Sherwood Forest.'

'Bow and arrow?' she says, sardonically.

'Shotgun. In the air. No one hurt.' She says nothing, knowing it's got to be hotter news than I'm making it sound. 'Two men appearing in court at noon, charged with conspiracy to murder. But that's just for starters.'

'Anybody we know?' she asks, interest mounting.

'One's a poacher-cum-security guard. The other's his uncle, a serving police sergeant.'

'Jesus.' Fascinated now. 'Where did this happen?'

'Behind one of Councillor Harry Laven's old folk's homes.'

She sucks air through her teeth into a whistle. 'That explains it. Just had London on. They were shooting a bit of mute on this Euro candidates photo call, working breakfast and all that. "No Laven," they report. Is he under arrest?'

Technically, yes, but I tell her to play safe and only say he's travelling back to assist with inquiries.

It's early days, just five or six hours into an investigation that will take weeks, but the vibes are bad. Ogden and nephew are saying, in effect, it was all a merry jape. They were trying to scare me out of competing with Bruce for security contracts.

Thin, true, particularly as everything said at the car had been caught by a voice-activated tape recorder which Heather Hann had strapped under the glove box. Malloy says she's heard dafter defences succeed.

She doubts whether a concussed recollection of the call Ogden made to Laven at his hotel will stand up in court. She doesn't doubt that she'll find much that's incriminating on Laven and Hedges Pharmaceuticals in the files when they're fine-combed. She fears that, with residents' wills witnessed and consent forms signed, Laven may have covered himself against criminal charges. He's open to lots of civil liability but that's not police business.

'We're short of one solid witness,' she'd summed up.

I feel depressed, like an author – Jacko, say – who thinks the midnight oil has burned brilliantly bright for him, then finds what he's written makes deadly dull reading in the cold light of the following morning.

'What can I safely say?' Emma asks, always wanting it libel-proof and free from contempt. 'Something like "Top Tory recalled from big party pow-wow to help police inquiries into a shooting incident at . . ."'

'Behind,' I correct.

'". . . behind one of his old folk's homes in Sherwood Forest. No one hurt. A police sergeant . . ." You won't give me his name?'

'You'll get it in court.'

'". . . and another man will be appearing at noon, charged with conspiracy to murder." Anything else?'

To go with this story, she means, but I offer another. 'You might drop in on the crown court at ten-thirty. If things go according to plan, there'll be a big settlement in that negligence case against Hedges.'

'Are they connected?'

I say nothing, answer enough for her, and she cottons on, seeing a way through the legal minefield she's about to tread, always does. 'We'll use the old Fleet Street trick.'

She laughs wickedly, music to my ears normally, but jarring with a headache that pills have reduced from pounding to nagging. 'We'll run them back to back and hope viewers make their own connection.' Her tone becomes tentative, soothing and concerned. 'OK for tonight?'

'Looking forward to it.'


The black clouds that brought the icy rain have scurried north on a stiff breeze that blows away the remains of my headache. The sun shines on lunchtime crowds milling through pedestrianised streets in their usual state of repaving.

Good to be alive, out and about. Twice now I've faced the barrels of guns. Still here, though. Still in the game. More than you can say for twenty-five old folk denied Gran's natural, peaceful ending. If Carole Malloy can't get Laven and HP, I will.

OK, you've a damaged leg, a bit of a limp that's slowed you up and ended hectic sporting days, so work on a decent golf handicap. Or suggest to Jacko that we take up bowls.

You've a date tonight with a lovely woman who, come on, face it, you still love and drinkie-poohs coming up with a stunner you – be honest now – fancy.

Spotting a chemist's shop, I wonder if I might break my New Year duck at some stage during the day, grin to myself, but don't go in.

A short cut down two escalators through a hot shopping centre and a cold bus station and the stylish pinkish cream brickwork of the crown court comes into view on the left.

I take a right over a pedestrian crossing, just a few more yards, and I turn beneath a golden Victorian lamp holder into a pub that backs on to the canal.


Michelle Fogan breaks away from her company, taking long, noisy strides over stained floorboards towards me, arms out, like Cantona after a goal.

'My hero.' Each shoulder is pressed down by dainty hands, each cheek is kissed; not the air kisses, mer, mer, which I hate. Big wet smackers.

Then, on tiptoe, she kisses very tenderly my forehead which looked like a squashed black ball in the shaving mirror. Now she is looking into my eyes and completes four of a kind on my lips, quickly and rather roughly.

She tastes faintly acidic. Her blue eyes are a bit misty, her broad smile slightly lopsided. 'You should have been there,' she gushes.

One arm round my waist, she ushers me to a corner where I'm introduced to her leading and junior counsels, both late middle-age and pin-striped, greying with the feyness you find in legal circles. They beam as they pump my hand.

I am gathered into the group standing around a waist-high round table, more of a shelf for glasses, really, a pole running through it from floorboards to cream ceiling.

'A celebratory drink,' the QC lah-di-dahs, emptying a champagne bottle which he replaces in an ice bucket.

'Four hundred and fifty thousand,' says Michelle gaily.

'Caved in after half an hour's negotiations,' hoots the junior. 'Well done.'

Allowing another half-hour for end-of-case paperwork, I calculate I'm about an hour late for the party. Michelle, in a well-cut slate grey suit with chalk stripes, looks to have enjoyed every minute of it.

'How did you do it?' asks the QC.

A highly censored version is offered. For all their pretensions barristers are just hired mouthpieces. This pair could easily be engaged to defend anyone involved in the conspiracy. Why give 'em ammo they might fire back at you?

Michelle goes on about all the money in the world being no compensation for what the Grimston family have suffered for ten years. She compares their lot to her own child's, a son.

The QC glances at her left hand seemingly in vain search of a ring. Soon he is looking at his watch, talking about home to the better half on the one-something and emptying his glass. He has the grace and, at a thousand guineas a day, the dosh to buy another bottle for the ice bucket, but departs as it's uncorked.

His junior goes with him after a hug that wrestles a giggling Michelle off her feet. The QC more formally kissed her hand.

The mouth-watering Sunday smell of roasting meat fills the bar and I suggest a hot roll. Michelle shakes her head and tops up both glasses from the new bottle. I order rare beef.

'Let your bill run,' she says mischievously. 'We'll stick it against HP's costs.'

I chew, say nothing, still standing.

'What about next week? Fancy a contract? Come in and we'll discuss it.' Can't be a staff job, she gabbles between sips, because there's not enough work for a full-time investigator, but she'd talk Jordan into a lucrative retainer giving the firm first claim on my services. She outlines some of the cases she wants me on.

'Difficult for a day or two,' I say, in deep difficulty, not knowing how to put this, where to begin.

'Why?' she asks, aggressively.

Attack, I decide, is the best means of defence. 'You may have solved your problem, but Heather Hann . . .'

Elbow on the small table, Michelle is helping herself to another, not really listening.

'. . . the sergeant in Missing Persons. You spoke to her on . . .'

'Oh.' She's distracted, as the glass overflows and puddles the polished table.

'I owe her.'

She's listening now. 'Why?'

I'm not going to tell her that she planted the gun that saved me last night. 'She was rather more help to me than she was to you.' I touch my nose. 'Old Pals Act.'

'Your former flame?' she asks rather truculently.

I shake my head. 'Happily married to a solicitor.'

'Oh.' She smiles brightly.

'Well . . .' A struggling shrug. '. . . Arnie Gillman's still on her missing list.'

'Work on it from our place for a few more days then.' She laughs wickedly, an answer for everything. 'We can charge Harbour Heights Residents Association.'

I have answers for nothing right now and go quiet.

She changes the subject. 'I've reported all on Dr Walls to Old Man Jordan, you know. Will they charge him, do you think?'

'They'll have a close look at him, I suppose,' I reply uncertainly. 'He was getting fees from Laven for giving out the jabs and at the same time he was under contract as a police surgeon.'

'They'll have to prove he was being paid hush money to keep quiet about the number of deaths,' she points out expertly. 'Otherwise, it's just a rap from the Medical Association.'

I nod. 'They're also going to have to prove that Ogden and Dunphy conspired together to save Deputy Chief Brooks from a manslaughter charge.' For the first time I tell her about the fatal caravan shooting and how I just managed to escape a rerun last night.

'Lord.' Her eyes open wide and some of the mist clears from them.

'Getting convictions on any of that is going to be a lot tougher for Heather than your case.' I don't have to tell her, a lawyer, of the higher standards of proof required by criminal courts compared to civil cases.

'Very difficult,' she concurs. 'Unless, of course, they offer Ogden a reduced sentence for plotting to murder you in return for a complete confession.'

Another gloomy nod. I disclose that Heather Hann's guess is Ogden will stick to his scare tactics story, say nothing more, fight the conspiracy charge and take his chance. Her fear is that By-the-Book Brooks will be retired early to take up his cushy post at Hedges Pharmaceuticals, that Dr Walls will lose his coroner's contract, but Laven and HP between them will make up any cash shortfall. 'She could end up with nothing.'

She empties the bottle into both glasses. 'You only get all loose ends tied up in naff detective stories.'

'Yes, but I feel I ought to help somehow.'

'How?'

'Dunno,' I answer, half truthfully.

Suddenly, she raises her glass, beaming. 'To Mrs Grimston and her children.'

'Cheers,' I say, anything but cheerfully.

'Drink up,' she commands.


Clip-clopping on the floorboards, she leads the way through a green door into the cold bright street.

At the traffic lights, she grabs an elbow to steer me over the crossing, away from the courthouse where I'd assumed we were bound. 'A coffee, I think.'

We stroll outside the bus station, into a tiled underpass, through the echoing main foyer of the shopping centre and emerge into a traffic-free, tree-dotted street that slopes gently up towards the market square.

Champagne usually lightens me, not the taste, the glow. But not today. Michelle seems to be afflicted with a similar feeling of flatness.

The media will run the damages award, she predicts, but not too big, as part of the out-of-court settlement was minimum details to be made public. There'll be little or no impact on the Stock Exchange either. 'A one-day wonder,' she says gloomily, the party mood gone.

Alongside a high curved wall, a church above it, she rummages in her shoulder bag, then purse for a pound coin and stoops, loose-limbed, to drop it in the cap of a busker playing a violin so badly he's close to begging. I tell her of the Mozart concert I'm going to tonight with Emma.

'So that business of splitting up is out of date?' she asks moodily.

No, I assure her, we're living apart, but don't go into why.

She smiles ahead. 'Another good friend, eh?'

Without consultation, she decides on our destination. 'The Bell.' It's an old haunt Emma and I used, just about the last place I want to be seen with a classy but semi-squiffy redhead.

We enter the market square with its grey-domed, colonnaded council-house, black hands of its clock at just gone two, looking down on stone lions and fat pigeons feeding by fountains on the wide, white-slabbed terraces.

She goes first down a flagstoned passage to the Bell Inn's long back bar, darkly panelled, names of past presidents of the university students' union on a board, mine not among them. She heads, rather heavy-legged, to an empty table.

'Black,' she says over her shoulder, 'and a brandy.'

I double the order which costs almost a third of an hour's pay. I tell her this when I sit on a red leather chair opposite her.

She doesn't laugh, a more important issue on her now-focused mind. 'Assuming they have to free Laven, how can we help to cook his goose? And HP's, for that matter?'

We, I repeat to myself. She wants in, wants justice, the whole truth to come out. 'Will Steve Grady help?' I ask tentatively.

The name jolts her. 'How?'

'Saw his name on Laven's computer.' I explain that Mrs Sharpe's old workmate Mrs Warminski had told him that a thousand was due from her estate to his dependants' fund. 'A letter from Laven to him was dated soon afterwards,' I add.

'Really?' A troubled expression.

'I didn't get the chance to break into the hard copy files to examine Grady's letters to Laven,' I go on. 'I assume the first was just a polite inquiry, for the reply merely pointed out that all her estate had been disposed of in accordance with witnessed last wishes. Grady must have queried that, either by letter or phone, because Laven's second letter was much stiffer. People in glass-houses shouldn't throw stones. That sort of threat.'

'What do you mean?'

'Laven said he was surprised to have his bonafides questioned by someone with the experience to understand the needs of medical research.'

'What's that mean?'

An honest headshake is my reply. We lapse into silence.

'Doubt it,' she says eventually and doubtfully.

Not sure what she is talking about, I stay quiet long enough to realise that so discursive has our conversation become that she's answered a question I'd asked some time ago.

'He's not much of a man.' A sad headshake. 'When the going got tough, he fled.'

Having told her a bit about Emma, I feel entitled to ask her about Steve Grady.

They'd first met during the pit strike. She was at university, an official of the students' Labour Club. Like many idealistic left-wingers, she devoted spare time to helping the women's support groups that blossomed all over the coalfields. Grady was on the trades council's welfare committee, doling out hardship payments.

'Hit it off straight away, did you?' I ask, teasingly.

'Not in the way you're thinking,' she says, unoffended. 'I was in head-over-heels with a lecturer at the time. Much older than me. Married, too, I'm afraid.'

I diagnose in her a weakness for mature men and don't know whether to feel safe or sorry.

Only when they met up again at an industrial tribunal three years later did they 'hit it off'. By now she was fully qualified. He was a councillor and chairman of the planning committee.

With their workloads, not too much time was left for hitting it off too often. 'But it was nice, you know. Not too heavy.' Pregnancy was a mistake. 'It was the day after the elections.'

'A celebration?' I ask.

'Sort of. He lost his seat. We thought it would give us more time together.'

Normally, she went on, serious again, she questioned her faith enough to take precautions, but was too Catholic to have an abortion. 'Besides I make a good mother. Love it – and him.'

Anxiety grips me. 'Still carrying the torch?'

'Eh?' A distant look comes closer. 'My son, I mean. Sod Grady. He abandoned us three months into pregnancy. Didn't want to break up the family etc.' She looked more puzzled than hurt.

'About sixteen months ago?' I check. 'Soon after you took on the case against HP?'

'About then. Why?'

I stay silent to draw an answer out of her.

'Yes. I first read the papers on summer hols in the Lake District.'

'With Grady?'

'Lord no. But he had a union conference at Morecombe and came a-visiting for a couple of days.'

'And about this same time Dunphy came to Jordan Associates on Ogden's recommendation?'

A slow nod, thinking. 'He'd been hired when I got back.'

'Did Grady ever mention Mrs Grimston's case against HP?'

'I told him I'd taken it on, of course. Thought he might know Grimston from the strike. Said he didn't. He didn't see the papers or anything. Unless . . .' An unsure shrug to tell me: unless he'd had a secret peek.

'Did he ever mention HP?'

'Only when they were moving from down south to Moorwood. He had to go to lots of planning meetings.'

'And that was – what – six months before your night of passion?'

188

'Lunchtime, actually,' she replies, working her lips, smiling cheekily. 'They opened HP's new plant two years ago.'

Confirms what I read in Laven's discs, I recall.

'There was a bit of opposition to it,' she continues. 'You know, no toxic chimneys in our back yard, but he was quite proud of the jobs it would bring.'

'Was Laven, though a political opponent, an ally in bringing HP up to Moorwood?'

'Think he was, yes. What are you driving at?'

'Just this. That New Year Laven and Grady go off happily together to HP's opening. I know that from last night's research. Your romance . . .'

'Affair . . .'

'. . . with him is blooming. A few months later you bring the action against HP. You're pregnant. He runs out on you. Dunphy starts spying on you.'

'What's the connection?'

'I don't know.' I tell her Grady was Dunphy's target when he tried to get into Special Branch files, but I can't work out why.

Neither can she. He had a 'good strike', she says, as if it had been a war, which it was, of sorts, I suppose. 'Why didn't your old boss Brooks, if he is involved, just look up Special Branch files on him and feed the info straight to Laven?' she asks logically.

'Because the computer records the caller's code. It's traceable. Brooks, I suspect, gave Laven or Dunphy Armstrong's code instead. That way he put a bit of distance between him and any dirty work. He's a past-master at that.'

I have a loose end. 'If you didn't know Dunphy was spying on you and your progress in the HP case, why did you fire him?'

'He'd been asking around about me and Steve.'

'How do you know that?'

'Steve phoned in a panic a couple of months ago. He was worried it would get back to his wife.' She giggles, rather maliciously. 'All my inquiry agents seem to panic him.'

Her face becomes pensive, lips pursed. 'I wonder . . .' She stops. 'What time . . .' She looks at her gold wrist-watch to answer her own uncompleted question. 'Let's ask him.'

'Where?'

The Peacock, she says, near his office, just a short, pleasant walk beyond the elegant Theatre Royal. Usually, she goes on, he's a late luncher. 'We used to meet up there sometimes when I was working round the corner in the mags or on ITs' – by which she means the city magistrates court in the imposing Guildhall and industrial tribunals in a not so imposing office block almost next door.

'He's got a tribunal hearing today,' I say.

'Let's sort this out then. He's used me. We'll use him.'

Well, it's justice of a sort, I suppose.

She drinks up and gets up. 'Game?' she asks. I nod. 'Must pay a call first.' She heads for the toilets downstairs.

'See you outside,' I call after her.

I use coins to make a call from a block of six glass phone boxes beside a flower stall on the wide pavement outside, not wanting to be delayed going through an operator with a credit card.

## 25

The lounge of the Peacock is a comfy place, all the more comfortable because of buttons on walls which you press for service. To save standing around, blocking the bar, you ring a bell to place an order which is brought to your table.

With students on holiday from the round-the-corner Poly, recently granted university status and a fancy new name, the place wasn't so full that we didn't find a table, or so empty that Grady spotted us coming in. Two brandies were belled.

Now it is thinning out as the BBC types, social workers and lawyers who also frequent it depart to their afternoon duties.

Grady is sitting at a table at the far end, back to us, facing a glass cabinet displaying pre-war tins for tea and sweets, talking to an elderly man. They finish their pints, stand and walk towards us, Grady turning to lead.

Passing in front of a marble fireplace with an ornate gold-plated clock, he mouths, 'Good Lord,' almost stopping in mid-stride, when he spots us. Michelle tips her glass to him. I smile.

He approaches, half turns again, excusing himself over his shoulder to his companion, who says, 'Thanks again,' and looks inquisitively at us as he shuffles behind him. Before he can open double doors to the street, two smartly dressed women walk in. Politely he gives way to them before leaving.

Grady is standing, staring down at us, as the two women pass his back in single file. 'What a pleasant surprise.'

A nasty shock, I'd say.

'Join us,' says Michelle, patting the bench with diamond pattern fabric on which we are sitting side-by-side, backs to twin windows with engravings of peacocks, feathers fanned.

The women – one very dark and petite, thirtyish, the other older with close-cropped red hair not as long or as coppery as Michelle's – don't take up what must have sounded like an open invitation. Neither do they trail the length of the lounge to the table just vacated. They take seats, much closer, near the fireplace.

The younger woman reaches behind her for the nearest bell on a square brass plate but is beaten to another by Michelle. It rings twice behind the bar to summon a waitress.

'What will you have?' Michelle asks Grady.

He looks at his watch. While he's deciding, the waitress takes the women's order for two Cokes, then Michelle's for two brandies. 'And?' She looks at Grady patiently. He settles for half a bitter and finally sits down, rather heavily, on a stool in front of us.

The barmaid departs with memorised orders.

'How are you?' Grady asks Michelle, ignoring me.

'Fine,' says Michelle with a tight smile. She gives him no chance to ask after their son. 'Just had a big win.'

'Me, too.' Grady inclines his head sideways at the door through which his drinking companion left – victory at the industrial tribunal, I assume.

'Remember the Grimston case?' asks Michelle brightly. 'Got his widow a tidy pay-out.'

'Good,' says Grady, looking anything but happy. He looks at me, his displeasure increasing. 'You on that, too?'

Michelle pats my hand which is doing nothing on the table now my brandy glass is empty. 'You've met my new sleuth, of course.'

'Another ex-fuzz.' He snorts in Michelle's direction. 'Thought you'd have wised up to them by now.'

Eventually Johnny Lawrence did get on to him, I realise, no longer sure how to play this.

'He's making further, separate inquiries about Hedges Pharmaceuticals and its business dealings,' Michelle tells him, openly and honestly.

'Nothing to do with me,' he grumbles.

'Today's settlement maybe,' I cut in. 'It would help to know how Grimston was prescribed the bronchitis drug in the first place.'

His head lowers slightly, shakes it. 'I'm sure I don't know.'

'Yes, you do,' says Michelle, suddenly serious.

'Grimston was, after all, from Wales,' I point out. 'His GP was there. How come he washed up in hospital here with an HP drug in tin foil in his pocket?'

'Ask her,' he retorts gruffly. 'She's his widow's solicitor.'

The waitress inconveniently returns with the order which stops Michelle from answering as she fiddles in her shoulder bag, then purse to find a ten-pound note. All three of us wait for the change to be counted out on a tin serving tray.

If she answers, 'Buggered if I know,' we're buggered, I fret. Instead: 'You tell him.'

'You serious?'

'Yes.'

'Why?'

She answers very soberly. 'It was an out-of-court settlement. There is the ethical question of client and chambers confidentiality here.' Now she's smiling sweetly. 'Of course, I could always leave my papers about for him to see.' His upper body is beginning to tip towards the table. 'And, believe me, there's a lot more in the file after eighteen months' hard work.'

He sighs deeply, shoulders rounded. 'No harm now it's all over, I don't suppose.'

'No,' Michelle concurs.

He straightens up. 'He came to me. Grimston, I mean. I was helping to run the strike fund. He was living up here, dossing, more like. Cold, late nights, standing around on picket lines. They lived like gypsies. Too much booze, not enough food. He developed a dreadful chest. I referred him to Doc Walls.'

'Why didn't you tell me this when we were together?' asks Michelle dully.

'How could I?'

Not wanting an ex-lovers' spat, I jump in. 'Better still, why not give him the money to go home again to Wales and bed, if he was that ill?'

'Doc Walls asked me to keep an eye open.'

'What for?'

'Don't you know?'

192

Michelle smiles scornfully. 'How can he? He hasn't seen the papers . . .' She pauses, then adds a menacing, '. . . yet.'

'For people with chest ailments.'

'Why?' I ask.

He is silent for a second or two, then surrenders. 'To put them on this so-called new HP wonder drug for chest troubles. There was a trial fee, fifty pounds, in it for them, see. But it had to be prescribed by a doctor.'

'How many similar hardship cases did you refer to Dr Walls?'

'Several.' A shrug. 'A dozen or so. There was a lot of illness about. Conditions for the flying pickets weren't good. But if they didn't picket they didn't pick up their extra union allowance to feed their kids.'

'And how many died from the side-effects?' asks Michelle sarcastically.

A groan. 'Don't say that, please.' He looks at her with begging eyes. 'No more that I know of. The first I knew about side-effects was when I took a look-see at those papers in the Lakes.'

'Why didn't you tell me?' she inquires, softly for her.

'Things had moved on too much.'

'There was fifty quid in it for the drug trialists,' I resume. 'What was in it for Dr Walls?'

'What lots of doctors get from pharmaceutical companies, I suppose. Golfing holidays in the sun disguised as conferences. Kind, not cash. That's the way they work it, isn't it? They're more interested in marketing than medicine.'

'And you?'

'Nothing,' he replies immediately and firmly.

'Not your fault then, any of that.' I smile understanding. 'Things moved on, you say. How?'

His head is hanging.

I try again. 'Anything to do with HP's move to Moorwood?' He won't look at me. 'When you were chairman of planning and overrode, with the backing of Councillor Laven . . .'

He looks angrily about him. 'Bastard.' A guilty expression now. 'Sorry.' I don't know whether he is apologising to Michelle or the two women within earshot. 'Questioned him, too, have you?'

I nod solemnly and lie shamelessly. 'According to the lunchtime TV news, he's now under arrest on conspiracy to murder.'

A longish pause to let the enormity of it sink in, which it does, draining all the crimson from his face. I go on, '. . . and overrode, you and Laven, all the local objections to get HP planning permission.'

Now he is looking at me, appealing. 'You owe me, you know, you coalfields ex-coppers. At least one of your old chiefs does.'

'Superintendent Armstrong?'

'Talked, has he?'

No, I tell him, but Johnny Lawrence, his trade union colleague from strike days, inadvertently had.

Then I'd know, he says, how he'd tipped off both Lawrence and Armstrong to some of the riskier excursions flying pickets were planning. Sick of it all, he became. The violence, the poverty that lasted a year. And what did it achieve? The end of the trade union movement as we knew it, that's all.

I suck up to him with a true tale from one mass demo when I heard these storm-troopers for socialism giving soccer-style ape calls to the one black policeman on duty and chanting to a woman TV reporter, 'Show us your tits.' I'd seen them throw darts at the rumps of police horses and half-bricks at police lines over the heads of mothers pushing prams.

'See what I mean?' Grady rounds on Michelle. 'You and your women's support groups. Stand by your man!' He grunts huffily. 'You should have seen what some of them were getting up to. Hooligans.'

I regret taking sides now and expect Michelle to monster him, the woman scorned. Instead, quite quietly, 'I stood by you when you lost your seat.' A sad sigh. 'Then, again, I didn't know then what I know now.'

'And what do you know?' he snaps.

'Plenty.' Their eyes are squaring up.

I step into the sullen silence. 'Things moved on after the strike to the opening of HP on the old pit site at Moorwood. You attended that ceremony with Laven.' That draws nothing from him. I press further on. 'Let's move to the summer of that same year when you two parted.'

Their eyes disengage.

'I told them, of course, naturally. Had to protect myself.' Grady dries up.

'Told who what?' I ask.

Nothing.

'Who?' asks Michelle.

'That Grimston's widow was suing via you.'

'That panicked them, I bet,' says Michelle pleasurably.

'Not really. I was called to a meeting there. At Laven's place. Dr Walls was there. So was a man from HP, some exec; don't know his name. He said not to worry. They'd fight it and win, if it ever got to court, which he doubted. Nothing about the trials need come out. I told them they didn't know you.'

He looks at her, very fondly. 'They said they'd assign a man to keep an eye on your progress. Frankly, I was for throwing in the towel, telling you everything, but . . .' His eyes drift off.

'But what, Steve?' prompts Michelle with a sad expression.

No reply.

I come in. 'Laven's thank you for his assistance in obtaining building consent and relocation grants for HP's plant at Moorwood was the new dorm added to the old house.' I pause deliberately. 'What was yours, Steve?'

'Oh, Christ.' He takes a deep breath, a drowning man.

'Come on, Steve,' says Michelle, smiling encouragement. 'It will all come out now. Half of them are being questioned. Get your side of the story in first. That's my advice.'

Her advice is tendered so tenderly, more personal than professional, that all and any resistance just melts from Grady's face.

'Seen it.' He sighs again, looking at me. 'You've seen it.'

Seen what? I think desperately. A six-year-old car, a humble bungalow.

'You stood in it yesterday.'

The expensive extension, I think.

He is looking despairingly into Michelle's face, disfigured by disgust now. 'I did it for us.'

'Us!' she exclaims, almost explodes. 'Don't you involve me.'

'It doubled the value of the property,' he explains mournfully. 'So, when I sold up . . . All I've got, that place. I didn't want . . .' He dries up before adding 'to become a kept man.'

Michelle looks quizzically at me for some clue to what Grady is talking about. Needing more, I give my head a quick, silencing shake and ask him, 'How was it paid for?'

'The way bosses get home improvements.' A short, dry laugh. 'Lost in the building costs of the new plant. Laven's extension, too.'

Well, I think, that's four of a kind – him, Laven, Walls and HP on corruption charges. Let's go for a full house.

I have to hear him out first, self-justification, mainly for Michelle's ears. 'I have no savings. How could I set up home with you? How could I even go on seeing you? Watching you beating your

195

head against a brick wall, a big multinational, to get compensation for Grimston, knowing the truth, not being able to help, say a word?' He gives his head a hopeless shake. 'It was hopeless.'

Having conned a confession out of him, her expression is unforgiving.

I play a new card. 'Know Dunphy?'

'Of him, naturally, from Johnny Lawrence.'

'He was Laven's man monitoring her.' I flick my head at Michelle. 'A corrupt ex-cop who went into security and surveillance. He got pinched a couple of months back trying to access on Laven's behalf a Special Branch computer file on you.'

'Lawrence alerted me he was on to us.' Grady circles his head to embrace Michelle.

'Don't say us,' she says, crossly.

No response.

'Alerted you to what?' I ask.

Nothing still.

'What did Dunphy hope to find?'

'They keep all activists on file.'

This I know. They used to spend hours, for instance, scouring newspapers for readers' letters critical of government policies, particularly defence, everyone left of centre a potential red under the bed. I don't see why I should deny it, so, to soften him, keep him talking, I agree with him, condemning the waste of manpower. I get back to the point. 'What happened in November?'

'October, actually,' he corrects me. 'For proof of my co-operation with the police in the strike, I suppose. To blackmail me.'

'For what purpose?'

'To frighten me off.'

'Doing what?'

'I was having a crisis of conscience. It's a trait with us uncertain socialists, you know.'

I persist. 'About what, Steve?'

'An old member of mine saw me at . . .'

I butt in. 'Wendy Warminski?'

'You know, don't you?'

Ambiguously I nod him on.

'She said a late workmate of hers, a Mrs Lillian Sharpe . . .'

Another nod.

'. . . should have left our dependants' fund some money which we'd never had. She told me she had died at one of Laven's

196

homes. I wrote to him, first contact with him in ages. He told me she had died in a flu epidemic, leaving nothing to us.'

'And then?' I ask quietly.

'It, well, sort of preyed on my mind. I knew from her Grimston case . . .' He flicks his head towards Michelle. '. . . that one HP drug had gone wrong. Was HP up to it again? Guinea pigs, you know. Paid trialists. Was Laven ripping off old people, my members included? I phoned Laven who got very aggressive and threatening. I told him unless he met her last wishes I'd consult her.' Another nod at Michelle.

'What was his reaction?'

'Very heavy. He said he knew about, well, Michelle and me, and, er, the extension and hinted that he knew what I got up to with the police and Lawrence in the strike and could prove it, if necessary.'

'What was your reaction?'

'What would yours be faced with that?' He looks down. 'Take the money and run.'

'And he sent it to you?'

'A thousand, yes, made out to me, not my union. I endorsed it to our account,' he says.

According to the discs I saw last night, he's telling a half-truth, but I'm not going to challenge him. 'And that was the end of it?'

'Not at all,' he says, gathering himself. 'All that had happened only confirmed my suspicions that I was being paid to keep quiet. I phoned him again and I told him point-blank what I thought, said I was seeing Michelle, taking advice, to hell with the consequences.'

'What did Laven do?'

'Him?' Surprised. 'Nothing himself. Sent round two cohorts to see me. At night. At my home.'

'Heavies?'

A grim snort. 'Smoothies.'

'Who?'

'One introduced himself as director designate of HP security. Said he wanted to assure me personally there'd been the most thorough inquiry into all aspects of the epidemic.'

'Did he give his name?'

'Don't you know?'

'You have tell him,' smiles Michelle. 'They're the rules.'

A deep sigh. 'Brooks.'

Got him, I think, holding back a jubilant smile.

'They'd called in the police, he said, a woman sergeant who'd found nothing suspicious with the treatment, wills, anything, he said. All the deaths were natural. Happens at that age in those living conditions, he said. Knew it was a load of soft soap, of course. Just didn't have the guts to stand up to them.'

'Did Brooks' companion say anything?'

'Confirmed everything. Publicity, he said, would only spread alarm through old folk's homes, damage trust, so there'd been no public statement, no need for inquests.'

Doc Walls, I'm thinking. But I've already got him. Still, every bit of evidence helps. 'Who was he?'

He looks at me with a pitying expression. 'Who else can order inquests up in Sherwood? Coroner Jordan, of course.'

I'm stunned into silence. Michelle drops her head, groans long and loud.

Unnoticed by her or Grady, the two women rise from their nearby table and come to ours. 'Mr Grady,' says the elder one. 'My name is Chief Superintendent Malloy and this is Sergeant Heather Hann. We are arresting you on suspicion of corruption and taking you to the Central police station for further inquiries.'


'Keep her busy,' Carole Malloy ordered at Central police station after I'd added a few more pages to my long overnight statement. 'Don't let her phone her office and warn Jordan what's coming.'

We stroll down the steps of the white-stoned station in the direction of Mansfield Road and the Peacock. I suggest one for the road.

'You've got to keep me entertained, haven't you, so I don't tip off the old man?' She smiles knowingly.

I hold up my hands in admission. She catches the left one coming down. 'Don't worry. Never liked him anyway. He never took on any cases. Look how he shuffled you off to me.' She squeezes my hand. 'Mind you, I'm pleased he did.'

In slow, even step, we ponder his motive. 'Money,' she decides. 'He's got a gorgeous place, landscaped gardens. And he took his social-climbing wife on a Caribbean cruise for Christmas.'

She resolves to push the other partners into demanding Jordan's resignation and renaming the firm. Then, when the bubble bursts on the public, they can say, hand-on-heart, that he is no longer associated with them.

She threads her fingers into mine. 'With him out of the way, everyone will vote for you joining us.' She laughs melodiously. 'Specially when I tell them how good you are.'

I clear my throat. 'I have a job.'

'Only till April and we can postpone payments till after then.'

'After April,' I say.

'Where?' she asks petulantly.

'Same job.'

She shoots a puzzled frown across her shoulder. 'Aren't you leaving?' I shake my head, looking ahead, not able to meet her eyes. 'Changed your mind?' Another shake. 'What then? We'll get you a good pay-out. Bound to.'

'To tell the truth . . .' I have to face her now. '. . . I never had any intention of quitting.'

'What?' Her stride slows to a dawdle.

'The truth is . . .' Pause, thinking: God, this is difficult. 'It's true that Sydney police asked for checks on Arnie Gillman when he failed to return home. Heather Hann . . .' I throw my head back towards the police station. '. . . traced his mother in next to no time to Laven Havens.'

I can feel my palm sweating in hers. 'Going through the records she rumbled just how many other residents had died in unreported circumstances.'

Grim-faced, Michelle nods dumbly ahead of her.

'The chief super ordered discreet inquiries into Laven and his associates. His connections with Hedges and Dunphy were easily established. They . . .' It's going to be hard to stop speaking of the East Mids Constabulary as an outsider but I let it go. '. . . had been having problems for years with Dunphy getting hold of confidential information.'

'Me, too,' says Michelle grumpily. 'Did they always suspect Ogden?'

No, to be honest, I tell her. By-the-Book Brooks and Armstrong were top of the list, because of their roles in Dunphy's murky past. The unmasking of Ogden was a surprise.

'They . . .' There I go again. '. . . couldn't raid Laven, could they? All that would have done was tip off everyone else to get the shredder working. And if the suspicion had been wrong . . .' A shrugging pause, no need to tell her of the writs that would have flown.

'No,' says Michelle, catching on immediately. 'I can see there was no real evidence at that stage.'

'Exactly,' I agree enthusiastically. 'So it had to be done surreptitiously.'

She stops, drops my hand as though it's infected and turns to face me. 'Are you telling me you're undercover?'

Yes is the honest answer to that. My confession is toned down a bit. 'Well, I am on sick leave, so they asked me to take Dunphy's place.'

'At our firm?'

I nod.

'You bastard.' She smiles, not unpleasantly, turns and begins to walk again, very slowly, head down, not taking up my hand. 'Why you?'

'Down to my mum really.' I swallow. 'Helen Myers.'

Her head comes up, eyes screwed fiercely. 'From Harbour Heights Residents Association?'

'Sorry.' My apologetic face.

She sighs, exasperated or admiringly; hard to tell.

'Well,' I go on, 'the chief super cast around for an in and knew my mum lived in Sydney.'

We have reached Mansfield Road and turn north. 'At Harbour Heights with Arnie as her janitor?' Michelle double checks, querulously. 'Too much of a coincidence, surely?'

'She lives on the other side of town, actually.' I grit my teeth. 'She's never set foot in the place. We just cobbled up that letterhead, typed up what was beneath it and I airmailed it for her to sign and send back to your firm along with that bank draft.'

'Timed', she says lowly, 'for when you knew we were short of one inquiry agent with Dunphy fired.' She gives me a sideways look, very cross. 'So all those consultations about compensation . . .'

'We'll pay you for your time,' I promise.

She breaks into a comically exaggerated limp. 'All this bloody business about your bloody leg was for the sole purpose of having you hanging around the office, on hand, for when the job came in from Australia. The right man in the right place.'

'But the sale of Gran's house is genuine,' I protest lamely. 'I still want you to handle that.'

She nods ahead of her to the square, biscuit-coloured BBC building. 'And that where-are-they-now business on the radio?'

I smile sheepishly. 'Briefed my mum on the blower, I'm afraid.'

'Good Lord.' She smiles broadly. 'She deserves an Oscar.'

I mount my defence. 'I had to look and act like a private inquiry agent . . .'

'You made a bloody good job of it.'

'. . . working entirely on my own. I was deliberately given the sketchiest of briefings and told to use my own initiative. I was expressly forbidden all info from state and Special Branch records or contact with HQ because a normal private eye wouldn't have access and Dunphy's informant could have found out and blown it. We didn't know what we'd got or who'd done what. There was no other secure way.'

So secure that, with Brooks a suspect, Carole Malloy had told him a dead-end admin job with no promotion prospects was all she could offer me, arranging an excuse to storm out and sue.

'So what about the mysterious Arnie from Arnold?' she wants to know. 'Is he dead or alive?'

'Alive . . .' Speculation, I realise. '. . . unless he's drunk himself to death with the three thou Laven gave him.'

'That I don't understand.'

'He didn't want Arnie engaging a solicitor or getting his old mum's union asking awkward questions about her estate.'

'Where is he then?'

'He missed the plane home, certainly. Sydney have since traced a fellow tourist who last saw him on the binge in Soho.'

She bridles. 'So you just used his disappearance to infiltrate our firm . . .'

There's no answer to that.

'. . . used your mum . . .'

She is, I fear, about to add, 'and used me to sweet-talk Grady into confessing.' I'd better break in. 'She quite enjoyed it.'

I tell her about my mum, confirming what I'd hinted at in her office last night. Apart from not liking politicians banging on about fatherless kids, I conclude, being illegitimate has left me with no hang-ups. 'I don't even mind being called a bastard.'

'Sorry.' She takes my hand again.

I nod towards the Peacock, in sight now, cream-painted brick-work, standing on its street corner. 'Fancy that flier?'

She shakes her head. 'If you've got to guard me, see me home.'

'Not the office?'

'I knock off early on Fridays.'

She's in no fit state to drive, I decide privately. The trouble is my car was impounded by the Scenes team in Sherwood, besides which, I'm over the top myself. 'I'll phone a cab from my place. It's only a couple of minutes' walk.'


'Coffee first?' I ask, closing the street door.

'If you like.' Ahead of me she is disappearing into the lounge. She sounds uninterested.

I go alone into the kitchen to fill and switch on a kettle. I can hear her moving about, not that there's much to see. Finally, she calls, 'Where's your loo?'

I direct her upstairs and spoon Nescafé into two mugs. No flush from the bathroom can be heard above the kettle coming to the boil. I pour and stir and pick up both mugs from the worktop by their stout handles. Elbows slightly crooked, I carry them before me at about groin height into the lounge.

She is stepping soundless down the stairs. It's not just her feet that are bare. Smooth square shoulders, slender freckled back, rounded bum, long shapely legs. All of her.

Am I this pissed? I ask myself. Am I seeing things?

Her broad hips pivot as she turns on the last step towards me.

What I'm seeing now is golden freckles on sloping ivory white breasts, then a waist that's not that slim and, yes, she's a natural redhead, right enough.

Why I should think this now, God knows, but there's this comedy duo, so rude they're on late TV. The tubby one did a short sketch, wearing nothing but a smile, his manhood hidden from view by an urn. A scantily dressed Greek goddess walked by. The urn shattered and flew in pieces across the screen.

Am I pleased these aren't priceless urns, hanging on to the mugs, nipping the handles, trying not to spill.

She walks, prowling, not that gracefully, a few steps towards me. She bends forward, throws her arms in a semi-dive around my neck, sticking her bottom well out to avoid any other point of contact with me – and, more importantly, the mugs.

Her lips press roughly on mine. Her tongue forces its way into my dry mouth.

Panic cools the animal passion: by no means entirely.

She releases my lips, but not my neck. Her eyes open. 'Your bonus,' she says throatily.

'Er.' I clear my throat. 'I . . . er . . . well . . . I've been living a celibate life just recently and . . .'

202

She lets go of my neck, turns, stoops over her shoulder bag on the brown couch, and offers a packet of condoms over her shoulder. I put the mugs on the Ladderex which takes a shaky second or two. I was expecting something like 'I don't do this for all the boys I meet' when I take the pack.

She says nothing as she drops the bag on the carpet and climbs on to the couch, turning, curling, chin propped by a cupped hand, the classic goddess pose. She watches me intently as I undress and prepare.

I kneel on the carpet beside her and lower my upper body over her. Eyes closed, I am kissing her softly and often, the way I like to start. I open my eyes for a peek. Hers aren't closed, staring at me vacantly, off-putting.

She takes her hand from under her chin and uses it and the other hand to push me back by both shoulders on to the carpet. She rolls off the couch on top of me. My right leg has landed badly or is trapped by one of hers; can't tell really. All I know is that it hurts.

With no more kissing, not a word exchanged, just rasping gasps, she is on me and I am in her, wrestling, writhing.

Short of match practice, it's not a great performance. A speedy conclusion more-or-less times with hers. I suspect that, without the urging of my leg, begging to be straightened, I might even have to have faked it.

It is over so quickly that the coffee is still quite hot as I sit beside her, both naked and sipping, not talking, me thinking, God help me, of Emma, praying that she never finds out.

The mug is in no danger of shattering now.


We don't dance, Emma and me, the slow minuet from the Paris symphony after the concert. Fond as I am of its pubs and its people, the Mansfield Road lacks some of the romance of the Rue de Rivoli.

We don't eat French either, just a quick pizza with a half-litre of house red at an Italian down from the Thai where we dined.

Over it, I tell all – well, nearly all – for her ears only and promise the rest when it's legally safe.

She bemoans what's becoming of the country – 'socialists who confuse perks with rights and capitalists whingeing about public spending unless there's a grant in it for them.'

'Yes,' I agree. 'Enough to make you vote Liberal, isn't it?'

'My goodness.' There's shock on her face. 'Things can never be that bad, surely?'

And we laugh.

Outside, I explain my car is off the road. 'Will you take me home?' I ask, heart in my mouth.

'Our home?' she asks tentatively.

'Please,' I say.

And we stand on the pavement in each other's arms, holding each other, whispering words of regret and forgiveness and love, and kissing for a long, long time.

Suddenly, the Mansfield Road is the most perfect place in the whole world, much nicer than all the Paris avenues rolled into one.

Odd, but my leg's not feeling a thing.

All the pain has gone.

# POSTSCRIPTS

16 March

To: Chief Inspector Phillip Todd,

Dear Phil,

Glad to hear of your impending medical all-clear.

The new deputy chief informs me that both you and Sergeant Hann will be receiving commendations for your outstanding work when all current legal proceedings have been completed.

Your long-overdue promotion to superintendent and transfer to Special Branch take effect on Monday, 5 April, Sunday the 4th having been your day off for the week.

Congratulations,
Carole Malloy,
Detective Chief Superintendent,
Head of East Mids CID.

PS  A postcard was recently received by a resident at Harbour Heights, Sydney. He handed it on to the NSW police who forwarded the contents to us. The attached copy might amuse you.

Bangkok – Feb 15
What a stuffing we gave those Poms. Seems a long time ago now. Been celebrating ever since, thanks to an unexpected family windfall. Taking slow route home. Delayed here by a beautiful bar-girl, aged twenty. Expect me when you see me. Cheers. Arnie.

Sydney, 21 March

Dear Phil,

Thanks for your long, lovely letter and Emma's later postcard from Jersey.

She's right. St Clements in February isn't Koh Samui, but the beach looked nice and flat for jogging. It's wonderful news that you're fighting fit at last.

I am thrilled you two are together again. You are made for each other. Believe me, with all my experience, I know. Nice that you have taken notice of your mum for once.

It was touching to learn that, at long last, I have been of some use to you in your career. Let's not do it again, though. I was petrified making my debut on air.

Your solicitor handled Mum's estate with speed and efficiency and I shall write to thank her. How do I address her? Do you know her well enough to tell me if she's a Miss or a Mrs?

With emergency trips to England to see first you and then Mum in hospital in such quick succession, I doubt that I can make another for some little time, so please bring Emma here again soon. On honeymoon, perhaps? Sorry dear. Just a happy thought.

Till we are next together you will remain, as always, in my thoughts and heart.

In haste as I prepare the Sunday barbecue,

My love,

Helen

xxx

10 April

Dear Sweeney,

Good news for me; not so good for you.

After fifteen rejections my first crime novel has finally been accepted, subject to heavy pruning, by Constable of London. (Nice name that for a publisher of crime, eh?) They also want a couple of follow-ups.

I found time to listen to your tapes. A good yarn, but, you're right, roughly told. Sadly, I'm too tucked up right now to rejig it.

I was about to suggest your Emma for the rewrite. She's certainly got a way with words. Her *News at Ten* exposure of all those goings-on at Moorwood was sensational. She must have a bloody good police contact somewhere to get in just ahead of the corruption charges; can't think who.

Didn't that new boy MP come across as a complete tit? And let's hope the police pension fund isn't invested in Hedges

Pharmaceuticals after the on-screen roasting your flame-haired lawyer friend gave them.

You're kidding me about her, aren't you? Artistic licence to disturb my old age, isn't it?

In case it isn't, I've decided on second thoughts against involving Emma. I'll hang on to the tapes and do the business when I've run out of ideas and need a new character.

Don't worry. When I get round to it I'll change all the names. Your sordid secret is safe with me, provided, of course, you keep on delivering. If not, well, matey . . .

Up the workers,
Jacko